CU00536941

UNLEASHED

EMMA SHELFORD

UNLEASHED

Kinglet Books
Victoria BC, Canada

ISBN: 978-1989677247 (print)
ISBN: 978-1989677230 (ebook)

www.emmashelford.com

First edition: August 2020

DEDICATION

To GG and Papa, for making this book possible in strange and fearsome times.

CHAPTER I

I scratch a red line through an offending sentence and wonder idly what profession I should choose next. I have had an agreeable time teaching for the past few years and envision a few more to come, but I thrive on change. Too much in my life stays the same, and variety keeps me sane.

It will depend on what Minnie wants, I suppose. Perhaps I can persuade her to open a scuba diving company somewhere tropical. My water elemental fiancée loves the ocean, after all.

A rap on my office door distracts me from my musings, and I look up.

"Merlo?" My friend Alejandro peeks his head through the half-open door. His round face wears its usual easy smile. "I finished the photocopying."

"Let's have a look." I hold out my hand, and Alejandro drops a stack of warm papers into it. My eyes rake over the picture and accompanying text.

Wanted: information regarding this individual. Dangerous—approach with caution. May answer to the name March or Xenia. If sighted, please call.

My phone number is on the bottom, and a picture of March Feynman is emblazoned on top. March—a well-to-do businesswoman and former leader of the power-hungry cult Potestas—is currently possessed by the earth spirit Xenia. Xenia is a reborn version of the elemental that possessed my father's body a millennium and a half ago. I never claimed that my past was a simple one.

Although elementals are without gender, Xenia chose her name while in a female body and has kept it since.

"Good." I slide a portion of the stack onto my desk and hand the rest back to Alejandro. "Paste those around downtown, and

I'll focus on South Vancouver. Get Wayne or Liam to do Kitsilano."

"I'll ask Liam," he says. "Wayne's been pretty busy this past week."

I nod sagely.

"It's time-intensive to have a new lover. I understand."

Anna Green, formerly March's righthand-woman but now without memory of that time, caught the attention of our friend Wayne Gibson. Alejandro twists his mouth.

"Do you think she's reformed? After all, she did try to sacrifice Minnie to gain powers. I know you changed her memory, but still, isn't she the same person?"

I sigh. It's a question I have also struggled with.

"That's up to Wayne to decide," I say finally. "I wouldn't date her, in his shoes, but I agree that people can change, given the right circumstances. Nothing is ever written in stone. If Wayne wants to give her a second chance, that's his prerogative."

"I guess." Alejandro's eye catches the photo of March in his hands, and he frowns. "Do you think this will work?"

"I don't know, but we have to try something. I think it's worth warning people. If our story weren't so outlandish, I would consider alerting the authorities. It would be helpful to have more eyes on the ground. However, we must bear our burdens as best we can."

"Yes." Alejandro taps his thumbs on the flyers. "We need to find her. Xenia is too dangerous to let run around in March's body. She doesn't understand morals or ethics."

"She understands, but she doesn't care. She seems to have access to the memories of her victims, but the knowledge is all theoretical. She's an elemental, through and through. I agree, she needs to be stopped."

"You're still searching the lauvan cables, right?" Alejandro asks. "Find anything yet?"

"Nothing."

Every evening since Xenia possessed March's body and escaped from us, I have dipped into the strands of energy that flow over the Earth and have sent my conscious to search for her. It's possible, given my abilities as a half-elemental, to look for Xenia through the lauvan. I can "see" the strands that surround every living person.

"I've combed the city every night for a week," I add. "And I still can't find Xenia's brown and burgundy strands. I don't know whether she's skipped town, or whether she's somehow hiding herself from view."

"Is that possible?"

I shrug.

"Who knows? This elemental world is new to me, too. Xenia likely has tricks that I've never even imagined."

Alejandro looks discomfited but shakes his head as if to rid himself of negative thoughts.

"I'm getting a new place," he announces.

"Oh? What prompted this?" Alejandro only moved into his current basement suite a couple of months ago.

"It's too dark, small, and expensive on my own." The strands that connect him to Jennifer Chan, his former girlfriend, twist with the direction of his thoughts. Jen helped him move into that suite, and I can imagine that the memories of happier times haunt Alejandro. He continues, "Liam was looking to get out of his place—it's a long commute for him—so we're going to be roommates. We have an apartment lined up already. It was empty, so the landlord let us take possession right away."

"It sounds like you've landed on your feet."

I'm happy for him. He has pined for Jen since the revelation of their past lives, where he was Arthur and she was Guinevere. She has no interest in repeating the past. Moving

3

out of the suite she helped him find must mean he's trying to move on, which I can only applaud. I may not agree with Jen's vow to avoid Alejandro based on their history alone, but she has the right to choose for herself. In any event, Alejandro is far more likely to win her back if he isn't moping.

"It will be good." Alejandro nods his head vigorously, then he looks at me with a hopeful, calculating gaze. "Now that you have a van…"

I laugh.

"You want help moving? I suppose I should have anticipated that kind of request when I bought the blasted vehicle. Yes, I can help."

I'm due to pick Minnie up from work soon, but I have a half-hour to spare, so I direct my royal blue Volkswagen van—retrofitted with an electric engine to satisfy my need for speed and Jen's environmental leanings—to the center of Pacific Spirit Park, near the university. I might as well get my searching for Xenia done for the day. I don't anticipate finding her—every search I have completed since she disappeared has been fruitless—but I must check.

It's worth repeating my endeavor, because with every entry into the network of lauvan that blankets the city like a carpet of glowing threads, I gain a deeper understanding of my elemental side. I have descended into lauvan cables for centuries, but exploring the finer strands that branch from the huge cable bundles is new to me. With every plunge, the journey feels more natural.

That can only be a good thing. If I have learned anything after confronting Xenia, it's that I am woefully underequipped to deal with full elementals. I have relied on my tried and true tricks for centuries, because I always have the upper hand against any human foe. Now that I'm fighting elementals, I need to up my game. If I am to meet Xenia in battle once more, which feels inevitable, I must learn from her. Learning from my enemies—adapting to fresh perspectives and new techniques—is what has kept me alive for so long.

It's also a new skill to acquire, and I can't deny the lure of the unknown. Living for so long, seeing the same things repeatedly through the ages, gives anything new a shining brightness that is impossible to ignore.

I walk along a quiet path, passing only one jogger commuting with a tight-fitting backpack, until I spot a patch of bushes thick enough to hide me from sight. I would rather not dirty my knees on the damp leaf litter, thick and soggy from autumnal rains, so I squat and press my hands against the ground. Earth lauvan are liberally crisscrossed over the leaves, and my own strands quest for connection. I close my eyes and send out my intention.

With a brightening in my inner eye, the strands of earth reveal themselves to me against a black backdrop of nothingness. My mind calms at the now-familiar sensation that was once so bizarre. Quicker than I can run or drive, my conscious races outward along tracks of lauvan, and it splinters into fragments that chase across the city in search of Xenia's distinctive strands. All the colors of the rainbow flit past, blues and greens and pinks, grays and oranges and silvers, but nothing matches the combination of Xenia's brown and March's burgundy. I eagerly aim my conscious at one multicolored cluster, but it's only Todd, my new half-elemental acquaintance. I briefly ponder why he and Minnie are the first half-elementals I have encountered in my long life, but my mind brings me back to task. I pass his silver-orange-peach cluster and scout onward.

There's nothing in the city. I can only check so many times before admitting this to myself. It's time to venture farther afield. Usually, I travel long distances within the confines of a lauvan cable, but I'm feeling confident. I have practiced so much in the past week, traveling within smaller strands that cross the city, that I feel ready to explore.

I gather fragments of my conscious—there's no reason to dilute my effectiveness on a trial—and soar eastward along the highway, which is visible from the fast-moving clusters in a line. It isn't long before I'm farther than I have ever been without a cable to guide me, but I'm pleasantly tethered to the earth and comfortable in my element. It's time to risk fragmenting, if I want to search the entire population of the Fraser Valley.

With a thought, my conscious splits into a dozen pieces and zigzags through clusters on either side of the highway. It doesn't take long to determine that Xenia isn't there. Disappointed, I gather myself together once more.

I'm bolstered by my distant foray. Why shouldn't I carry on? I turn around and race back to Vancouver and past, sending myself over an expanse of blue water strands and lauvan-coated islands in the Strait of Georgia, then beyond to Vancouver Island and Seattle.

After an unknown amount of time flitting from cluster to cluster, I admit defeat and return to my body. Xenia is nowhere to be found. She must be far from Vancouver.

My chocolate brown lauvan beckon me with a warm glow of home, and I enter my body with a gasp of relief. Not for the first time, I am glad that I didn't abandon my body to Xenia. My knees groan in protest at holding their folded position. When I check my watch, half an hour has passed. Damn it, Minnie will be waiting. I jog back to my van, but in the back of my head, there is one thought.

Just because I can't find Xenia now doesn't mean she won't come back one day. I must stay vigilant.

CHAPTER II

On Friday evening, a brisk wind blows and the pattering of rain on my coat makes me draw the hood closer around my head. Minnie hunches her shoulders.

"It's too bad we have to learn about the elements while being out in the elements," she says over wind whistling in the trees above. "The beach is going to be freezing."

"We'll keep it quick tonight," I promise. "But Todd was so eager to do another lesson that I didn't have the heart to postpone due to rain."

"You love teaching him, don't give me that." Minnie grins at me.

"You know me well."

I take her hand, and we walk down a long staircase to the beach. Todd waits for us at the bottom with his hood swept back and his eyes closed. An expression of contentment rests on his face.

"What a great breeze," he says when he notices our arrival. "A storm's brewing. It feels like a wild one."

"Plenty of air lauvan to play with," I reply. "Let's get to work."

I start them building a barrier to stop the flow of wind around their bodies. Todd grasps it quickly and plays around while I guide Minnie in constructing her wall. When Minnie finally achieves a passable barrier, she looks relieved at the reprieve from the constant wind. When she is finished, Todd waves me over.

"Look at this."

Todd has created a hardened shell of air in front of his face. It's so dense with air threads that I can scarcely see his features. He leans out from it and grins.

"Throw something at me," he says. "Go on. A rock or something."

I shrug and pick up a pebble from the beach. With an accuracy born of centuries of practice, I lob the missile directly at Todd's air shield. Minnie gasps, but the pebble ricochets and bounces harmlessly to the ground.

"What do you think?" Todd raises his eyebrows and waits for me to comment. I nod, impressed that he managed to come up with the notion by himself. His imagination has held him back in the past. Perhaps, with the frequent new ideas that I present to him in lessons, his mind has broadened.

"Nicely done," I say, and he beams. "How much force do you think it can take?"

"It's pretty strong." He looks at the square of air threads dubiously. "I don't know. I haven't tested it much yet."

"Stand back," I say.

Todd scrambles to the side and I lift a rock the size of my head into the air then twirl it around like a hammer throw using its strands. When I let go, it soars through the air with momentum, straight to the silver square.

On impact, the square shivers. The rock cracks in two and drops to the ground. I pace forward to examine Todd's handiwork.

"That's remarkably sturdy, Todd. I would be hard-pressed to construct one as strong as this."

Todd's mouth works as he tries not to visibly react to my praise.

"Good," he says nonchalantly. "I am part air elemental, after all. I've been working on my skills in the evenings. I want to make up for lost time."

"Here." I point to a corner of the square where the strands appear woven, like a fabric. "Did you weave this together by hand, or use your intention?"

9

"A bit of both."

"Good, good." I examine it further. There are some differences in the wall to how I would normally build a structure like this, and it excites me to think that I can learn from Todd and Minnie. I relish the chance to grow. If I can become more effective with my elemental abilities, perhaps I can hold my own against Xenia and her kind. It's also a novel experience to learn something new from someone else. Too often, I am the teacher.

"Look at this, Merry." Minnie holds up what looks like a rope, and it takes me a moment to recognize blue strands of water. "I separated water lauvan from the water. Usually, they stick together much more than earth lauvan do."

"Excellent." I admire her accomplishment. "The essence of water, without the liquid itself. Helpful when hiding your actions in combat with humans. They'll never know where the water came from once you release your hold."

"Always back to fighting with you, isn't it?" Minnie says. Normally, a comment like that would be accompanied by a teasing smile, but her expression remains serious. "That's fine. I want to learn how to fight, to defend myself. I'm tired of being meek and mild. You'll have to get used to that."

"I've never considered you meek and mild," I say in astonishment. Where did that comment come from?

"Oh, come on," she says. "I've always been your compliant woman. Maybe this time I want to be different."

I can only blink in surprise. Minnie's strident tone is unlike her, and I don't understand where her opinion comes from. I am not certain how to react to this combative stance, so I clear my throat and change the subject.

"Shall we all try Todd's air wall, but with water?"

Alejandro calls me on Saturday to wheedle a furniture pickup out of me, so Sunday afternoon finds me pulling up to the curb of a brown clapboard house in Burnaby, Alejandro beside me and Liam in the back.

"This is it," Alejandro says doubtfully. "I think."

Liam slides the back door open and jumps out. He pulls his hood over his head with a baleful glance at the weeping sky.

"Glad we're only picking up a table, not a mattress or something. Tables can be wiped clear of rain."

"Neither of you has one that will suffice already?" I ask. "What have you been eating on until today?"

"I want something bigger," Alejandro says with an evasive air, but his strands crackle with suppressed excitement. I wonder what this table looks like. "It's not fair for Wayne to always have us for dinner, is it?"

"Very considerate." I wave him forward. "After you."

Alejandro and Liam traipse up the walkway, and I follow at a leisurely pace. By the time I'm at the bottom of the cement steps, an elderly woman has opened the door and ushers the others inside.

"It's a good thing you're strapping young lads," she says in a hoarse, accented voice. "It's a heavy brute, it is. Sturdy as the day is long, mind you, you'll never need another. Your children will be feeding their grandchildren on it, I have no doubt." She laughs with wheezing breaths, and Alejandro smiles politely. She gestures him inside. "Have a look, it's in the dining room. I'm downsizing, you know how it is. There."

Alejandro breathes in with a hiss, and I poke my head over Liam's shoulder to see what caused him to react so.

A table fills the tiny room with a presence that can't be

denied. Its wooden surface, stained a deep mahogany, is lined with scratches and dents. It's clearly well-loved but polished and clean. The imperfections merely highlight its sturdy nature and long history.

I take all this in with one glance, but what really strikes me is the shape.

"It's a round table," I say with a raised eyebrow at Alejandro. He grins at me.

"Yes, it is. That's why I wanted it."

Liam looks from me to Alejandro. He must sense the subtext, for his brow contracts in confusion.

"Why? What's special about a round table?"

I glance at Alejandro again, unsure what to say. Although Liam knows about the elementals and my abilities, he doesn't know about our shared history as Arthur and Merlin. There was a round table there, of a sort. The silence stretches, and Liam's expression grows from confused to suspicious.

"You can fit as many people as you need at a round table," the old woman pipes up. "No matter how many wee ones my children pop out, there is always room for more."

"Excellent point," I say to cover the awkward moment. "Well, Alejandro? Pay the good woman, and we'll take the table off her hands."

It takes all three of us, grunting and straining, to shuffle the huge table through the hallway and down the steps. Once at the curb, it's clear that the table won't enter my little van in one piece, so Alejandro dismantles it via the split for a leaf down the middle, and we squeeze it in with merely a hair's width to spare. Liam crawls in beside it and I direct my wheels to their new place.

I pull up to the curb, and Alejandro jumps out with excitement to show me around. They have a garden suite in the bottom of a big old house divided into apartments. It's

12

surprisingly bright and large, despite its position on the bottom floor. There are French doors that open to a patio and a small backyard. I point to it.

"Sword practice?"

Alejandro grins at me.

"Of course."

"That was a major selling feature for him," Liam says. "Who knows what the upstairs neighbors will think? I'm happy there's space for a barbeque."

Moving the table into the eating area is smoother on this end without stairs to navigate. When we finally drop the beast on the floor and Alejandro assembles the two halves, we stand back and catch our breath. The table dominates the room, looking as immovable as a tree.

"Somehow, it fits," I say. "I like it."

"It's massive," says Liam. "But there's lots of room for games night. Good find, Alejandro."

Alejandro rubs the edge of the table. Liam notices the movement, and his eyes narrow at the reminder of its roundness.

"I'm heading out," he says abruptly. "See you two later."

I stare after him. Knowing what the issue is—Liam feels left out of an inside joke—and knowing what to do about it are two separate matters. How many people should we tell about our histories? Is it fair to keep it a secret, now that so many are involved?

Alejandro is oblivious to his friend's coolness and continues to gaze at the table, deep in thought. His strands droop with sadness.

"What's wrong?" I ask.

"What's the point in bringing back memories of the past?" Alejandro says without looking at me. "When one of the most important people from my history won't be with me? What am

13

I supposed to do without her?"

I sigh. I thought giving up the old apartment and moving here with Liam was a good sign, but it appears the process of getting over Jen will be a long one for Alejandro.

"You might have to accept that being with Jen is not in the cards for you this lifetime." I press on despite Alejandro's wince. "Not every life has resulted in happily-ever-after for you. Remember your time as a sailor in the sixteen hundreds? We figured that you had only one night with a version of Jen while on shore leave, and that was it."

"And I thought about her the rest of that life," Alejandro says, his voice gloomy.

"This is your chance to recognize what is actually happening. You didn't know why you were drawn to her then, but you do now. And that knowledge can help you set your feelings for her aside, because it's what she wants. If you love her, you'll want her to be happy in her choices. And, if her choice is not you, so be it. This is your chance to move on with full understanding."

Alejandro looks unconvinced. I take my leave a few minutes later, but I hope he thinks on what I said. I still haven't lost hope that Jen will change her mind, but there's no way I will tell Alejandro that. For his own sanity, it's best if he can leave her behind and move on to greener pastures. He deserves someone who wants him.

CHAPTER III

Monday passes uneventfully, filled with classes, marking, and a departmental meeting that has me yawning pointedly at the organizer. When the day is finally at an end, and I am shrugging my coat over my shoulders, Wayne knocks at the door.

"Heading home?" he says. A laptop is under his arm. "I wanted to show you something."

Wayne sets his computer down on my desk, types a few lines, then turns the screen to face me. I lean in, interested to see what Wayne has been up to.

"Our memoirs," Wayne says with a chuckle. "Categorized and organized. The website is password protected, so no one else can see it. Any one of us can edit these, write our own memories, add notes to someone else's section, and organize it by date and person. I hate the thought of all this history locked away in our minds. If we can get it out, hopefully we can trigger each other's memories and create a clear picture of what the past was like."

He looks at me in expectation. I consider him.

"You know you'll be at it for decades, right?" I say finally. "Do you know how long fifteen hundred years is? I hope your fingers are up to the task."

Wayne grins.

"I'll do my best. Look, I have a special section for you since you don't have discrete lifetimes."

"I'm breaking the mold again."

I look at Wayne's website and then at his hopeful expression. It feels strange that we could reduce our lives, all of them, to a few words on a page that are supposed to evoke all the wonders, terrors, joys, fears, sorrows, and delights of life. I don't know how successful we will be. But the sight of Wayne's excited face convinces me that he and the others will benefit from this endeavor. Even if I don't understand it, I can support his aspirations.

"It looks good," I say, and Wayne's face loosens with relief. "No guarantees I'll jot down more than brief notes, though. I have a lot to get through."

"Your sections are your own," Wayne assures me. "This is just for us." He closes the laptop then looks at me with a serious expression. "There's something else."

I turn to Wayne fully while I button my coat. His strands are twisted with concern and determination.

"Spit it out."

"I want Anna to know about this," he says in a rush. "It's eating me alive, knowing that there's a huge secret part of me that I have to hide from her. I know we've only been dating for a few weeks, but I don't think I can keep going without being honest with her."

"You're in that deep, are you?" I look him over with interest. His agitation is apparent from his strands. He's not lying—not telling Anna weighs on him heavily.

"I really like her," he says. "There's a true connection there. I won't deny that knowing she also has a past is appealing, but that's not the only reason. We really click." He looks out the window with his brow furrowed. "What if she's the one? I don't want to drive her away because I can't share everything. I hate lying. I'm terrible at it."

"I know. You always have been."

I drum my fingers on the chair beside me. What are the repercussions of Anna knowing about Wayne's past lives? Presumably, she will want to find out more and discover that she was Vivienne and other people before this. That doesn't bother me as much as the possibility that the grail will undo the memory-block I put on her, which prevents her from remembering her time with Potestas. That would spell the end of Wayne's burgeoning relationship, not to mention open a whole host of new problems. Would March's wing-woman, and an avid supporter of elemental powers for humans, attempt to find Xenia and help her with whatever she plans? It's not something I am eager to risk.

"What did you tell her about her memory loss, the cave, all of it?" I ask.

"I told her the truth about the cave and her involvement. It wasn't a fun evening, but she needed to know. Especially before I introduce her to the group. I didn't tell her that you messed with her memory, though. She thinks she fell and hit her head."

"How convenient. What if she regains her memories of Potestas and her motivations for joining? Despite your feelings for each other, she might feel obliged to help her friend March, who is currently possessed by Xenia."

"I don't think she would," Wayne says, but I can see the hesitation in his eyes.

"What if she changes into a person that you aren't in love with?" My words are blunt, but I need Wayne to understand the risk. Anna, before I manipulated her memory, was conniving, at times ruthless, and entirely obsessed with gaining elemental powers. From Wayne's account, she is different now, perhaps closer to the woman she was before her involvement with Potestas.

"I don't see why the grail would mess with whatever you did to her head," Wayne says. There's a desperate note to his voice, but he has a point.

"You're probably right. The mechanism for each type of memory loss must be different. But it's a risk, nonetheless. I want to make sure you understand that. At the end of the day,

17

it's your decision. I'm simply the guardian of the grail. Get the others to weigh in, but for my part, I'll leave the decision to you. We're all equals, now."

Wayne gives an unexpected laugh.

"That's something Arthur would have said."

I smile at that.

"True words don't grow old."

"Thanks, Merry." Wayne wrings his hands together as he thinks. "I'll call Alejandro."

"I'm going to Alejandro's now. I plan to leave the grail at his house. Come by with Anna if you decide tonight."

Wayne nods and pulls out his phone as he leaves. I sigh and sling my satchel over my shoulder. Will we have a new initiate to the history circle tonight? I don't look forward to telling Minnie that the woman who tried to kill her might join us.

After a few quick texts, I jump into my van and race to Minnie's office. She waits for me at the curb, tapping her watch pointedly. I grin and give her a smacking kiss on the lips when she climbs into the passenger's seat.

"Just keeping you on your toes," I say. "Ready to help Alejandro unpack?"

"I'm ready to order pizza," she says. Her grumpy tone surprises me—she's usually mild-tempered—and I glance at her.

"Is everything all right?"

She shrugs.

"Yeah, it's fine."

Her lauvan show that she's telling the truth. There are no swirls of lies or sharp edges of discomfort. She's merely moody. It's odd, for Minnie, but a bad mood is no crime. I am sure she puts up with enough from me.

I give Minnie a minute of quiet for her to process whatever she's thinking about, but eventually I break the silence. She needs to know what she's getting into tonight.

"Wayne might bring Anna by for dinner," I say. "He wants to tell her about his past."

Minnie stares at me incredulously.

"What? Are we talking about the same Anna? Anna Green, the murderous Potestas member?"

I nod. She peers at me, searching for my reaction.

"And you're okay with this?" she says finally.

"I don't think she'll remember her Potestas past if she touches the grail, only her previous lifetimes." I'm not at all certain of this, but it seems like the right thing to say in the wake of Minnie's reaction. "Wayne's tearing himself up about it. He really thinks she's changed, and he wants her to know him better."

"Typical man, thinking with his lower brain." Minnie crosses her arms and looks out of the side window.

I frown. Minnie has no love for Anna, and rightfully so, but the way she's acting is not like her at all. I have known Minnie for months, and her previous incarnations for centuries, and this behavior is inconsistent with all versions of her. Am I seeing a side of Minnie that has been hidden from me? Perhaps her current body's personality is coming out more strongly than it has before.

"I'm not enamored of the idea," I say carefully. "But I do feel that it's Wayne's right to choose. As long as Anna doesn't remember her Potestas past, I can't see that it will do us much harm. If we do see signs that she's recovering her current lifetime's memories, I can fix her again."

"Fine," Minnie says, still not looking at me. "Just don't

19

expect me to be her best friend."

We drive the rest of the way in silence. I'm confused by Minnie's reaction but chalk it up to a bad mood and the reminder of a painful episode in her life. It was only a few months ago that she was almost sacrificed by Anna and the Potestas cult. I can't expect her to brush it off as nothing.

Alejandro opens the door to my deliberate knock when we arrive, and he ushers us in with an eager wave.

"Come in, come in. There isn't much, yet, but we've found enough chairs, at least."

"Can I help unpack something?" I say. There aren't many boxes around, given that he and Liam only moved in a day ago, but there must be something that needs to be done.

"There are a couple of kitchen boxes, but other than that, it's all away." Alejandro gestures around the empty suite. "I don't have much. Liam's already set up his room."

"Kitchen it is."

"How many others are coming?" Minnie asks, her phone open to a pizza app. Alejandro counts on his fingers.

"You two, Liam, me, Wayne and Anna." Minnie's face darkens at the mention of Anna, but Alejandro doesn't notice. "Jen and Cecil, too." His strands twitch, but he keeps an admirable composure.

"How are we going to discuss Anna's involvement with Liam and Cecil here?" I ask. "Will we talk in code?"

"Talk about what?" Liam stands at the door of his room with his arms crossed. "What's going on that's so secret? Don't make me regret moving in with you, Alejandro. I hate secrets."

Alejandro looks at me with a pleading glance. I rub my face with one hand.

"If we're telling Anna, I don't see why Liam can't know," Minnie says, her fingers selecting pizza options on her phone. "I'd rather him than her."

20

I look at Alejandro, who shrugs with a twitch of his shoulders. I sigh.

"Let's wait until everyone is here," I say. "I know Jen wanted to tell Cecil, too. Then we can have a great big reveal party. Will that suffice, Liam?"

Liam narrows his eyes and glances at each of us in turn.

"I guess it will have to," he says finally. "Let me know when the others are here."

He retreats to his room and shuts the door. Moments later, music drifts over his threshold. Alejandro heaves a sigh and sinks into one of the mismatched chairs that encircle the round table.

"This is moving fast," he says. "Another three added to the group."

"We should set up the grail in front of city hall," I say. "Put out an advertisement, let everyone check if they have a past."

Alejandro snorts.

"It might be easier."

A knock on the door brings Jen and Cecil inside Alejandro's new home. Jen clutches her purse and Cecil rubs his neck awkwardly until Minnie takes pity on them. With a return to her usual, empathetic self, she engages the two in conversation and leaves Alejandro and I to unpack cutlery and plates into the empty kitchen. By the time there's another knock on the door, the kitchen is unpacked enough to find important items, and Jen is at ease with Minnie at the round table.

"I'll get it," I say and walk with unhurried steps to the front door, where a young woman with a visor and a branded shirt holds a stack of pizza boxes.

"Delivery for—" She frowns at the label. "The Lady of the Lake?"

Inwardly I chuckle, but my face remains stoic.

"You've come to the right place."

21

I hand over a few bills. Wayne and Anna approach from the road and move aside for the departing delivery woman, and I greet them with a smile. Anna has her hair down, but her makeup and expression are far more fresh-faced and open than I ever remember her having. I can see why Wayne is falling for her. I can't remember how far back I erased her memory, but if I took away all references to Potestas, she won't remember me, either. I hold out my hand.

"Hello, Anna."

"Nice to meet you," she says automatically and shakes my hand with a light but firm pressure. With hesitation, she says, "I knew you before, right? Wayne told me a little of what happened during that blank part of my life. It's hard to imagine, really, but I trust Wayne." She smiles at him, and he beams back. Another two strands join their collection of connected lauvan.

"Yes, we knew each other." I don't elaborate. Nothing useful would come out of rehashing our relationship, such as it was.

"I'm sorry for any hurt I did to you," she says. Her eyes are wide with her earnestness. "I don't remember it, but it sounds pretty terrible. I don't know what I was thinking. I really don't understand what happened to me."

She sounds sincere, and her strands reflect the same. I recall the cage of lauvan that Anna and March had trapped Minnie in during the botched sacrifice in the cave, and I look away for a moment to collect myself.

"It's in the past," I say finally. "This is a fresh start for you. If you use it wisely, all will be forgiven."

She nods fervently.

"I plan to."

I wave her and Wayne inside. Anna hovers near the door and tugs on Wayne's hand.

"Maybe this isn't a good idea," I overhear her whisper to

22

Wayne. "Everyone must hate me, and for good reason. Your friends don't have to like me for us to date."

"They don't have to," Wayne says. "But please give them a chance, for my sake. They are a big part of my life, and you are, too."

Anna sighs then strokes Wayne's arm.

"For you," she says. "It must be the new-boyfriend endorphins."

Wayne chuckles and pulls her forward. I drop the pizza boxes on the table.

"Everyone, this is Anna," I say. Minnie folds her arms but otherwise stays quiet. Jen looks to me for direction, and I nod with a half-glance at Wayne, so she takes her cue and stands to greet Anna. Wayne looks relieved.

After a few introductions, or re-introductions for most, I raise my voice.

"Eat up, folks. Pizza's getting cold. Alejandro, where did we put those plates?"

Despite the number of people crammed into the suite, there is enough room for everyone around the table. It's quiet as we chew pizza. I'm never one to be bothered by silence, but the tension is thick enough to cut with a knife. Anna and her past billow around us like a thundercloud, and the Alejandro-Jen-Cecil triangle contributes its own breezes.

I'm contemplating what to say when Anna breaks the quiet.

"I know many of you don't want me here," she says with her hands clasped under the table. "After what Wayne has told me, I get that. I did some terrible things, unforgivable things. Even though I don't remember them, it doesn't take away my guilt." She swallows then glances at Wayne, who nods his encouragement. "I know I can't make things right, but I want to apologize for my actions. And to thank you for having me here. It's a mark of your friendship to Wayne that you're

23

allowing me to be here, and I'm glad he has you in his life. I don't want to get between you and him."

No one seems to know what to say. The silence lingers for a moment before I speak to ease Wayne's pained look.

"Well said, Anna. We all have a past, and none of us is spotless. If you're sincere in your desire to use your second chance for good, then I'm happy to support you."

"Me too," Alejandro says, and the others murmur their agreement. Minnie stares at Anna with her arms crossed.

"It's going to take a while for me," she says finally. Anna gulps but meets Minnie's hard gaze. "You almost killed me, and that's hard to forget. However, I'm willing to reserve judgement until you have a chance to let your actions prove your words."

"That's all I ask," Anna whispers.

Minnie nods and looks away. I frown. This isn't like Minnie. She is usually the first to empathize and the first to understand. Seeing through another's eyes is practically in her job description as a psychologist. I know that the cave incident was more than anyone should have to endure, but her reaction is not what I would have expected from her.

"Do you remember anything from Potestas?" Jen asks. Although it's not a neutral subject, I appreciate her distraction from Minnie's prickliness. Anna shakes her head.

"Not really. A few things, dribs and drabs of memory that feel more like a dream. I remember meeting March for the first time, but not what we talked about. It's strange—I remember some faces but not names, and I remember a few places. I can see Potestas headquarters, although I didn't remember the name until Wayne told me. And I can picture all three of March's houses, quite clearly."

I lean forward in my interest.

"Do you know addresses?"

"Yes," she says. "But that's all. I don't remember anything that happened at them."

"That would be useful," Alejandro says. "We could make sure Xenia isn't hiding at one of them."

Alejandro is correct, but there's another prize we might glean from March's holdings.

"Do you think the Potestas library is at one of the houses?" I can barely keep excitement from coloring my voice. With access to the library, I could expand my knowledge immeasurably. My elemental contacts are invaluable, but they don't know everything. March was able to prepare her body for Xenia through the knowledge from her books, which was a procedure that the elementals knew nothing about. Jen glances at me.

"March must have hidden it somewhere. Why not in her house?"

"Why not, indeed.' I lean back, absorbed with the thought of the secrets waiting for me. Anna pipes up.

"I might have keys. There are a few on my keychain that don't match anything else."

"If you can get me access to March's spirit library, I'm happy to forget the past."

Anna flashes me a grateful smile, and my heart squeezes from memories. I hope we did the right thing, letting her come here. One glance at Wayne's besotted face reminds me that we did.

"Speaking of the past and things that are hidden," Wayne says. "Are we ready to talk about that?"

Liam leans forward, his pizza forgotten.

"Finally. I hate secrets. Are you going to spill whatever you've been dancing around?"

I look at Jen.

"Have you told Cecil yet?"

25

She shakes her head quickly.

"It never seemed like the right time. Are we doing this now?"

"I guess we are," I say with trepidation in my heart.

CHAPTER IV

I stand and retrieve my coat from a pile on the floor. In the inside pocket, a hard lump resolves itself as the grail. The stemless cup gleams with enamel in peacock blue, rusty red, and aquamarine, and it swirls with multicolored lauvan.

Everyone's eyes fix on the cup. I place it in the center of the round table and sit down.

"Who wants to do the honors?" I ask the others. They all look wide-eyed at the proposition of being asked to divulge our secrets.

"It should be you," Alejandro says quickly. "You started it all."

"We haven't proved that yet." I sigh and stare at the grail. Its strands wink at me. "Fine, I'll do it. Liam, Anna, Cecil, you all know that I have strange abilities, and that elemental spirits dwell in a parallel world that touches our own."

They nod slowly and glance at each other in confusion.

"What you don't know yet is that I am immortal and have been alive for fifteen centuries." I ignore their incredulous looks and plow on. "Although the bodies of Minnie, Alejandro, Jen, and Wayne are not immortal, their souls are reborn again after death. They can trace the memories of their past lives to the time of my earliest memories, back when I was Merlin, and they were Nimue, Arthur, Guinevere, and Gawaine. We have connected with each other during most of their rebirths, although I don't understand how."

I place my palms on the table and take a deep breath.

"I know this sounds incredible, unbelievable, but you've all seen unbelievable things lately. We wanted to tell you, partly because we don't want to keep secrets from our friends, but also because we want to give you a chance to find out if you have past lives like us. All you have to do is touch the grail, this cup, here." I point to the vessel, and all eyes stare at it.

"If you don't want to know," Jen says quickly. "We totally understand. It was really hard for me to learn about all this, and I get it if you want to keep things simple."

Cecil stares hard at the grail. His russet strands twitch with curiosity and confusion.

"I can't believe I'm believing all this," he mutters. "But I thought elementals were nuts, and they're real. If I touch that cup, I'll really get memories of whoever I was in the past?"

"Perhaps," I say. "We don't know if everyone has a past. It could be that nothing happens when you touch it, in which case you will remain the same as you were before."

"I'm out," Liam says. His strands twist with concern, and his brows pinch. "For today. I need to think about it. Seriously, Merlin and Arthur? And I don't know if I want other people in my head."

"That's a good idea." Jen nods vigorously. "Sleep on it. You too, Cecil. Think about it for a bit. The grail's not going anywhere."

Jen pushes them to wait because of her own experience, but I agree. It's a big decision with far-reaching consequences. Neither of them appears as eager as Wayne was when he first heard.

"I'll leave it here, with Liam and Alejandro's permission," I say. "I can hang it under the table, out of the way."

Cecil doesn't look convinced that waiting is the best choice, but Jen's hand on his arm steadies him. Liam looks relieved to defer his decision.

Anna, who has been quiet until now, stands.

"I'm ready," she says. "Wayne told me earlier, and I know I have a past. I have enough memory loss. I'm okay with not remembering the atrocities I did in this life, but I want to see my history."

I look her over. Her strands are tight with resolve. She thinks she's ready. Who am I to say otherwise? I wave at the grail.

"So be it. Welcome to your past, Anna."

Anna glances at Wayne, who gives her a nod and a tight smile of encouragement. She looks at the grail, takes a deep breath, then grasps it firmly around the bowl.

The strands of the grail react instantly. They stream out from the cup and down Anna's arm. Her own lauvan intertwine with them and flutter out from her body in a cloud of static threads. Her eyes squeeze closed, and she shakes.

"Help her sit," I say to Wayne. He grasps her around the middle and guides her to the chair. She follows, unresisting, her focus clearly elsewhere.

Liam looks horrified, and Cecil fascinated.

"Is she downloading her memories now?" he murmurs. I let out a huff of surprised laughter at the analogy.

"It's more like she's plugging in, making the connection," Alejandro offers. "The 'downloading' comes slowly, later."

"She's okay, though, right?" Liam asks.

"She'll be fine," Wayne says, but he looks like he reassures himself as much as Liam. He has never seen this process, only felt it himself. "It should be over soon."

Within a minute, the grail's strands shrink back to the cup and slide calmly over its surface. Anna lets go and breathes heavily with her eyes closed.

"Anna?" Wayne whispers. "Are you okay?"

"Yes," she says slowly. "I think so."

"Do you remember anything?"

She opens her eyes but only to look at her hands.

"I'm not sure. Maybe. It's all a jumble."

I break the silence that follows with one word.

"Vivienne."

I say it as an experiment in triggering memories. Anna winces and gasps, then she looks into my eyes. Anna is there, but a hint of Vivienne lurks behind.

"Yes," she breathes. "I think that was my name."

"Do you remember anything about Potestas?" Minnie says with narrowed eyes. I look at Anna with my breath held and am relieved to still see the knot in her strands that blocks her memories. She shakes her head with a frown.

"No, I don't think so. Nothing more than before. Only memories that look like they're from the history channel."

I breathe a sigh of relief. I would erase her Potestas memories again in a heartbeat, but I suspect Wayne might take issue. After all, others have reacted badly to my meddling, and he was never keen on my mind manipulations. It's easiest if the grail has no effect on her current body's memories.

"I think that was enough excitement for one night," Jen says. "Thanks for the pizza. Let's head out, Cecil."

Cecil stands but gazes thoughtfully at the grail. Wayne and Anna murmur quietly to each other, and Liam retreats to his room without another word. Minnie grabs another slice of pizza, which leaves me to listen to the exchange at the door.

Alejandro follows Jen and rummages in the pile of coats for hers. He holds it out so she can slide her arms in.

"Take care of yourself," he says quietly. Jen searches his face, but Alejandro never hides anything. His heart is on his sleeve, as always.

"I'm ready, Jen," Cecil says. He eyes Alejandro as he grabs his coat from the pile, then he puts his arm around Jen's shoulders possessively. Jen looks down in confusion.

I have a flash of sympathy for Cecil. Not only is Alejandro Jen's ex-boyfriend, but he was her husband in another life. That's a hard pill to swallow, and I don't blame him for feeling defensive.

30

"Bye," Jen says to the room. I hold up my hand in farewell, and they exit quickly. Alejandro's shoulders and lauvan droop in unison.

"Want to spar for a bit?" Wayne calls out to Alejandro. He must have witnessed the incident at the door. Alejandro perks up at the thought of his favorite activity.

"Yes. I'll get the swords."

"I'm not feeling great," Anna says. She's pale and looks tired. "I think I'll head out."

"That's fine, I'll take you home," Wayne says quickly, but she shakes her head.

"Don't worry about me. You stay and have fun. It's a quick bus to Bethany's."

Wayne's forehead puckers, so I interject.

"We can give you a ride, Anna."

Minnie raises an eyebrow but doesn't protest out loud. Anna smiles tentatively.

"Thanks, Merry. That's great."

I catch Alejandro in the kitchen before we leave as he grabs a glass of water.

"Jen still seems set on Cecil," I say bluntly. "If you're not careful, you could drive them both away if you're too cozy with her."

Alejandro's face closes in a mulish expression.

"I didn't do anything."

"I know, but I can see more than most. It's hard, but you need to move on. Remember what you said a couple of weeks ago about wanting her to be happy, with or without you?"

"That was when I figured she would come around," he says. "But how long do I have to wait?"

"That's what I'm saying. You can't wait, can't put your life on hold. Perhaps, in this life, you and she are not meant to be. Don't waste your precious time on Earth pining over someone

31

who doesn't want you."

The words are harsh but necessary to push through Alejandro's stubborn refusal to see the truth. Jen may still have feelings for him, but she's determined not to give into them. Alejandro may come back, life after life, but each lifetime is still so short, compared to my own. I hate to see the people I care about waste their youth on something they can't have.

"I've heard enough tough love," Alejandro says bitterly. "Go on, Minnie's waiting for you." There's enough emphasis on Minnie's name to highlight the fact that I have my beloved and he does not.

I nod and retreat. I've said my piece. He will have to come to his own conclusions, and that will take time. Hopefully, not too much time.

Minnie and Anna stand awkwardly together at the front door when I sweep toward them.

"Ready to go? Good." To Anna I say, "Let's get you home to rest. I'm sure it was an overwhelming evening."

"Yes, but it felt right," she says. "I'm glad I did it. I don't want to hide from who I am."

"Says the woman who has forgotten what she did," Minnie mutters as she passes out the front door. I shrug in apology at Anna, who nods as if that reaction is all she deserves to expect.

Minnie climbs into the front passenger's seat and slams the door shut. Anna slides into the back and perches on the bench with unease. In the driver's side, I put my wallet and phone on the console and press the ignition button. The electric van starts with a quiet ping and silence.

We are equally silent on the drive to Bethany's house. Anna

is staying with her friend's aunt until she gets her feet under her, and it eases my mind that Bethany is keeping a watchful eye on her. Anna seems sincere, but she has fooled me before. Just because I want to give her a second chance doesn't mean that I won't keep an eye out for regression.

Minnie plays on her phone to ignore Anna's presence in the back, and Anna doesn't break the silence. My mind is too full of the evening's events to strike up a conversation with either woman, and I'm not certain what I would talk about if I did speak. The only things they have in common are Potestas and me. Anna remembers neither, and Minnie has no fond recollections of Potestas.

My phone pings with a text.

"Check it for me, would you?" I ask Minnie. I have no secrets from her. She puts her own phone down with a sigh and picks up mine.

"It's Todd," she says after a moment. "He wants to meet for a lesson."

"Are we doing anything on Sunday? See if he's free at ten." Minnie nods and types my answer.

"What do you teach?" Anna says from the back in an attempt to make small talk.

"Normally, English literature. Todd is a special case. He's also half-elemental, like Minnie and I are. We meet to practice our skills, since he's new at it." I glance in the rearview mirror. "Wayne told you about elementals, right?"

"Yes, Wayne explained everything." She frowns in thought. "That's what I was after, before I lost my memory. Some way to get those elemental powers."

"You got it," Minnie mutters.

"That's amazing you have those powers," Anna says as if she didn't hear Minnie's response. "How do half-elementals happen?"

33

"As far as we know, Minnie and I had fathers possessed by an elemental, and both of Todd's parents were possessed."

Anna is quiet after my answer, and I sneak another look in the mirror. She gazes out the window, deep in thought. Her strands carry the faintest hint of twisting jealousy. I wonder if talk of elementals triggers Potestas memories in her, despite my manipulation of her memories. Or is she curious because it is in her nature to desire more than she has, and being a half-elemental looks like a path to greater things? It's what started her on her Potestas journey, after all. She is still Anna, even if she can't remember her actions of the recent past.

Minnie reverts to her usual self away from the influence of Anna, and the rest of our evening is peaceful.

"I'm finished with my last client at three today," she says in the morning as we brush our teeth in the tiny bathroom. "What's your schedule like? Do you want to play hooky with me?"

"Always," I say through a mouthful of toothpaste. After I spit and rinse, I ask, "Did you have something in mind?"

Minnie twists her mouth in thought.

"Just spending time with my love, I guess."

I kiss her cheek.

"Good answer."

"We could talk wedding plans," she says with a mischievous glint in her eye. "Do you think a venue for two hundred guests would be too small?"

I choke.

"Two hundred? Do you even know two hundred living people? I certainly don't. We've done this so many times before. Can't we swing by city hall at lunch instead?"

Minnie puts her hands on her hips, but she can't keep mirth from escaping her in a smile.

"I always expected a large church wedding, white ballgown, tiara, the works. Pretty sure there was a chocolate fountain in there somewhere. Are you going to deny me the poufy white dress that I dreamed about as a little girl?"

I sweep her into my arms and twirl her out of the bathroom in a wild Viennese waltz.

"For you, I would endure a thousand poufy white dresses. If I must."

Minnie finally dissolves into the laughter she was holding back.

"I have no desire for extravagance," she says after her fit of giggling subsides. "My wedding in Italy as Zanetta was enough to last me a dozen lifetimes."

"That was worthy of a queen, wasn't it?" Zanetta was the only daughter of a wealthy merchant who wished to advertise his fortune to the entire city of Venice. It was a celebration of overindulgence as much as of marriage, and when Zanetta and I finally escaped to the nuptial chamber, it was with relief. "I'm glad to hear you don't wish for a repeat."

"City hall and dinner with friends is fine by me," she says. "We've done this dance before. I only want to hear the words of promise from your lips again. They are so sweet, every time."

"No chocolate fountains?"

Minnie leans closer and twists one of my strands around her finger. The intimate sensation ripples through me.

"I'm sure we can arrange something with chocolate."

I grin then check my watch. "As much as I would like to continue this conversation, we should leave soon. I have an idea for this afternoon, though. Would you like to meet the spirit of the Fraser River?"

Minnie's face lights up and she throws her arms around my neck.

"Yes! I would love to meet a water elemental. I have so many questions."

CHAPTER V

I pull into the parking lot next to a stretch of swampy grassland beside the Fraser River and above the Massey Tunnel.

"Don't be too disappointed if the elemental doesn't show," I warn Minnie. "This one was a lot more nervous about breaking rules than the wind elemental Ailu. If it feels like it's being watched, it won't visit us."

Minnie nods her understanding, but her eyes flash with optimism.

"We won't know until we try. Lead the way."

I grasp Minnie's hand and we meander to a stream that intersects an earth cable where I first encountered the river elemental. My feet pause when we near it. Is this really the most effective way to contact the elemental? It's the spirit of the river, so presumably touching strands of the Fraser will make it easier to communicate than through threads of a stream.

We change direction until we are on the muddy bank of the river. I scan the shore until my eyes spot a half-submerged log emerging from reeds, then I tug Minnie toward it. When we are balanced on the rough-barked trunk, I plunge my hands into the water.

"Is this what you did before?" Minnie asks in confusion.

"No, I was in the earth cable when the elemental jumped up from a nearby stream, but I thought it would be easier for it to find us this way."

She nods and waits with tense shoulders. I close my eyes and send out my lauvan and intention to meet.

There is a long moment when I think that no one will answer my call. Then, blue water strands grow into a human figure between my wet hands. Minnie inhales sharply.

"Greetings, earth child," the elemental says in a burbling voice.

"Are you the elemental of the river?" I ask. It's worth making sure that this is the same elemental I spoke with a few weeks ago. The elemental's head-shape nods slowly.

"We spoke before," it says, and I relax. "We are still not being watched closely, so I may visit with you for a time."

"I would like to introduce you to Minnie. She is also a half-elemental, but with an affiliation for water."

"A water child?" The elemental peers in Minnie's direction. "Place your hands in the river, water child. Let me feel you."

Minnie glances at me until I nod, then she slides her hands into the cold water that sloshes against our log. Her navy-blue strands eagerly reach into the river in a dark cloud of flowing threads. The elemental pauses for a long moment, then it nods slowly.

"It is a pleasure to meet you, Minnie," it says. "I haven't experienced a water half-elemental for many, many rebirths."

"You, too," Minnie says, her cheeks flushed with excitement. "I would love to know more about our element. This is all very new to me."

"Firstly," I interrupt. "Can we give you a name if we're having a social visit? It's so much simpler for my human brain."

"As you wish," the elemental says smoothly. Minnie wrinkles her nose in thought.

"What about Shannon?" she says. "It means 'wise river' in old Irish, if I recall."

"Shannon," I repeat reflectively. "That will do. Let's make her female, since she's your element, Minnie."

"Shannon." When the elemental says her new name, she does so in a soft, flowing way that mimics the sound of water over rocks in a brook. "How fascinating it is to commune with humans. Minnie, will you consent to travel upstream with me? I wish to introduce you to my river."

"Oh!" Minnie looks at me, startled. I nod with encouragement.

"Go for it. It will be enlightening. I'll wait here and guard your body."

Minnie swallows but says clearly, "I would like that very much, Shannon, but I don't know what to do."

"Do not resist," Shannon says. "And I will guide you."

With that, Shannon disappears from between my hands and flows toward Minnie's. Slender, navy-blue lauvan streak down Minnie's arms and disappear, leaving only the thicker human strands with her body. Her eyes are closed, and she is unnaturally still. When I poke her arm, there is no response.

"How strange," I whisper to myself. Minnie gives no sign that she can hear me. I shuffle around on the log to get comfortable. Who knows how long she will be?

I'm cramped and sore by the time Minnie finally returns to her body with a rush of lauvan and a gasp, but the wide-eyed delight on her face makes me swallow my complaints.

"That was incredible," she gushes. "I've never done anything like it. It felt so natural, and the sensation—I can't describe it. Is that what traveling through the cables is like for you?"

"I imagine it's an equivalent experience," I say with a smile. "Was Shannon a good guide?"

"She showed me everywhere along the river. I don't know how far we traveled—I need to look at a map, now—but she told me everything about it, and even showed me a few tricks that I would never have guessed to try."

"Could you teach me?" It feels odd to ask for lauvan advice from someone who only discovered her abilities two weeks ago, but let it never be said that I am too proud to learn. The only way to adapt and survive is to learn from others.

"Of course," she says. "All of it. And she said I could come back anytime. If no one on her side is watching, she'll teach me more."

I help Minnie off the log and hug her shoulder with one arm as we pick our way between mud puddles and back to the path. I'm overjoyed, truly, that she has found another mentor on her journey of discovery. A twinge of sadness, almost jealousy, creeps in at the thought that I can't provide everything for her, but I banish the feeling. It's unworthy, and not what is best for Minnie. And, this way, I can learn water skills from a river elemental so that the next time Xenia rears her head, I can surprise her with tricks she doesn't excel at.

Early Thursday morning, I wake with an uneasy feeling in my chest. The apartment is quiet, and Minnie sleeps peacefully beside me. It's so early that the sun hasn't yet lightened the eastern sky.

What woke me? I rub my chest and roll over, intending to drift back to my dreams, but the uneasy feeling persists and won't let me sleep. I sigh loudly in exasperation then hold my breath. Did I wake Minnie? She continues to breathe quietly, and I exhale softly in relief.

Lying here won't help anything. I might as well get up. Perhaps I can do my daily lauvan check for Xenia, get that out of the way before my day starts. I don't expect to find anything—she must have left town, and good riddance—but I need to do my due diligence.

I slip into clothes, including a warm coat against a chill mist that dampens the concrete far below, and ride the elevator to the main floor. Once out the door, floating earth strands swirl around my ankles. They are truly everywhere, and it's so easy to tap into the vast network anywhere I go.

There's no one up at this hour, so I sit on a bench near the door to perform my checks. It's too early in the morning to not be comfortable. I slip into the connection, easy as cutting butter, and spread my conscious in a lazy search of Vancouver. It's not exhilarating now that it's familiar, but it's effortless. Natural, as Minnie said. The cliché "in my element" has never rung so true.

I relax into the sensation and enjoy flowing around the city, past endless lauvan clusters in all the colors of the rainbow. The uneasy feeling that woke me grows stronger the farther south my conscious travels. I pull all the parts of me together to examine my findings.

A huge knot of lauvan pulses at the northern arm of the Fraser River, identifiable by shimmering blue strands that flow past me in a vast swath across the fluid black landscape. The knot contains mostly shades of blue. It throbs with light and movement, and my unease intensifies the longer I look at it. What could it possibly be caused by? I don't recall ever seeing such a thing before.

I memorize the location of the knot then pull back to my body. I shiver, partly from the cool air and partly from the unease the knot awoke in me. What could occur on the physical Earth that would correspond to such a disturbance?

I need to find out.

Minnie groans awake when I gently shake her in the pre-dawn light.

"There's a disturbance in the lauvan," I say by way of a morning greeting. "I need to see it in person."

"Is it Xenia?" Minnie sits up in bed, instantly awake. I shake my head.

"No, but I don't know what it is. I've never seen anything like it."

"I'll come with you. Give me a minute."

By the time I have brewed coffee and poured it into mugs to take with us, Minnie is dressed and by the door. She takes her mug with a murmur of thanks, and we ride the elevator down to the van. Traffic is light at this hour, although a few early commuters have started to emerge from shuttered houses.

"Where are we going, anyway?" Minnie blows on her coffee to cool it down.

"North Arm Fraser River," I reply. "On the Vancouver side, across from Mitchell Island."

"I could see if Shannon knows anything," Minnie says in an eager tone. I nod.

"Good thinking. I'll drop you off close to the water then go investigate."

The road is congested with commuters by the time we pass the Knight Street bridge, but I turn right to escape traffic and enter a tiny neighborhood sandwiched between industrial lots and an overgrown train track. We're close, now, and the van trundles to a stop where the road ends at the river.

"Is it just me, or is the river much higher than usual?" I say. Water laps at a pier, which I'm certain was not intended to be submerged in places. Minnie frowns.

"Seems like it. If there's flooding, it usually happens during the spring melt, not now. It hasn't even been unseasonably rainy this year."

"Call me if Shannon tells you anything interesting," I say

when Minnie opens her door. "I'll be back soon."

Minnie's strands fizzle with her excitement at contacting the river elemental. She waves her understanding and I race a few blocks to the disturbance's location.

Exactly where I expect the disturbance, a police cruiser is parked outside a row of narrow houses that face the river, which is filled with log booms at this junction where the north arm of the Fraser River divides to pass around Mitchell Island. It's a working part of the city, and these houses are old and ill-kept, their paint peeling and roofs mossy. The river, which must normally lap serenely at the end of their yards, now gurgles at their doorsteps.

It's still early, but a commotion out front is enough to wake the neighborhood. Two men shout at each other across a low fence, while a police officer waves a clipboard and attempts to regain control of the situation. She is in her mid-thirties, with her black hair pulled into a tight bun. Her face must be quite pretty when relaxed and happy, but now she only looks resigned and annoyed.

"If you had fixed your pipes when I told you to, my basement wouldn't be floating right now," the man on the left screeches. His distended stomach jiggles in his indignation. "My old record player, ruined!"

"It had nothing to do with me," the rightmost man shouts back, his narrow face red in anger and a large bruise forming on his cheekbone. A frightened-looking woman peeks out from the curtains of his house. "And don't keep your crap in your moldy basement. Can't you see the river rose in the night? Use your eyes, idiot." He turns to the police officer. "Can't you restrain him? He attacked me because he's too dumb to see the river, and he blames me for his damp crap."

"It's more than damp," the other man yells. "The water is knee-deep!"

43

"I need a statement from both of you," the police officer says loudly. "Either do it here, or I'll take you to the station in cuffs to make a statement. We take assault seriously."

"Assault?" The portly man scoffs. "Just because he can't take what he's due."

"You see what I have to put up with?" The red-faced man points a shaking finger at his neighbor. "I'll tell you everything. This man is deranged."

"Deranged?" the other man yelps.

The police officer sighs audibly as the two men shout at each other some more, and she extracts a pair of handcuffs from her belt.

I have watched the drama with interest, but since it looks like it's about to wrap up, I walk toward the end of the row to examine the water's edge and find evidence for the disturbance. I wonder if I should enter the lauvan network again to check its location.

My movement catches the police officer's eye. She frowns and looks me up and down. Presumably she finds nothing of interest, although she studies my face with narrowed eyes before turning back to the shouting men.

Her attention leaves me unsettled, although I don't know why. I shake my head and focus on my own task. What is the disturbance doing to the physical world?

I duck behind a parked car and quickly thrust my hands into the earth lauvan surrounding me. Sure enough, the swirling ball of blue strands is near. In fact, it is in the river, directly behind portly man's house. When my strands draw back to my body, I frown. What is the disturbance doing here? And did it have anything to do with the altercation out front? The lauvan of the disturbance were blue, and the river rose inexplicably overnight. Could they be connected?

My phone rings, and I pick it up quickly.

44

"I can't find Shannon," Minnie says, disappointment and worry lacing her voice. "Do you think something happened to her?"

"I doubt it." I try to comfort Minnie, although I don't have any answers. "Perhaps someone was watching, and she didn't feel safe visiting you. Don't forget, it's against their rules for elementals to visit the physical world. Shannon seemed fairly law-abiding when I spoke with her earlier."

"Yeah, maybe." She sounds appeased. "Anything on your end?"

"Nothing obvious." I pause. "I wonder if the river rose because of the disturbance. There is some flooding here."

"Maybe. The bigger question is, why?"

I'm silent. Why would the river rise due to elemental interference? Who is behind it? I have a sinking feeling I know who, but why is another question.

Friday passes without incident. Mid-morning on Saturday, my phone rings. I frown at the display.

"Who is it?" Minnie asks.

"Anna Green." I answer the phone. "Hello?"

"Hi, Merry?" Anna's voice is tentative. It's bizarre to hear it so. Before her mind-wipe, Anna sounded confident, coy, or determined, never tentative. "It's Anna."

"Yes?" I don't give her more than that. She clearly had a purpose in calling, and I don't need to engage in small talk. I accepted her into the group for Wayne's sake, but that doesn't mean I wish to welcome her with open arms. It's too soon to forget her kidnapping of Minnie.

I can almost hear her deflating at my tone, and I regret my

45

monosyllable answer.

"It's the books you were interested in," she says in a small voice. "I found them. I thought you'd want to know."

"What? March's library?"

My body tenses with anticipation, and Minnie's head tilts in question. This is a coup, indeed, if Anna found the library. Access to those books would be a huge boon to my understanding of the elemental world. If March could learn how to prepare a body for possession by a strong elemental— something that my elemental contacts couldn't even find out— what other treasures lie in wait for the discerning?

"Where?" I say, my eagerness barely masked.

"I can show you, if you like." Anna's voice has regained some of her confidence now that she has my attention.

"Absolutely. Are you free now?"

We arrange a meeting place and I hang up with my nerves jangling. Minnie raises her eyebrows.

"What's up?"

"Anna found the Potestas library. She's going to show me right now."

Minnie nods, but it's with less enthusiasm than I exhibit.

"Good. Maybe Anna will prove useful after all."

"I know you're still not enamored of our new recruit."

"No, and I'm surprised you are, after what she did to us."

"I'm not pleased with the development." I shrug. "But you should have seen the sad puppy look Wayne gave me. It would have taken a sterner man than I to say no."

Anna waits at an intersection in the residential neighborhood where she used to live. I park on the street nearby and stroll toward her. She wears her curly hair down and a quizzical expression on her face.

"I feel like I know this place," she explains when I ask what she's thinking. "More than other spots in the city."

I debate whether to tell her, but the knots trapping her mind are still intact, so I don't see the harm.

"You used to live here." I point to a large white house in the middle of the street. "Right there."

"That's where the library is." She looks at me. "How do you know? Did you ever visit me?"

"Once. It devolved into knife threats and ended with me tying you to the kitchen counter with lauvan while I rescued Alejandro from Potestas." I gaze at the house. "Good times, I'm sure you can imagine."

Anna winces and her purple strands squirm with discomfort. I don't mind. She certainly didn't feel guilty at the time, so it's only fair that she feels a portion of it now.

"How do you know the books are here?" I ask.

"I don't remember much, but I remember March's houses. I have a key to this one. No one seems to be living here, so I let myself in and snooped around for clues."

"Clues to what?"

She shrugs with a jerk.

"Who I am, I guess. It's hard having a chunk of my life gone. Anyway, one of the rooms is stuffed with books. They look like they were stashed there in a hurry, and no one has sorted them out since."

"When Potestas disbanded, I suppose." I stare at the house for a moment in contemplation then wave Anna forward. "Lead the way."

Anna walks unhurriedly down the sidewalk with her bottom shown to full advantage in a tight pair of jeans. I look away with a grin, imagining both Minnie's and Wayne's reactions to my glance. Although Anna may have a more hesitant demeanor, she hasn't lost her confidence in other departments.

We traipse up the front steps, past a wicker swing that shifts in the autumnal breeze, and Anna slots a key into the door. It opens with a click. She glances at me with worry in her eyes.

"What if there's someone here?"

I gently push her to the side and enter the hallway first. Silence cloaks the house, almost as thickly as the dust on the floor. There is a trail of footprints, but when I point them out to Anna, she whispers that they are hers. No lauvan drift through doorways or hang on knobs. The house is deserted.

"No one is here," I say at a normal volume. "Which room has the library?"

"This way." Anna speaks quietly despite my assertion of solitude and points to a room on our right. When I swing open the door, it stops halfway, blocked by something I can't see. I squeeze through the gap and my mouth drops.

It's a small room brimming with books. There might be a window opposite, but the only hint I have is a few chinks of light glinting through piles of texts. Towers of books climb nearly to the ceiling, and there is limited room to walk. Behind the door, preventing it from opening fully, is a spilled pile of books.

"Just a little light reading," I breathe. Anna chuckles.

"It will keep you busy for a while."

My heart sinks when I contemplate the hundreds of hours needed to even make a dent in the knowledge housed here. Normally, I'm not concerned about time, but Xenia's presence in the world makes me nervous that I won't have enough of it before she makes a move. I snap my fingers when a memory hits me.

"There used to be two notebooks written by Potestas members filled with important things they found in these books. A summary of spirits if you will. Have you come across anything like that?"

"The only thing handwritten I found was this." Anna reaches to the top of a desk stacked high with books and slides out a leather-bound notebook from between two piles. "I didn't read much of it, but it says it was March's, so there might be information there."

My greedy fingers rifle through the pages, and it's a moment before my eager eyes comprehend what I'm seeing.

"Is it a diary?" I ask in curiosity.

"More like a logbook, I think." Anna puts a hand on her hip in a pale imitation of her old flair. "She mentions Xenia, so it's a recent thing."

I flip to the last entries and devour the words. There is mention of Xenia's growing power, March's preparation of her own body, and Xenia's refusal to possess it. That entry bleeds resentment and bitterness. An earlier entry catches my eye.

Xenia found my collection of amulets. She took a few of the most powerful ones for herself, of course. I don't know what she plans for them, but those ones were reputed to function as conduits between the world beyond and this one. Of course, their previous owners assumed the world beyond was the land of the dead, but given Xenia's interest in them, I imagine that she sees a different use.

"This is good, Anna." I snap the notebook shut and slide it under my arm. "Thanks for showing me. We should move the books to a safer location soon. This resource is too precious to lose. There's a small chance that Xenia will come back for them, even though she doesn't need more information about the elemental plane."

"Of course," Anna says quickly. "Anytime, just let me know when and where. Hey," she says when I turn to leave, my mind searching for suitable places to stash a roomful of books. "I

49

was curious about Minnie discovering her half-elemental nature. How did you find that out?"

"Another elemental told us," I say with a wry grin. "I hadn't noticed before then. He has keener eyes than me."

"What did he see?"

I gaze at Anna's face. It's open and genuinely curious, but her coils of lauvan are tight and waiting for my answer. She really cares about what I will say next.

"Half-elementals have two sets of lauvan: thicker human strands, and thinner elemental threads. It can be difficult to see the difference unless one looks very closely."

"Can you—" Anna pauses, and her strands squirm. "Can you tell if others are half-elementals just from looking at them?"

It hits me—Anna wants to know if she is one. I try my best not to smile at the absurdity of her question. Only I can see that her strands are purple, not one of the four elemental colors of silver, blue, orange, or brown.

"Sorry, Anna, you're fully human."

Every one of her lauvan droops in despondency, even as she chuckles lightly.

"Oh, I was just curious how it works."

Anna still craves elemental powers, even if she doesn't know what they arc or how they work. I make a mental note to tell Wayne. He's sensible enough to stay on guard for the return of Anna's dark streak, even if he won't like my warning.

A sense of uncase rolls over me, the same feeling that woke me up a few mornings ago. It was a prelude to the disturbance by the river.

"Hold on for a moment," I say to Anna then drop to my knees to grasp the nearest earth lauvan that snake over the floor. "I need to check something. I won't be long."

"What are you going to do?"

Anna's puzzled face is the last thing I see before closing my eyes and sending my strands into the earth network. The pull of this newest disturbance is unmistakable and draws me east. Not far from where we stand, a bright ball of orange lauvan sparks and fizzes in the darkness. The sight fills me with foreboding, and I quickly pull back to my body.

"I have to go," I say. "There's something strange with the lauvan that I need to check out."

"Do you want help?" Anna asks. "I can come, if you like."

I hesitate then nod. It can't hurt to have backup or an extra set of eyes. I don't know what I'm approaching, so a different viewpoint might be invaluable.

"Sounds good. Let's go."

Anna traveled to March's house by bus, so I gesture her into my van, and we drive eastward. The blare of sirens soon alerts us to the disturbance. I park as close as I can to the tumult, and we run forward to see better.

A residential house is on fire. It's not a tiny blaze, but a conflagration that reaches skyward. Wind buffets the flames and spurs them to higher heights. Sirens wail and firefighters shout instructions to each other. Policer officers push gawking spectators out of danger.

"Is it normal for you to feel big events like this in the lauvan?" Anna asks. I shake my head.

"No, it's not. Something else is happening here, and I don't know what it is." I hail a nearby spectator, an elderly man in a winter coat that he might have been large enough to fill in his prime. "Excuse me, do you know how the fire started?"

"Tea towel caught fire on the stove," the man says in a hoarse voice. "That's what I heard. Nothing too big. Everyone got out, called the fire department in good time. No one expected it to take over like this. Must be a perfect storm. You'd think the house was made of straw, the way it lit up."

The faces of the firefighters, those that don't look grimly

51

determined, are baffled and wary. Something about this fire doesn't add up to them, either.

"Merry," Anna hisses. Her fingernails dig into my arm even through my coat. "I see someone I recognize." Confusion passes over her face. "I think. I don't know, now."

"Who was it?" I follow her finger toward a man lurking in the back of the crowd. He is unremarkable in every way except for three things: his expression of satisfaction, his familiarity, and the orange lauvan that writhe between his green strands.

It's an elemental possessing a human body. I recognize the person as a former member of Potestas. It's worrisome that Anna can remember him, even if only vaguely, but it's not as concerning as the possession.

"Damn it," I mutter and pull Anna toward the possessed man. "Another elemental got through, just like Xenia. Come on, I need to catch him."

I break into a jog with Anna at my heels. The crowd shifts, and when a sightline emerges, the man is gone. I pull up short and scan the crowd, but no one's strands match the green and orange combination of the man I hunt.

"He's gone," I say in disbelief.

"Why is that police officer staring at you?" Anna says to me. "She's kind of intense."

I whip my head around to look in the direction of Anna's gaze. Engaged in crowd control is the female police officer from the riverside assault feud. She gazes at me with a pointed appraisal, as if she is trying to figure out how she knows me. It's not a friendly stare.

"Come on," I say. "Let's get out of here. I missed my opportunity to catch the elemental bastard, more's the pity, but at least we have evidence."

"Evidence for what?" Anna half-jogs beside me, her face worried. Mine is set in grim lines.

52

"Evidence that Xenia is recruiting followers."

CHAPTER VI

Once in the van, I text everyone to come to Alejandro's. This is too important to say over the phone.

Emergency round table meeting. Come to Alejandro and Liam's place right away.

"Round table?" Anna tries and fails to hide her grin. "Really?"

"Alejandro's new table is round, is it not?"

I pull into traffic and race toward Alejandro's. It's not far, and when I stride around the side of his house with Anna at my heels, Liam opens the door with a look of concern.

"What happened? Is it Minnie?"

"Nothing that dire." I enter the suite, where Alejandro paces around the table. Wayne looks up from his drumming fingers.

"What the hell, Merry? Did someone die?"

"Possibly," I say. Anna looks at me in puzzlement.

There's a knock at the door, then Jen and Cecil enter. I check my phone.

"Minnie can't make it for a while yet," I say. "So, it looks like we're all here. Anna and I saw another possession."

Jen gasps and Cecil pales. Alejandro grips the nearest chair with whitened knuckles. Liam sits heavily onto another, and Wayne sighs before his eyes narrow.

"Where? What were you doing?"

Belatedly, I realize how the situation might look to Wayne given our history, and I hasten to clarify.

"Anna was showing me March's library, all the Potestas spirit books, and I felt a disturbance in the lauvan. We rushed to the location, and there was an uncontrolled house fire raging. The fire fighters were flummoxed by how fast it had spread. Then we saw a former Potestas member."

54

"I think I recognized him, but I wasn't sure," Anna says. She taps her forehead. "Buried memory, maybe."

"He had fire strands among his human ones. What's more, this isn't the first disturbance I've seen. There was a similar one a few days ago at the river." I exhale and take a seat. The rest follow my example. "The only explanation that makes sense is that Xenia is recruiting."

"Damn." Wayne leans back, his suspicion over my meeting with Anna dampened by the unwelcome news. Jen and Cecil glance at each other with identical expressions of worry.

"Now what?" says Liam. I shake my head in question.

"That's why I called you here. Between the seven of us, I hope we can create a course of action."

We sit in silence for a long moment. Wayne drums his fingers again.

"At least we can look for the possessed man," he says finally. "If he used to be a Potestas member, we still have the list. We're pretty good at finding them, these days."

"You recognized him?" Jen asks me.

"He was at the cave."

"That must mean that he remembers it?" Liam says with worry. "Why would he accept an elemental possession otherwise?"

"Xenia must have fixed my memory manipulation." My heart sinks. Anna frowns but says nothing. Belatedly, I recall her belief that she lost her memory from a blow to the head. Let her think what she will. "The people in the cave were all willing, eager even, to become hosts to elemental parasites. Xenia, using March's memory, must have recognized the simplicity of using those bodies. For her, it would be a trivial matter to restore their memories and convince them to join her. And, since March figured out how to prepare bodies for possession, nothing is stopping Xenia from bringing her

55

strongest followers to Earth."

Wayne pales.

"Does that mean she'll come after Anna?"

We all turn to look at Anna, whose lips tighten. Her strands writhe with discomfort.

"Xenia, this ruling elemental in my former friend's body, might come to my door and offer me powers in exchange for my memories back." She gazes at Wayne. "You're worried I'll say yes, aren't you?"

"No," Wayne says quickly, but his strands say otherwise. Anna clearly doesn't buy his hasty answer.

"I was given a second chance." She crosses her arms. "I'm not going to waste it. I won't lie, having a part of my life completely blank isn't all roses, but I like being in control of my body. I'm not interested in giving it up to a weird spirit."

Wayne looks both mollified and apologetic. He reaches under the table to squeeze Anna's knee. She doesn't respond, and he leans back with a guilty expression.

"Merry, why don't you look in the lauvan for Xenia's new minions?" Alejandro says to break the awkward silence.

"Minions?" I'm amused despite the situation. The side of Alejandro's mouth quirks up.

"It's a new word I learned. It works, though, doesn't it?"

"Perfectly."

"Good. Then find the minions. They're not as powerful as Xenia, right? And, besides, I have that protection spell we found weeks ago that stops them from possessing us. Tell me what type they are and where to go, and I'll hunt them down. They need to be stopped."

There's a recklessness to his words and strands that I don't like. I glance at the gold and green threads that connect him to Jen, and the green ones show signs of fraying. Alejandro feels hopeless about the situation with Jen. I fear those feelings will manifest in a show of careless behavior to his own safety.

"Even with the protection spell, they are still elementals. They have abilities that can overwhelm you, even if they can't possess you."

"We'll go together." Liam says to me. He must have caught the underlying message in my words. I wonder whether Alejandro has confided in Liam. Whatever the case, I'm glad Liam is looking out for Alejandro, because it doesn't appear that Alejandro will prioritize his own safety.

Cecil glances at Jen with concern, and his strands curl protectively around her. He doesn't want to see her chase after elementals. Jen's face is determined, but I'm not worried about her. Between Cecil and her own common sense, she will stay safe.

"Good," I say. "It's a great idea, Alejandro. I will search in the lauvan for the new recruits—minions if you will—and we can hunt them down. We need to decide how to stop them from coming to our world in the first place, but reducing their numbers will be a start."

"What will you do with them?" Anna asks. "The people, I mean. Can you get the elementals out without hurting the people, or will they die?"

Her eyes are big with her concern. How much does she remember of the possessed people? Or, does she realize she was so close to becoming one of them that their fate is a frightening echo of what hers could have been?

"I don't know what will happen to them," I say honestly. "I'm still not certain how to force the elementals back to their world. I'll have to ask my elemental contact. I expect he can help us from his end. The best we can do for now is to capture them and keep them away from Xenia while we figure it out." I stand. "I'll do some searching now."

Anna nods with relief, then she stands with me.

57

"I forgot my phone in your van." To Wayne, she says, "I'll be right back."

Jen and Cecil speak quietly together, and Alejandro walks to the kitchen sink for a glass of water. Only Liam stays in his seat, his eyes boring a hole in the center of the table, and his forehead creased. I suspended the grail underneath the round table a few days ago. Does the question of touching it weigh on Liam?

His existential crisis will have to wait until after I check the lauvan network for Xenia's followers. I move toward the back door, where the small yard beckons with its ample earth strands, but Wayne stops me before I step outside.

"Do you think Anna's remembering more?" he says quietly.

"Perhaps. Not much, though. That Potestas member that we saw, she truly had no idea who he was. It was a momentary flash of recognition. I assume she used to know him well, as an involved Potestas member."

Wayne stares at me. His strands wriggle with indecision.

"Do you think I'm crazy, bringing her into this? Dating her, knowing what she used to be?"

I let out a long sigh as I consider what to say.

"It's a risk, but you knew that. It's possible that she will remember everything at some point. She might even be enticed back into the elemental world and convinced to become a host to an elemental, and you will lose her."

An unwelcome thought emerges. What if she remembers, but doesn't tell us she does, so that she undermines our resistance by being a mole for Xenia? This seems unlikely, but I resolve to watch her lauvan carefully for future duplicity. Anna is adept at it, after all.

Wayne waits for more with a raised brow.

"But," I continue. "I think the chances of that are low. Despite the introduction to her past, and plenty of talk about

Potestas and her former world, she doesn't seem any closer to regaining her present-life memories. I will keep watch for changes if it would make you feel better."

"It would." Wayne dithers for a moment. "What also worries me is that she will want her memories back, that she will think she can handle them, and then she'll turn into a different person." He shakes his head as if to dislodge his intrusive thoughts. "Don't mind me. Don't borrow problems from tomorrow, right? Live for today."

"Today is all we have." I pat his shoulder once. "Enjoy it."

I take a deep breath of fresh air once outside. The grass is damp from a recent rain, and by the look of heavy clouds overhead, more is on the way. I choose a central spot on the weedy lawn and sink to my knees with a wince of annoyance at inevitable wet patches on my pants. My fingers spread into the dense threads that hover a handspan above the ground. My eyes close, and I sink easily into the network of lauvan that surrounds me.

My heartrate slows at the sensation, then it disappears as I leave my body fully. My conscious flies through the strands, instantly dispersing into dozens of separate parts to search Vancouver quickly and efficiently. I'm alert to every lauvan cluster that is blue or orange, given that water and fire are the two elemental disturbances that I'm aware of.

I don't know how much time passes, but I estimate that my search through the Greater Vancouver area is half-complete when there is a tremendous tug on my conscious. It pulls my disparate parts back to my body with impossible speed. I open my eyes with a gasp, and magnified blades of grass greet my vision.

"Why am I lying on the ground?" I mutter. Cecil's horrified face appears in my field of view.

"I'm so sorry, Merry," he says. "We were sparring, and I lost my balance."

He holds out his hand and I regain my feet. My clothes are wet on one side and liberally streaked with mud and grass stains. I hear a titter from the house and turn. Minnie and Jen sit on the steps to watch the others swing their wooden swords around.

"Are you all right, love?" Minnie calls out. She must have arrived while I was in the lauvan network. I wave her off.

"I didn't realize I'd set up shop in a battlefield." I walk to the fence and kneel once more. "Try to avoid fighting over here, will you?"

"Of course," Cecil says with apology in his voice.

"Ready?" Wayne calls out to him. Cecil raises his sword and meets Wayne's swing with a powerful block of his own. Alejandro leans against the house, his expression disgruntled as he watches Cecil. His strands are rough and point menacingly toward his rival. Beside him, Liam still looks preoccupied about his grail decision.

I shake my head and close my eyes. I don't have time to placate Alejandro about his love life nor counsel Liam on his past lives. I have minions to find.

I descend into the network once more and spread myself thin to find the elementals. It isn't long before I am successful. Intertwined with recognizable green lauvan are flickering fire-orange threads. I memorize the location then pull back to my body.

"Got one," I shout as soon as I have control over my throat. I spring to my feet. "The same one Anna and I saw. It's on the corner of Alma and Sixteenth, moving east slowly, probably on foot."

"I'll go." Alejandro jerks upright.

"I will, too," I say, then an uneasy feeling overwhelms me, and I clutch my stomach with the sensation. Minnie stands up, her face pale.

"What's wrong?" she says.

"Something else is out there. Perhaps another disturbance. I need to check it out." I glance at Liam, who nods.

"I'll go with Alejandro," he says. I point to the door.

"Show Anna the pictures you have of Potestas members from the cave ceremony so she can identify the correct one. And be careful. He's dangerous. If you can follow him, find out where he frequents, that might be the safest course of action."

"But not one that will solve any problems," says Alejandro. "Leave him to us, Merry."

He disappears into the house. Liam throws me a shrug of uncertainty and follows him. I sigh and close my eyes once I sink to my knees. I hope Liam can temper Alejandro's reckless streak before it lands him in trouble. I would do it myself, but another disturbance means another elemental possession. Our best bet is to capture as many as we can, and if I can get this one as it crosses over, perhaps I can have the advantage for once.

CHAPTER VII

It doesn't take long to pinpoint the disturbance. Uneasiness emanating from a swirling cloud of silver threads draws me inexorably. It's small but rapidly growing. I identify the location and pull back to my body.

"I have it," I say to the others and leap to my feet. Anna has emerged from the house by now, and she looks at me with anxious eyes. "It's near forty-first and Granville. The elemental might not even have crossed over yet, because the disturbance is still growing. I'm not sure how this works."

"I can come," Anna says quickly. "I just looked at the pictures of the Potestas members, and I can help identify."

"Are you sure?" Wayne frowns. "It's dangerous."

"And it's partly my fault it's happening," she shoots back. "I'm not going to sit on my ass and let everyone else clean up my mistakes."

Wayne glances at me in mute appeal, but she has a point.

"I'll keep her out of trouble," I say to appease him. "I'm concerned about Alejandro, though. Could you follow him and Liam and make sure they don't bite off more than they can chew?"

Wayne looks at Anna with indecision but then nods.

"I can do that."

"What can I do, Merry?" Jen asks. Cecil's face darkens.

"It looks like they have it covered, Jen. Call us if you need us?" he asks me. His strands flow outward and form a barrier between Jen and the others. Knowing Jen, she won't appreciate an overprotective boyfriend, but this isn't the time to address it. We have an elemental to catch.

"Will do. Come on, everyone. Let's ambush the enemy."

It's a quiet trip to the location of the air disturbance. I drive as quickly as I can through traffic-clogged streets, cursing my van. Why didn't I go first as a bird, and Minnie and Anna could have followed in the vehicle? The silence in the van reminds me that I probably shouldn't leave Minnie and Anna alone. Minnie's lauvan are in a spiky configuration aimed at Anna.

I'll be frustrated if we miss this elemental, though. I press my foot to the accelerator and pass a slow-moving jeep before the oncoming cars race by me. Minnie clenches her hands over her knees but doesn't say anything.

When I see a parking spot a block away from our destination, I yank the wheel over and pull into it. This is close enough. We will be faster on foot.

I run in the direction of the disturbance. When I turn the corner around an apartment block, my feet skid to a stop.

The road is littered with asphalt shingles. They flap in strong gusts that swirl along the street, despite the calmness of the rest of the city. A police car, lights flashing red and blue, is parked in front of a freshly painted house with a manicured front yard. It has only half the shingles it should.

"What the hell happened?" Minnie breathes beside me.

"Air disturbance. Quick, Anna, look for Potestas members."

There are several onlookers marveling at the spectacle of a localized windstorm strong enough to rip apart a roof. I scan the gathering. I have only a passing recollection of Potestas members from the cave, but my memory is usually accurate. It doesn't matter, though, since I'm looking for lauvan.

"There," Anna hisses. "That woman with the blond hair and red shirt. Straight ahead."

She's about thirty, with a trim body and long, straight hair.

She gazes at the house with a curved smile and runs her hands over her hips as if testing out her new body. Sure enough, her petal pink strands are interspersed with fine silver threads.

"I'm going in," I mutter. Before the others can say anything, I stride forward with intent. She's close, and it's time I get a handle on these elementals. Hopefully, this one will give me some much-needed answers, so that I can stop these disturbances from happening again.

"Hey!" A shout jolts me from my single-minded purpose. I glance around in confusion. Was someone hailing me?

The police officer from the last two disturbances walks quickly toward me. Her face is set with determination, and she waves at me. When she's close enough, she speaks.

"I'm Officer Lee. I have some questions for you."

I don't have time for this. I look back at the elemental woman, but she is walking away. She pauses long enough to look at me and wink.

"I'm in a rush," I say desperately. The woman is getting away, and she knows it. "I can come right back."

"I'll need you to answer the questions now," she says doggedly, but her eyes flash with annoyance.

I glance at the elemental once more, but she has vanished. My shoulders slump. Damn it. I was so close. What could the officer possibly want to talk to me about?

"Yes?" I say with ill-disguised impatience.

"I've noticed you lately," she says. "It's Merry Lytton, isn't it? You have a knack for turning up at scenes of interest."

"How do you know my name?" Curiosity wars with fear. Why does she have me in her sights? I live a blameless life, as far as anyone in this city is aware. I did manipulate a few minds to their breaking point, but nothing that can be traced. I haven't killed anyone for decades, so I really ought to be commended.

The officer doesn't answer my question right away.

"I'm asking the questions. Why are you here today?"

It's fortunate that I have centuries of practice at deception.

"McNeill's makes the best doughnuts in town," I say. "Have you tried them? If I don't get my fix at least once a week, I get very grumpy."

Officer Lee's eyes narrow.

"What was your reason for being at the waterfront at seven thirty Thursday morning?" she fires back. I pretend to think.

"Oh, the shouting match, when the river was flooding? Strange business, that. I was waiting for my fiancée. She's a psychologist, sometimes does house calls."

"What was the address of the person she visited?"

"Doctor-patient confidentiality, officer," I say with a hint of reproof. "I can't divulge that without a warrant."

Officer Lee's lips tighten.

"And the house fire on Saturday?"

"I heard the sirens. I must admit, I never lost my fascination for fire trucks from my boyhood. I was driving by and couldn't resist a quick peek."

I can tell that Officer Lee wants to heave a huge sigh of frustration, but she refrains with admirable composure.

"Last question. What were your movements on September twenty-ninth?"

I'm genuinely flummoxed.

"You'll have to remind me—was it a Tuesday?"

"A Friday," she says through gritted teeth. I glance up and tap my foot in thought, then it comes to me.

"Ah, that was the day I went to the museum in the morning. There was a fascinating traveling exhibit on Dark Ages Britain. You really should visit, it's spectacular. Is it still there? I'm not certain. In the afternoon, I was at work."

Officer Lee's eyes light up.

"You were at the museum that morning. Do you recall any

65

unusual activity that day?"

"You mean, apart from the priceless sword going missing, and alarms ringing throughout the building?" I raise my eyebrow. "Nothing beyond that."

"I'll need you to come down to the station for questioning about that incident," she says with almost-concealed glee. She thinks she got to me. She knows there is some connection—her lauvan tell me that she doesn't buy my innocent act—but she can't understand the links. How could she? I'm certain there's no module for elemental powers in police training. She doesn't even know what questions to ask, beyond ascertaining motives for my presence.

I pull out my calling card and hand it to her. No point in being uncooperative if I want to maintain my innocent façade.

"Please, call me for a meeting anytime. I'm happy to help." I wait for a beat. "Is that all?"

"Yes." She sighs and turns to the mangled house. The wind is dying down now, but the mess of shingles remains. "Thank you for your time."

I pity her—her frustration is palpable—but I'm more concerned for myself. I don't want to leave town to avoid confrontation with the law. What's more, the elemental woman got away. I hope Alejandro and Liam had better luck.

"What did she want?" Minnie asks after she and Anna join me. I run a hand through my hair.

"I keep popping up at disturbances, and she noticed. She's trying to connect the dots, but she's missing a vital piece."

"Hard to explain without elementals," Anna says with a nod.

My phone pings, and I pull it out. It's a text from Alejandro. *We lost the elemental.*

My heart sinks. We were so close to catching two, and now we have none. I will have to go into the lauvan network once more and hunt them down. At least we have that option.

"Find me somewhere quiet, and I'll search for the elementals," I say. "I refuse to go home empty-handed today."

We stride away from the scene of destruction. Minnie points westward.

"There's a park over here. Plenty of lauvan and benches."

"Can you see them too?" Anna asks Minnie. She nods brusquely in reply. Anna pauses for a moment before asking, "Can I come with you both, the next time you do a lesson with the other half-elemental you met? I would love to take notes. It might really help us dealing with elementals, if I can see what they are capable of. It's all theoretical to me right now."

"Sure," I say, my mind already planning my search for the blond elemental woman. When Minnie's glare bores into my head, I draw my attention back to my companions. I shrug at Minnie. "It's not a bad idea. Knowledge is power."

"That's what I'm afraid of," Minnie mutters.

At the park, I drop onto the center of a waiting bench and close my eyes. A soccer game is in full swing, but I ignore the shouting and cheers. Minnie and Anna sit on either side of me, and I'm grateful for their watchful eyes while I descend into the strands.

My conscious scouts around the neighborhood, but no pink and silver strands cross my path. Perhaps she drove away. I expand my search, but there is still no sign of her unique cluster. Where could she have disappeared to? I look for any double strand cluster, including the green and orange one that Alejandro and the others chased after, but there is nothing.

I check and double check, but the city is devoid of elementals possessing humans. My strands flow back to my body, and I open my eyes with a gasp of air.

"Nothing," I say. "Not a damn sign of any of them."

"She can't have gone far." Minnie looks around as if she will spot the elemental woman from our bench. I shake my head.

"There is no signature of them anywhere in the lauvan network. My guess is that Xenia taught them how to mask their signal just like she does. That's why I haven't found her in my nightly searches."

"She can do that?" Anna says in wonder.

I sigh in irritation.

"Apparently, but I have no idea how."

Minnie and I have separate plans this evening, but before she leaves for drinks with friends, there is a knock at the door.

"There's Gary," I murmur to her. "You almost made it out unscathed."

Minnie laughs.

"Gary's a sweetheart," she says. "Although he does like to talk."

I open the door. My elderly neighbor Gary Watson beams at me, ready for our game of chess. We have played sporadically for years, and I value him highly. He even joined us in freeing Minnie from Potestas at the infamous cave ceremony, and he knows about my abilities, if not my past.

I'm sure he would love to be involved more, but he's on the other side of seventy. He deserves a quieter friendship than I can offer.

"I hope your brain is sharp tonight." Gary taps his temple with a sage nod. "I got moves fresh in my mind from the book Mrs. Watson bought me. They're doozies, all right." He notices Minnie behind me and smiles even wider. "Minnie. How are you, my dear?"

"Wonderful, thanks, Gary." She wiggles her left hand in front of him, the sapphires on her ring winking in the hall light.

"We got engaged since I last saw you."

Gary guffaws with real delight and slaps my shoulder.

"You're making an honest woman out of her. Good on ya."

I shrug.

"One can only endure constant hints for so long."

Minnie smacks my shoulder playfully as she and Gary switch places.

"Have fun, you two," she says as she walks down the hall. "Put him through his paces, Gary."

"Yes, ma'am," he calls out. As I shut the door, he rubs his hands with glee. "I got some whoppers for you, Merry. Moves you never seen before. Wait." He scowls at me, the expression mitigated by a glint of amusement in his eyes. "You're not going to pull any funny business during our game, are you? Is that how you always win?"

"Gary, my friend." I drape my arm over his shoulders and steer him to the table. "My genius at chess has no need of aid. No excuses for you, old man. You'll have to bring everything you have to beat me."

"Such a cocky whippersnapper." Gary chuckles and shrugs off his cardigan in preparation for playing. "Put your money where your mouth is."

We set up the board and start to play. Gary moves his white pieces with careful deliberation which contrasts sharply with his stream of words. Gary is a talker, but tonight I'm happy to let his words wash over me, since my mind is preoccupied with the elementals. Gary almost captures vital pieces a few times, and he crows over it.

"Did you see that, youngster? I almost had your queen. It was the rook and bishop working together that did it, and with that pawn blocking you, too. Lone wolves are overrated."

Gary finally departs—he lost, but as usual is happy anyway—but his words about working together echo in my mind until I drift to sleep.

CHAPTER VIII

Dreaming

No one is seated yet, and the din of argument makes my head pound. Tensions are high this spring from endless rains and a dispiriting campaign season last year. The lords and warriors attending this meeting of Arthur's are frightened and angry, which results in squabbles over trifling insults to mask the real issues.

Arthur attempts to reason with Erec, a local lord who points toward a seat at a table closest to the fire, where the highest-ranking nobles usually sit with their host.

"You're placing Madoc over me?" he says, his already high-pitched voice rising with an unseemly shrillness. "What has he done for Gwent that I haven't done five times over? Who supplied warriors for the riverside skirmish at midsummer? It certainly wasn't Madoc."

"It's only for supper," Arthur says firmly. "You are an esteemed warrior, and we are glad to have you and your men on our side. Please, sit and enjoy the meal. Placement doesn't matter."

"If it doesn't matter, then why doesn't Madoc sit at a lower table?" Erec demands. Arthur sighs with growing impatience. When Erec turns to his neighbor for validation, Arthur slides toward me and turns his back on Erec.

"I swear," he says to me in a low voice. "They care more about their status in this hall than anything else. Why won't they focus on the critical issues? Don't they realize that Angles are arriving on the southern shores, in addition to the Saxons that will surely come? And, now that Morgan has removed her support, we need as much unity as we can scrape together." He rubs his forehead in frustration.

"They focus on what they can control, instead of the looming dragons they don't know how to," I say. "But we won't get anything done until they stop squabbling like infants."

Arthur stares at the group, where multiple seating arguments are evident. He taps his foot with a frown on his face, clearly thinking.

"That's it," he says at last. "If they all want prominence, I'll give it to them all."

Before I can ask what he means, he strides to the nearest trestle table. They are lined up in rows in the great hall with benches on either side. Each one is long and heavy, but Arthur pushes the nearest at an angle to the others with an energy born of his frustration. He muscles the next table into configuration, and the hall silences at the sound of screeching wood against flagstones.

Gareth comes up beside me.

"What is he doing?" he asks in a conversational tone. I shrug.

"No idea." A thought dawns on me when Arthur pushes another table into place, his face gleaming with perspiration. "Wait, he's putting the tables into the shape of a circle."

Gareth grins in understanding.

"No high table. That's Arthur for you." He chuckles. "I never would have thought of it. I would have plied the malcontents with more ale and asked them a riddle to distract them instead. That's why Arthur is our leader."

He walks forward to help Arthur with his furniture rearrangement, and I follow. We place benches around the perimeter of the tables, and I gesture for servants to bring candles. We leave a small gap in the circle for servants to enter the inner part. When it is complete, Arthur stands on a bench and addresses the quiet crowd.

"No one is higher or lower than anyone else at my table. We are all Gwentish, and we are all equal in the face of our common enemy. I invite you to set aside your grievances against each other and place your anger where it belongs: on the heads of invaders who would kill us for our land. Sit, eat, and remember who is friend and who is foe."

Gareth leads us in a shout, and everyone in the hall follows with enthusiasm. Arthur's words must have struck a chord, as they often do, for the warriors milling around the room find places at the newly created round table with gusto. When Arthur looks at me, I nod my approval. He smiles and invites me with a wave to sit at his right hand. I suppose there is still one exalted place at this table of equals.

CHAPTER IX

Now that I can't track elemental possessions via the network of earth lauvan, I'm at a loss of how to move forward. I spend Saturday night pacing the apartment, with Minnie alternately joining me and trying to calm me down. A text from Todd early Sunday morning distracts me from my sleepless thoughts.

Still up for our lesson today?

Minnie still sleeps beside me, but I know she has no plans for today. I'm of half a mind to say no—I should be focusing on scanning the network for disturbances—but with elementals on the loose, I want Minnie to have as much control over her powers as possible for her own protection. I reply.

Ten o'clock at the beach.

I hesitate, then text Anna as well. I did say she could join us. Even though Minnie gave me a death-glare yesterday, it's still a good idea for Anna to learn more. Perhaps she can see weaknesses that I cannot fathom from my half-elemental perspective.

Anna waits for us when Minnie and I roll into a parking spot in the van.

"Good morning," she says. "Looks like rain. I hope you brought your raincoats."

Minnie nods curtly, pulls her hood over her head, and stands at the railing to look through the trees. I try to be more gracious.

"Good morning, Anna. Did you sleep well after our tumultuous day yesterday?"

"I had some memory dreams," she said. I look at her with interest.

"What were they?"

"I was in a large room," she says in a wandering voice. "Standing on a stool? I was trying to hang something, greenery, maybe. You were there, too."

"Ah," I say. Perhaps I don't need to rehash my relationship with Vivienne in front of Minnie. We have no secrets, but that doesn't mean I need to flaunt my past dalliances in her face. "Interesting. What else?"

"I dreamed I was pregnant." Anna puts her hands out to indicate a belly. "Really huge. I was sitting in front of a fire, talking with Morgan. I don't remember what about, now, but it was a peaceful dream." She shakes her head and smiles ruefully. "I thought the memories would come back faster than this."

"It's different for everyone. Alejandro likes to talk a lot about his memories so he can trigger more. Wayne practices sword fighting for the same reason. You'll find your groove."

Anna throws me a coy grin.

"I always do."

It's such a Vivienne-like sentiment that I am taken aback before smiling in reply. She might not be receiving memories rapidly, but her past selves are inside her, nonetheless.

Todd's dented pickup truck roars into view and coughs to a stop beside my silent van. Todd unfolds himself from the driver's side and lopes toward us.

"Hi," he says then looks at Anna with misgiving. I reassure him.

"This is Anna, a friend of ours," I say. Minnie's raincoat shifts audibly. "She knows about the lauvan. There are more elementals possessing people, like Xenia did, and she wants to take notes on our tactics to learn how to gain an advantage over the elementals."

"Okay," Todd says. He sounds mollified, but still looks slightly suspicious of Anna.

75

We traipse down the stairs to the beach which is deserted from the cold breeze off the ocean. I wonder if my air elemental acquaintance Ailu is present, but I resist the urge to check. I will speak with him later. I need to find out what he will do from his side to prevent more elementals from crossing over. Perhaps he can alert the fundamentals since the disturbances are caused by one of their own. We're at a loss to prevent disturbances on our side. I look forward to Ailu clearing up this mess.

We start with warm-up exercises—Minnie and Todd perform feats with each element to remind themselves of how the elements differ—then we practice each element in turn. Both have improved drastically since their first lessons, and I learn as much as they do when we feature their elements.

Minnie wades into the surf and plucks out a thick rope of water strands. It glistens with blues of every hue and undulates gently in her arms.

"Told you water cables exist," she says to me with a smile. I bow.

"I stand corrected. What can you do with it?"

In reply, she closes her eyes and grows still. My heart beats fast—I don't like her standing in the crashing waves, so vulnerable—but after a minute, she reopens them.

"Just surfing the waves." She grins. "What a rush."

Minnie lowers the cable gently to the water's surface and wades back to the beach. It's a matter of moments for her to strip the water strands off her legs until her clothes are dry once more.

"How do you find the water cables?" Todd asks. Minnie scrunches her nose in thought.

"They run along the currents, mainly," she says. "I don't know, I can feel them, I guess. The network of water lauvan touches my strands and I can sense where they are, if they're close."

"I get it," Todd says eagerly. "I can feel the air cables, especially if I close my eyes."

Anna sits on a nearby log and scribbles furiously in a notebook. Wisps of her hair are tucked behind her ear.

"Minnie," she says with a distracted air. "How did you first start to sense the lauvan? I know this is new to you."

"It came upon me in flashes. At first, it was only flickers at the edge of my vision, then the flickers grew and grew. It was terribly distracting. Then, Merry took away the strands over my eyes that had stopped me from seeing everything." She smiles at me. "Now, I can interact with them fully."

"Could you feel the water cables before that, do you think?" Anna taps her pen against the notebook. "Any strange feelings or awareness?"

"I don't know. I've always been drawn to the water, which must be related. Maybe I was feeling the pull of water cables without realizing what was happening."

"What's all this in aid of?" I ask Anna. I applaud learning in any form, but her thoughts clearly have a direction.

"I'm interested in how Minnie came to be like she is." Anna bends over her notebook. "That's all. It could be useful later, you never know." She looks up, as if pulling herself out of her thoughts. "The possessed people are feeling similar things, I assume."

I nod and turn to the others. It's true that any information we glean that might help us in our fight is useful, but Anna's inquiries feel more pointed than she lets on. She's thinking more deeply about this than I expected. I always had the impression that March was the brains of Potestas, and Anna was simply a high-ranking cult member. Now, I wonder how involved Anna really was in her Potestas days.

I let the matter slide from my mind as I focus on the lesson.

"All right, Todd, let's harness some wind."

"Finally." Todd rubs his hands together in anticipation then raises them to grasp air threads more easily. The breeze picks up, slowly at first then increasing rapidly at a steady rate. Todd's face is tight with concentration. Minnie's hood flaps, and Anna closes her notebook in haste to avoid pages tearing from it.

Moments later, I can scarcely breathe from the wind whipping past my face. My eyes water uncontrollably. Trees above us creak and groan at the force battering them.

This is awe-inspiring, no doubt, but frightening as well. Does Todd know when to stop? Does he have control over it? I heave my foot forward to get close enough to stop Todd, but a blurry Minnie reaches him first. She raises her hand and pushes his shoulder roughly.

Todd lowers his hands and the wind instantly calms from a hurricane to a gentle breeze. He glares at Minnie.

"What the hell?" he says. "What was that for?"

"Someone had to stop you before you destroyed the forest." Minnie's face is hard with anger and disgust. "Did you even think about the ramifications of all that wind? What you might have destroyed?"

"I had it under control." Todd looks at me mulishly for support.

"It was intense, Todd, but you seemed to know what you were doing," I say to placate them both. "Perhaps tone it down next time. It's important to think of the consequences of our actions since we have far greater reach than most."

"That's it?" Minnie stares at me incredulously. "A rap on the knuckles? Don't you think that was beyond excessive?"

"We're learning here. That's why we're on a deserted beach. Things might get out of control, but if we don't test our limits, we won't know what they are."

"Whatever." Minnie throws up her hands. "I'm out for today. You and your protégé can finish up together."

I stare after Minnie as she stomps toward the staircase. What is going on with her lately? This isn't like her at all.

Perhaps I'm expecting my lovers of the past, and not accounting for the present Minnie. I still don't know where the line is drawn.

When I turn back to Todd and Anna, they look like they're walking on eggshells. I ignore Minnie's exit and continue our lesson.

Minnie waits for me in the passenger's seat of the van. I slide in the driver's side but don't start the vehicle.

"What was all that about?" I say quietly. "I know Todd went too far, but it felt like an overreaction on your part. Is there something bothering you? Talk to me."

Minnie shrugs. Her strands are bunched in clumps of self-consciousness.

"He was being a tool," she says. "But, yeah, maybe I went overboard."

"Is there something more going on?" I probe. "Something with work, friends? Me?"

"No," she says slowly. Her strands don't react to my suggestions, but there is something bothering her that she's not confiding in me. I hope she does soon. She reaches out and strokes my hand. "Not you."

I give her a reassuring smile.

"Good. Although that's the only thing I have complete control over fixing."

She laughs lightly.

"I don't think you've changed much in centuries. I can't imagine you'd do it now." She sighs. "My moods have been a bit off lately. I don't know. Maybe my hormones are out of whack. I could go to the doctor, I suppose."

I scan her body carefully.

"Everything looks in order, but it can't hurt to get a second opinion if you don't trust Dr. Lytton."

She squeezes my hand then releases it.

"Never that."

I start the engine and back out of my parking spot. When we turn onto the main road, I broach the sticky Todd subject again. I feel like a dog with a bone, but I want to understand what's going on.

"Do you think your disagreement with Todd might be fueled by your opposite elemental leanings? You're water, and he's fire and air. According to historical teachings and common idioms, fire and water don't mix."

"Maybe." She stares out the front windshield. "I don't know, I don't trust him. He doesn't feel as balanced as I would like a person with power to be. He's too eager to learn his maximum capabilities and push the envelope. I worry that he doesn't have the willpower or the values to use his abilities properly."

"Perhaps." I recall my storied past and chuckle. "I was never the epitome of restraint, though, so I can't judge too harshly."

"Yeah, well, maybe you should have been restrained," she says with a bite in her voice. "I can't believe I'm saying this, but I swear you're getting more trusting as you age. I know you've felt alone for a long time, but that doesn't mean you should embrace everyone who stops to say hello. We know nothing about Todd. What's his story, really? What has he done in his past?"

Minnie is talking about Todd, yes, but there's a strong subtext of Anna in her words. I don't want to mince around.

"Is this about Anna? You think I'm being too trusting, letting her into the circle."

"This is not about Anna," she says impatiently. "This is about you letting your guard down. But, yeah, let's talk about Anna. You're getting pretty friendly with her. Are you willing to forget her transgressions just because she's good at pulling a pouty, innocent face? What's next, a fight to the death between you and Wayne, using your wooden swords?" Minnie crosses her arms. "It's not like you and she don't have history. She was around a hell of a lot in the years you weren't with me, after all."

"You've never had a problem with my past relationships before. Did you really expect me to wait for you, when I didn't even know that you kept coming back?" Anger pulses through me at her presumption. She has no idea what I went through. In every one of her lives, we found each other. She didn't have to bear the loss of her lover again and again, an endless spiral of grief. "I had no idea about any of this. Did you want me to hold a candle for Nimue for centuries? I would have ignored over a dozen of you. I won't take responsibility for not recognizing the pattern. In no religion on Earth was the process of an immortal being reunited with reincarnations of his first love explained."

"Fine," she says with her arms crossed. "You're blameless and pure of heart. Good to know. Drop me off at the beach, please."

I glance at Minnie, but she looks resolutely out the side window. I heave a sigh and direct my van toward the beach. My heart still pounds from anger and confusion at our fight. How did it devolve into an argument? While I might have fought occasionally with previous incarnations of Minnie, none ever acted like this. What is causing this behavior? Where is the Minnie I fell in love with?

CHAPTER X

We barely speak until I drop Minnie off at the beach, and my disgruntled mood causes me to fly through amber lights with more recklessness than usual. I flip off the honk behind me and squeal into the parking garage of my apartment, thinking longingly of the throaty roar of my old sportscar. My electric van doesn't have enough growl for my current attitude.

Before going upstairs, I wander into the landscaped grounds of my apartment complex. It's been a few hours since I checked for disturbances. I haven't felt any uneasiness, my first indicator of a disturbance, but I should stay vigilant.

I sit on the edge of a cement wall surrounding raised gardens and plunge my hands into lauvan that spill over the edge. Within seconds, I am flying through the network of earth strands.

In here, I can't feel my body, and it's blissful to switch off the elevated heartbeat, adrenaline, and foul mood residual from my fight with Minnie. Here, it is only my mind, unaffected by my body's sensations. I can dissociate from the physical and look at the situation objectively.

Minnie is different lately, and I don't think even she knows what's wrong. I need to be patient while she figures it out and try my best to help her, if she'll let me. I hope she knows that she's the only one for me. While I might have a long history of other lovers besides her, she's the only one who ever captured my heart.

My questing conscious picks up a tingle in the lauvan. I focus my wandering thoughts and bring my disparate parts together to examine my finding. Sure enough, there is a tiny ball of blue strands. It's not a human cluster, since it's made of many different hues, and its constant movement and incremental growth indicate another disturbance. It's small but won't be for long.

I return to my body in a rush of strands and race to my van while my fingers text Alejandro the location. I don't have time for anything more if I want to catch this elemental as it enters our world.

I screech to a halt at a parking lot in Stanley Park. There's no room, not legally, but I have more important issues. I hastily splash Minnie's water bottle on the ground beside the van and twist the strands until a white line forms. It's unskillfully done and will have parking attendants scratching their heads, but it will have to do.

My feet pound along a path to the water's edge until I burst out of the trees onto a walkway that circumnavigates the park. I look around frantically for signs of elemental shenanigans. Joggers on the path eye me with suspicion as my lungs heave for breath.

Is it simply my fancy, or are the waves higher than expected? I don't remember this height of swell at the beach earlier. Peaks crest into foamy spray that curls over itself and splashes into steely gray troughs.

A bright red kayak crowns a wave and slides down the other side. Its rider, a young woman with highlighted hair tied back in a braid, looks panic-stricken as she navigates the suddenly rough seas. A kayak is stable, but even a seasoned paddler would have difficulty today.

There are a scant few onlookers, and none has the distinctive two-tone lauvan signature I've come to expect with possession. Where is the elemental? Has it not yet emerged from the divide?

The kayaker screams as a large wave almost rolls her over. I curse and survey the scene. While I'm waiting for the elemental to show, I might as well help the distressed woman.

What are my options? There isn't anything I can do with my earth lauvan network since the kayaker is on the ocean. Increasing the wind will only make matters worse.

It will have to be water strands. I leap over the barrier and wade into frigid water. Waves splash my thighs, and I plunge my hands into the ocean and seek out strands with chilled fingers.

I can do a few things with water—capture fish, flatten a small pond, steer a rowboat—but calming an ocean is out of my usual scope. Water strands are so dissolute and slippery compared to earth. Perhaps if I found one of the water cables that Minnie showed me, I could make a greater difference. With one hand, I pull as many strands as I can reach to calm the seas, and with the other I search for a cable. The seas quiet only marginally, and my fingers find nothing resembling a cable.

I wish Minnie were here. If there were a cable near, she would find it. Despite my centuries of practice, I'm not skilled enough for this situation.

The kayaker screams again, and laughter rings out down the shore. My head whips around. Holding onto the railing, a hand and leg in the water, swings Esme Rotari, a former Potestas member with whom I had a passing acquaintance. She chuckles with a wild look in her eyes as she watches the kayaker. Blue threads swirl lazily among her mauve strands. With a sharp tug, she yanks a handful of blue water lauvan into the air, a maniacal grin on her face.

A rushing roar fills my ears. I turn to the sound. A huge wave curls over the kayaker. Her desperate scream and frantic paddling are swallowed by the frothing ocean.

I hesitate with indecision. A woman is drowning, but an elemental is so close. I could save one—possibly—and lose the other, but then how many more might suffer the

84

amusement of possessed Esme?

Before I can decide, a splash covers me in water. I peer through wet eyes. It's Alejandro, cutting through the sea like a fish, heading straight for the upturned kayak.

With the kayaker taken care of, I vault over the railing and run to where I last saw Esme.

"No!" I shout and spin on the spot. Somehow, somewhere, Esme has disappeared. Was I dithering for that long? She's not that fit—surely, she didn't go far. I close my eyes and reach into the earth network, but Esme's mauve and blue strands are nowhere near. She must had hidden herself from my sight already.

Should I pursue? In what direction? I pull myself back to my body and hear shouting.

"Merry! Come help!"

Alejandro calls for me. I can't forsake him for a chance. I run to the railing and peer over. Wayne stands in the water, helping a bedraggled Alejandro support the kayaker. She's pale and unconscious. I reach my hands through the railing, and we feed her through gently.

"She's not breathing," I say urgently. Alejandro crawls through with impossible speed and leans over her. With one hand he plugs her nose, and the other tilts her head up. He presses his mouth to hers and blows gently in a rhythm.

It only takes four breaths before her chest heaves. Alejandro rolls her onto her side, and she coughs up a lungful of salty ocean water.

"You know, I could have done that with lauvan," I say conversationally. Alejandro glares at me.

"Then why didn't you?"

"You looked so purposeful. I couldn't spoil your heroics."

Alejandro throws me a withering look but is distracted by the woman, who struggles to sit up.

"What happened?" she croaks.

"Your kayak tipped over," Wayne says. "Alejandro here fished you out and resuscitated you."

She turns reddened eyes to Alejandro, who looks sheepish, his hair plastered to his head and his shirt dripping wet.

"You saved my life," she whispers then throws her arms around him. He looks surprised but gratified, and I suppress a smile.

The wail of a siren filters through the trees. An onlooker must have called an ambulance.

"I'm going to make myself scarce," I mutter to Wayne. "I'm already on the police watchlist."

"What have you done now?" Wayne says in surprise. I wave him off and retreat to the shelter of the trees. A quick pull of errant water strands, and I'm simply another unremarkable, dry walker.

The ambulance packs away the kayaker and leaves Wayne and Alejandro to lean against the railing, looking out to sea. I join them and we contemplate the now-gentle rollers.

"That was stupid, Alejandro," I say finally. He looks at me with indignation. "Reckless. But brave. And you saved the woman in the end, so all's well that ends well."

Alejandro deflates and looks out to sea again.

"I know it was stupid," he says. "But I couldn't leave her to die. Especially since it was caused by an elemental, and we're the only ones who can deal with them. It's almost our fault she was in danger."

"Whoa," I say. "That is very convoluted logic. I hope you don't feel responsible for every natural disaster ever, simply because elementals might be behind it. That thinking will lead you down a very dark path."

"We're doing our best," Wayne says, his voice warm with reassurance. "Don't beat yourself up for things out of your

86

control."

Alejandro sighs, but it's a contemplative sound.

"What's happening over there, do you think?" he says. "On the elemental side? I thought your river elemental was nervous about being caught, Merry. Why are these ones so bold?"

"I don't know. I wish I did. I would ask Ailu, but I gather that he's not high enough in the ranks to know important details. Are the other fundamentals hunting for their missing compatriot? Clearly, the elemental plane is not on lockdown, or these elementals wouldn't cross the divide. There is so much I don't know. All we can do is react and hope that the next disturbance will yield an elemental that we can capture for answers. I'll speak to Ailu soon and see what assistance the elementals can provide us. Surely, if we alert them to the issues, they will aid us."

Silence reigns, interrupted only by crashing waves against the shore. Wayne is the first to speak again, and it's clear that his thoughts have strayed from elementals.

"We've found a lot of our past fellows," he says. "But not everyone, not yet. If we assume that everyone living then has a modern-day counterpart, what happened to my wife back then? I know she isn't Anna because Anna was Vivienne. And what about my relationships in other lives? Were they all the same, like they were for you two? Is dating Anna a waste of time when we might uncover my soulmate any day?"

"Soulmates aren't all they're cracked up to be," Alejandro says darkly. "Don't hold your breath."

I consider Minnie's strange behavior lately and our fight this morning. I sigh.

"None of us can know the future, despite all our past. Don't throw away happiness for the elusive chance of a different future, or you might be very lonely. Tomorrow will bring what it will."

Wayne nods slowly but doesn't respond. I nudge Alejandro with my elbow.

"Speaking of women, that kayaker was grateful for your heroics. Did you get her number?"

Alejandro jolts with surprise and stares at me.

"What? No."

I shrug and face the ocean again.

"Lost opportunity. Oh well, with your reckless streak and drive to do the right thing, there will be more damsels in distress in your future."

Minnie still hasn't arrived home when I get there, so I pick up my harp. I don't play it often these days, but occasionally it calls to me. My fingers pluck a lyrical Scottish ballad from the thirteenth century, meant to be danced to, then a lively drinking song in Russian. Halfway through the last, there's a knock on the door and Jen enters. I nod at her but continue to sing until the end.

"It's so rude." Jen giggles. "If I didn't know the language, I would have said it was a beautiful tune."

I grin.

"The neighbors won't call me in if they don't understand the lyrics." I put my harp beside my bookshelf and stand. "Coffee? Tea? Something stronger?"

"Midafternoon?" Jen looks scandalized.

"A drinking song calls for a drink. No? Coffee it is."

Jen follows me to the kitchen, where I put a pot of water on the stove and find mugs in the cupboard.

"I've been looking through Wayne's history website ever since he gave me the login info." Jen's lauvan twitch with her announcement. I don't react, although my heart leaps. She's finally embracing her past, and I couldn't be more thrilled. Perhaps Guinevere is coming back to me.

"Anything interesting? I've put a few lines in, but it's overwhelming when I remember everything, not dribs and drabs like the rest of you. It will take me a hundred years to fill out in detail."

"Just do names, places, and dates to start," she says. "That would be helpful when we want to cross-reference. For example, I've had memories of myself as a woman named Jeanine. Empire waist dresses and speeches straight out of a Jane Austen novel have me thinking it's Regency-era England. I dreamed about her last night, and I'm sure you were there."

"Indeed." I lean against the counter and marvel at the revelation. "Lord Meryton of Steele Hall. Minnie was Lady Celeste Meryton at the time."

Jen winces.

"Another memory hit you?" I ask, recognizing the signs.

"Yes, when you said the names. I remember—she was your aunt?" Jen's brow wrinkles in concentration. "She died, and you were far more upset than you should have been. I suspected you two weren't what you seemed. Did you never tell Jeanine your history?"

"No." I look down and fidget with the tea towel in my hands. "It's never been easy to relate that, and we couldn't be close, given your station and our genders. By the time you had more freedom after your husband's death, I had to move on. Questions would have been asked about the ageless Lord Meryton. And it was too difficult to stay when reminders of Celeste abounded."

Jen touches my elbow briefly, her face empathetic.

"That makes sense." She retreats and fishes her phone out of her purse. "I'm going to write that connection on the website."

She scrolls and types for a moment while I remember the past. The others delight in recapping our shared history. I'm happy for them, and thrilled that Jen has finally come around, but it doesn't come as easily to me. Their pasts are vague memories that aren't as connected to their current lives as mine are.

To me, every memory, whether it was made yesterday or a thousand years ago, is equally relevant. So much has passed—so many people loved and lost, so much wandering—that it is difficult to disengage my emotions from the memories. Even though I know now that I never truly lost those I loved, still, the hurt was real and is terrible to recall. Even though I know Celeste came back to me years later as Josephine, I still endured her death, not knowing the truth of her rebirth.

"Isn't it weird how Guinevere was so bad at languages," Jen says thoughtfully. "And I pick them up so quickly? I thought we would have more in common."

"I don't know how much Guinevere and the others shape who you are today. Perhaps her struggle with language propelled you to improve your linguistic abilities in this life. Or, perhaps her abilities have no bearing on you, and only your deeper soul attributes are similar." I shrug helplessly. "I really know nothing. It's incredibly frustrating."

Jen chuckles.

"Poor Merry. You're so used to knowing everything, aren't you? This is probably good for you. An opportunity to experience being humble."

I snort.

"No, thank you. You can keep your humble pie. It's a taste I haven't acquired nor wish to."

Jen looks at her phone again and hums in a contented way while she scrolls through the entries. Even her golden strands loop in lazy spirals.

"You really feel better about this, don't you?" I say quietly.

She looks up with a wry smile.

"I do. Don't get me wrong, it's weird and bizarre and I have to pinch myself frequently, but still. It's kind of fascinating now that I've stopped fearing destiny. I know I can choose what I want. It's liberating to think of it like that. And I've always been interested in history—no surprise, I guess—so to have insight into different times and places is amazing. I think Wayne's enthusiasm might have rubbed off on me, too."

"Enthusiastic might be too mild of a word for Wayne's passion."

Jen grins. She grabs a lock of her loose hair and tugs at it absentmindedly while she skims her phone. I gaze at her in wonder. I distinctly remember Jeanine Vernon with the same habit. Jen glances up and catches me scrutinizing her.

"What?"

"You're pulling your hair. I've never seen you do that before."

She drops her hand, but her mouth twists.

"Yeah, it's one of those things that has cropped up since I touched the grail. More of my past lives are coming through. Sometimes I don't know where I end and they begin."

"What does it feel like?" I'm genuinely curious since my experience is so different. "Does it feel like you and them?"

"Less and less. It used to feel that way, like the memories were intruding into my real life. Now it's becoming more real, like they are true memories and not some movie I watched a long time ago. And the more real it gets, the more they take over and become me." She exhales with a puff of air. "I used to be scared that I would lose myself, lose Jen, in these other people, but the more they take over, the less scary it is. It's starting to feel right."

"Fascinating," I murmur, scanning her face for signs of the

others I have known. Jen swats at my arm.

"Stop it," she says with a playful tone. "You're trying to see the others. I'm still me, mostly. Don't forget that."

"I know, and I'm glad you're you."

"Aww, too sweet. Hey, I also noticed something when I looked through Alejandro's website stuff." She shakes her head in disbelief. "He's so thorough. There are pages and pages of history."

"He's relentless in triggering memories. It's his new favorite hobby."

"It's working. Anyway, I couldn't help notice that so many of his names and places are familiar." Jen wrinkles her nose and her strands spiral with agitation. "As in, we were together a lot. Not every lifetime, but often enough. Even when we weren't married, we were in similar locations, or had chance meetings that neither of us remember much about yet—he was a sailor at one point, and I distinctly remember a brief encounter with a sailor of his description at one of the ports he visited." Her cheeks color, and I grin.

"An 'encounter.' Is that what the kids are calling it these days?"

Jen aims a kick in my direction.

"You get the point. It's unnerving. This whole fate thing seems inevitable."

"Truer words were never spoken."

"But I never knew the truth, before. This lifetime is my chance to decide for myself. I've been trying hard to not encourage Alejandro when he reaches out. It feels cruel, but false hope will only make it harder to get over me. I'm trying to do the right thing."

Jen gazes at me earnestly. She believes her words, and in any other circumstance, I would agree with her. Stringing a lover along only delays the inevitable and makes the heartbreak hurt more. In this case, though, I'm not sure if Alejandro will ever get over Jen. There have been a few times in the past that he never did. I knew the sailor that Jen mentioned, years after that brief romance on the docks. He still pined for the Spanish baker's daughter that he left behind. As far as I knew, he never married another.

"It's hard to know what the right thing is," I say. "But it's the best we can strive for."

Jen sighs then turns to rinse her coffee mug in the sink.

"Speaking of joining the fold, has Cecil decided if he wants to touch the grail?" I ask. "He seemed interested."

"I haven't encouraged it," she says without looking at me. "He's dithering, and that's okay. A part of me wants desperately to know if he was—" She swallows. "Anyone from my past, and the other part wants to keep my relationship with him simple. It's already opened a can of worms since he found out that Alejandro was Arthur to my Guinevere. I had to do some serious unruffling of feathers."

"The grail is at Alejandro's, whenever Cecil decides." I put my palms up. "It's out of my hands, now, and I like it that way. Everyone can decide for themselves what is best for them."

I spend much of the evening connected to the lauvan network in my apartment's gardens, but no disturbances present themselves. I'm in bed by the time Minnie opens the door, bringing with her the scent of the sea. We don't speak, and I drift to sleep to the sound of the shower. I'm frustrated with her, but my time in the network removed the worst of the feelings, and now I'm simply tired and unwilling to fight.

93

CHAPTER XI

Dreaming

I'm so close to Arthur's villa, but not close enough that I can delay my midday meal. It's not much—some bread and cheese, both older than I might wish—but it will do until I arrive home. Food at camp is never as palatable as at the villa.

I will stop at the next open meadow I see. It's a sunny day, welcome after weeks of overcast skies, and I don't want to waste a moment of precious sun. My stomach can grumble for a while longer. If I remember correctly, there is a patch of open grassland close to here. It will make an excellent site for a quick meal.

When I come out of the woods, blinking in the bright light of a noon sun, someone is already in the meadow. I squint at the figure until her form and strands hit me with a pang of recognition. It's Vivienne, picking berries with her young daughter sitting on a shawl by her feet.

I had forgotten that Morgan's dwelling is near here. I rarely visit since I am not welcome there.

Vivienne starts when she hears hoofbeats then relaxes when she sees my face. She props her bucket on her hip.

"Merlin. It's a surprise to see you here."

"Vivienne." I slide off my horse and lead it the short distance to mother and daughter. "I'm on my way home with a message, but I planned to eat my meal in this meadow."

"Don't let us stop you." She puts her bucket on the grass and sinks gracefully to sit next to her little child, who raises her arms in a wordless request for comfort. I suppose she doesn't see many strange men. Vivienne tucks her on her lap and rummages in a nearby sack. "Shush, it's fine. This is only

94

Merlin. Here, eat your bread."

She offers a piece of loaf to the child, who gnaws it while staring at me with an intense gaze.

I sit distant enough to avoid frightening the child further and pull out my bread and cheese. I tear into it with gusto.

"How do you fare, Vivienne?" I say between mouthfuls. "Does Morgan treat you well? Does Mordred?" I give a pointed glance to the small girl, Mordred's daughter. Vivienne smiles.

"Morgan is wonderful, as always. I don't have much to do with Mordred, which suits me well. My child is healthy, and I could not wish for more." She smooths back a curl from the child's forehead.

"I'm glad to hear it." I am genuinely happy for her, despite her alliance with troublesome Morgan. It isn't easy for a woman with a child to not have a husband—my own mother was lucky to have a brother to take her in—and I appreciate that Morgan takes care of her own. It's unfortunate that her stance on Saxons is so inflexible.

Vivienne is about to say more, but a rustling from the path makes both of us turn our heads. An old man, clearly a beggar from the state of his ragged clothes and the haunted look in his eyes, shuffles out of the woods. He looks far too bent to be wandering the forest.

Vivienne tightens her lips then plunges her hand into the sack at her side.

"Here, grandfather," she calls out. "I have bread for you."

The man's eyes light up, and he toddles in our direction. The smell of his unwashed body travels before him, and I command my nose not to wrinkle. Vivienne smiles at the man and hands him the half-loaf of bread. The man bows a little lower than his natural bend.

"Thank you, kind woman," he rasps out. "Goodness is

rewarded. May the sun smile on your beautiful face always."

He shuffles back down the path and disappears, leaving his scent lingering in the air. I look at Vivienne with a new appreciation for her character. She catches my eye and rolls her own.

"I know you think I'm evil at heart," she says. "Foiling your precious Arthur's plans, aligning myself with Morgan. But everything I do is done for a good cause, and usually because I care. You might not understand my reasons, but they are there." She opens the sack wider and pulls out a piece of cheese for the child but exposes the emptiness within to my eyes. "Besides, how can I teach my daughter compassion for those in need and respect for elders if I don't show any myself?"

I nod slowly, pleased and surprised at this new facet of Vivienne I haven't seen before.

"You have no more food for your meal," I say. Vivienne shrugs.

"I will have supper tonight. He will not. I can survive a few hours without food."

I rip my bread in half and offer it to her. She accepts with a smile stripped of her usual coyness. It suits her well.

I have completed my physician duties for the day. Queen Christina now rests after my adjustments to her lauvan. Her illness is a tenacious one and has required four adjustments in as many days, but I'm confident that a few more will make it retreat for good.

It is too late to explore Stockholm before supper—a long repast hosted by the queen's unstable, overbearing mother and her simpering courtiers—and the only part I look forward to is

96

sneaking in as many insults to the queen's mother Maria Eleonora as I can manage without her courtiers noticing. She has disliked me from the start, and although I have been in Sweden for less than a week, she has made no pretense about her true feelings. In her mind, I have usurped her favored physician, and I am not welcome as a result.

Her dislike doesn't bother me. If she persists in ruining my supper, then I will happily ruin hers.

After supper, then, I will explore the city more. It has been many years since I have ventured here, and I'm always fascinated by how places change. My Swedish, although antiquated, is passable enough for a tavern.

I can pass the time before supper most comfortably in the library. The queen is very well read, and I understand that the library is her place of tranquility and the source of her many tomes of instruction. I run my fingers over leather spines on a shelf at head height, noting which titles I have read. There are not many I have not.

"You must be the famous Dr. Pierre Michon Bourdelot," a low female voice behind me purrs. I turn my head to view the newcomer. Her flaxen hair is gathered in a loose cloud that frames full lips and large eyes. A sumptuous dress shows her décolletage to her advantage. "The queen has told me much about you."

From that comment, and from the finery indicating her elevated position in court, I can guess to whom I speak.

"La Belle Comtesse, Ebba Sparre, I presume." Ebba is the queen's best friend, and likely one reason why the queen refuses to marry another. I turn fully toward her and bow. She responds with a curtsey, but her eyes never leave mine. "I hope she spoke of only good things."

"The queen speaks her mind," Ebba says with a laugh. "She said many things, but I gather that you are a man worthy of

97

respect. Indeed, the queen is nearly healed, and I understand that we have you to thank for that."

I give another shallow bow in acknowledgement.

"Will she grace us with her presence at supper, do you suppose?"

Ebba wrinkles her pert nose.

"She dislikes her mother's courtiers. She will use her illness as an excuse for as long as she can."

"It is good to be the queen," I say with a sigh. Ebba laughs.

"You dislike them too, I presume. Don't worry, the feeling is mutual, from what I understand." She puts her finger on her jawline in thought. "Perhaps I may be of service? Since I am returned from my uncle's house, I will join you at supper. Together, we can fend off the barbarous hordes."

I smile. Already, I like Ebba, and I understand why Christina prefers her to all others.

"Although I am a formidable opponent to the barbarians, I would be grateful for a comrade-in-arms."

Ebba steps toward me and slips her delicate hand into the crook of my arm.

"Come, let us battle together."

Supper is full of barbs, as usual, but my humor in the situation increases tenfold with Ebba by my side. Her sharp retorts and witticisms are couched in such demure glances and a sweet demeanor that no one knows how to react to her remarks. I haven't had such fun in ages, and her sparkling eyes tell me she enjoys our antics as much as I do. It's with difficulty that I retain my composure until we rise from our seats and exit the banquet room together.

Ebba bursts into laughter as soon as we are out of earshot. Her laugh is low and alluring, and even as I join her mirth, I can't help admiring the curve of her neck and her bright cheeks. Her breasts jiggle as she gasps for air, and I look elsewhere to avoid staring.

"That was too much fun," she says finally. "I miss Christina for that. Her wit is so sharp. I am grateful you are returning her to me. It has been too long."

She takes my hand in her soft fingers and grips it tightly. Her bright eyes meet mine, and she pulls me closer. I don't resist.

"Too long," she repeats softly and draws me toward an open door in the dimly lit hall. Inside is a dark room that might contain divans and a cold fireplace, but I am too preoccupied to examine it fully. With a burst of strength that I have no intention of fighting, she pushes me against the wall and presses her lips to mine. She tastes of the butter cookies we nibbled at the end of our meal, and I meet her kiss with equal fervor. Her hands roam my body then descend to interesting places. I release myself from her mouth.

"What of the queen?" I gasp, my breath vanished along with my objections to the movements of Ebba's hand. "I thought you and she—"

"She has been ill for so long," Ebba whispers. "Although she slowly recovers, I can't wait another day. The fire in me must be sated however it can. Will you deny a poor, suffering woman her relief? I didn't realize you were so cruel."

"Never accuse me of being cruel to a woman in need." I grip her bottom in both hands and twist her around until her back is against the wall.

When we are finished and our breathing has quieted, I help Ebba adjust her dress, although nothing can hide the color in her cheeks. Before she leaves, she turns.

"Why are you truly here, Dr. Bourdelot?" she asks. "It is a long way to come for a medical consultation. What were you promised?"

Ebba is astute. I have no wish to tell her of the true reason I came—my eighth wife's wedding ring is in Christina's

99

possession, and her advisor promised to secretly obtain it for me if I would heal his queen—but I didn't expect her to question me. She is a match for Christina, after all.

"Treasure to make the journey worthwhile. It appears I have an avaricious streak."

Ebba considers me for a moment.

"Most do," she says at last. "It's those who have a reason for their greed that are the interesting ones. Goodnight, Dr. Bourdelot."

She disappears in a swish of skirts, and I sag against the wall. The high of intimacy drains away, leaving me awash in thoughts of Khutulun. I'm here for a promise to a long-dead lover, a woman I treasured as much as any gold. Suddenly, my dalliance with Ebba feels tainted, as if it tarnishes Khutulun's memory. I try to banish the thought—that way lies madness, for once I start down that path, there is nowhere to stop unless I hold a candle for Nimue my entire life—but it is a persistent one. I wonder if I will ever reconcile my string of loves and lovers to myself.

CHAPTER XII

Minnie's hand on my chest wakes me the next morning.

"Hey, you," she whispers and kisses my cheek. "I'm sorry for yesterday. I don't know what's up. I must have been tired or something."

"I'm sorry, too." I return her kiss, happy to reconcile. Her hand sneaks under the sheet. She smiles wickedly.

"Looks like you're ready to kiss and make up." She slides her leg over my hips and settles with an alluring sigh.

Before the sensations take me over, the memory of my dream—the reason I'm ready for Minnie this morning—interrupts my thoughts. Why was I dreaming of Ebba? Was it from anger about my fight with Minnie yesterday? I don't tend to dream of others when I'm living my life with Minnie or her past counterparts.

I would contemplate further, but Minnie is very distracting. I put the dream aside to ponder another time and focus on the flesh-and-blood woman on top of me.

Once we're eating breakfast, the weight of my failures yesterday weighs me down. Two more minions evaded capture and hid themselves from being found. That brings Xenia's minion count to at least four. What's more, we have still never successfully captured one, and even when I arrived early enough at the site of a disturbance, I was waylaid by a maniacal elemental freshly in possession of a human body and excited to experiment with newfound abilities.

"What time is your first class?" Minnie asks over her coffee.

"Nine." I check my watch. "I should get moving. I want to plug into the network first and check for disturbances."

"I need to stop by my old apartment and give the landlord my keys, so I'll take the bus. It runs straight there. Let me know

101

what you find." She rises to kiss my forehead. "Good luck."

Once downstairs, I stride to my now-favorite bench and drop onto it with my eyes closed. Descending into the earth strands is like sinking into a warm bath, comfortable and easy. My strands spread out in a familiar search pattern, highly attuned to changes in the network. Any hint of uneasiness, and I am ready to gather myself and head straight for it.

I search for some minutes—or what I figure must be minutes, since time feels abstract in this space—until something tickles my conscious. It's not uneasiness, exactly, more like the foreboding of uneasiness to come.

Have I pinpointed the site of a future disturbance? I eagerly zoom toward the spot, where the faintest hint of silver threads coalesces. That's it, I'm certain.

I memorize the location and pull back to my body then whip my phone out and call Alejandro. My fumbling fingers dance over the screen in my excitement.

"Alejandro," I gasp when he answers. "I have another one. And it's only just starting—we might catch this one. Two blocks east from your house. Wind-related."

"Wayne's over," he says. "He and Liam and I are on it, Merlo. We have the Potestas photo list. We'll get this one, I have a feeling."

He hangs up and I nearly leap to my feet in excitement, but instead I plunge my hands into the lauvan. I want to check the growth of the disturbance before I join the others.

The silver threads have doubled in number, but the cluster is still small. With any luck, Alejandro and the others will see the wind destruction materialize and catch the elemental as it enters our plane.

A sensation tugs on my focused conscious. If I had a face to control, I would frown in confusion. What was that? My conscious races toward the new disturbance, and its rapid growth frightens me. How did I not notice this before?

A cluster of brown strands pulses with angry movement. It's large, and I fear the physical effects have already happened. I must get there as fast as I can to catch the elemental.

I pull out of the network, take a quick glance around to make sure I am alone, and yank on my strands. A moment later, I'm flapping my wings with furious intent to the earth disturbance.

Even if I didn't know where to go, it wouldn't be hard to guess. Sirens wail toward an intersection where a gaping hole in the asphalt leers up at me like a satisfied smile. I glide lower and scan emergency workers and onlookers below for signs of brown lauvan intermingled with their colorful strands.

After three passes over the crowd, I land on the ground a block away and transform, feeling useless. What's the point of having these abilities if they don't allow me to gain the upper hand? I might as well follow sirens around town. I would have as much luck that way.

As a half-elemental, I feel my lack of abilities keenly when encountering beings that exist in the elements. There is only so much that I can do on this side. I need to contact Ailu for help, and he can alert the other fundamentals about our plight. They can control their own. Feeling better with a plan, I spread my fingers into air threads that lazily drift in the still air.

Ten minutes pass before I admit defeat. Did something sinister happen to Ailu? Perhaps he was caught sneaking around the physical realm too many times. Was he sent to dormancy and replaced by a different air elemental? The thought upsets me. I have come to rely on Ailu's help. There is so much I don't know about the elemental plane, and he was willing to teach me. In addition, I rely on him to find a solution to our Xenia problem. I'd better not have seen the last of him.

My phone rings, and I answer it with dull fingers.

"Yes?"

"We got him," Wayne says, his voice crackling with energy. "We actually got the son of a bitch. He's tied up in the back of my car, blindfolded. What do we do with him now?"

My heart leaps. We have an elemental, a minion of Xenia, someone to question and get answers from. We now have a chance to get ahead of this mess instead of trailing behind.

"Let me think," I say, then my phone beeps with another incoming call. "Hold on."

"Merry?" Anna says when I answer. "Nothing urgent. I have a couple of theoretical questions about the elemental world."

"Anna. Are you still staying at Bethany's house?"

"Yes." She sounds confused. "She's away right now, though. Holiday in Spain. Why?"

"Does it have a basement?"

I arrange with Wayne to meet me at Bethany's house, and I fly there with light wings and a lighter heart. Finally, we are getting somewhere. I hate the thought of Xenia gathering her forces unchecked. Until Ailu responds with reinforcements, capturing Xenia's elementals will slow her down.

Wayne's car is already parked when I alight on the sidewalk, although they must have recently arrived. Liam emerges from the passenger's side as I transform.

"Man, that's cool," he breathes. "I wish I could do that."

"I can take you up some time," I offer. "But not today. Today, we have a prisoner to interrogate."

Wayne opens the back door for Alejandro, who watches the blindfolded prisoner with unmoving eyes.

"Pull him this way, Arthur," Wayne says. He catches himself and chuckles. "Sorry, Alejandro. I'll haul him out this side."

Liam hears the slip of name and looks downcast. His strands droop, and I wonder if he has decided to touch the grail. It appears to be a momentous decision for him, as it should be. I can't predict what he will choose, although it looks like it pains him to be out of the loop.

Anna runs down the path toward us.

"Don't let the neighbors see," she hisses. "Does he have to be blindfolded and tied up?"

"Yes," I say. "But I can make it appear not so."

A few quick knots later, our prisoner wears sunglasses and gloves to cover the ropes and blindfold. Wayne and Alejandro shuffle forward with the man between them, and Anna runs ahead to open the door.

Bethany's abode is a compact, two-level house. A weathervane twists on the roof, the porch is hung with windchimes, and the garden is filled with whirligigs and windsocks. I raise an eyebrow. Normally, I wouldn't give the house a second look, other than to consider the owner eccentric, but Minnie's obsession with all things water has me on high alert for similar tendencies in others. When Bethany returns from her holiday, I might pay her a visit.

Anna waves us inside with an urgent flapping of her hand. Wayne pulls the prisoner over the threshold, and the rest of us follow. The interior of Bethany's house is light and airy, painted in pale grays with large windows draped with breezy sheer curtains. Her décor consists of an eclectic assortment of crystals, scarves, and what appear to be traveling souvenirs.

Anna leads us to the end of a short hall, which descends through a doorway and down a rickety staircase. The basement is unfinished with the exterior wall insulation covered only by plastic sheeting. One wall is filled with stacks of cardboard boxes, another corner contains a washer and dryer, and the floor is coated with gray paint for a more finished surface.

"Set him down here," Anna says. She points to a corner with a wooden chair, and Alejandro pushes the man onto it. I affix his hands and feet to the chair with lauvan then rip off the blindfold. The man blinks at the sudden light.

He's familiar, although it takes me a moment to recall his name. It's Ben Hart, a passing acquaintance at Potestas. He was eager to embrace his spirit traveler and intent on stopping me when I journeyed to the cave to free Minnie. It doesn't surprise me that he succumbed to the temptation of whatever Xenia promised him, although my heart sinks at another life taken over by a rogue elemental.

Shaggy brown hair flops over his forehead, and his gangly limbs look uncomfortable wrapped around the chair. His eyes, however, gleam with knowledge and appraisal.

"Merry," he whispers. "I've heard so much about you."

"And I haven't heard nearly enough about you." I cross my arms and gaze down at him. "It's time to tell us what you know. How many of you are coming through the barrier? Why now? What is the earth fundamental planning?"

The elemental in Ben laughs lightly.

"You think I'm going to tell you everything? It will take more than capturing me to betray the earth fundamental. You'll have to do better than that."

I smile, but there is nothing friendly in my expression.

"You are new here, so I'll forgive your lack of knowledge. Human bodies are quite frail. You haven't yet experienced cold, hunger, thirst. They are hard to ignore, especially when it is so easy to appease your body's needs by giving me a few simple explanations. If your endurance is greater than I expect, there are other ways of persuading you to speak." Anna glances at me, perhaps guessing what I mean, but I keep my eyes trained on Ben. A flicker of confusion passes over his face. "It won't be comfortable, I assure you. Would you like to reconsider your stance?"

"No," he says. "I will hold."

"For now." I turn to Anna. "Don't bother feeding him or giving him water, not yet. I want to give him a chance to think about his situation."

I bend and pull earth strands from the floor. My fingers fashion them into a cage of brown threads. Ben watches with narrowed eyes. When the cage completely covers Ben on his chair, I step back.

"That should prevent him from communicating with other elementals. It's not as foolproof as Xenia's barrier was when she captured me, but it should do the trick."

Wayne looks askance at the empty air but doesn't comment. Anna leads the way upstairs, but she turns to me in the hall.

"How long am I going to have a prisoner in my house?" she says with a trace of annoyance. "Bethany will be back in a week. And am I supposed to take him to the bathroom?"

"I'll be back after my classes to deal with that," I assure her. "If I hurry, I can catch the last few. And if it's too much for you, I can move him somewhere else."

"No, no." Her lauvan twist with a mix of annoyance and contrition. "If I do this, I can prove myself to the others. I know most in your little group are having trouble forgetting, let alone forgiving. I need to do what I can to win their trust." She nods decisively. "And, this way, I can ask him questions about the spirit world. Maybe he will talk to me."

"You can try," I say. Perhaps she can be the good cop to my bad cop, but I sense that elementals think differently than we do. "Best of luck."

CHAPTER XIII

I return to Anna's house after my final class to lead the prisoner to the bathroom and back again. Anna gives me a key and goes to work, and I return that evening for another bathroom visit. It's inconvenient, but the frequent visits give me a chance to evaluate Ben's state of mind. So far, he hasn't budged from his silent stance, but I caught him looking longingly at the bathroom sink. He must be thirsty.

Anna didn't get any information from him before she left, to her exasperation. I suspect she wanted to have a breakthrough to prove her usefulness. I'm not certain for how long her desire to atone will last, but I'm happy to benefit until it fades.

The next morning, I dress early. There is a lot I must accomplish before work today. The lauvan network needs to be evaluated for disturbances—although I feel large-scale uneasiness without being plugged in, I can sense faint stirrings of disturbance at its earliest stages if I travel through the strands—and I need to visit the prisoner.

Todd texts me while I brush my teeth. I spit then glance at the screen.

Lesson soon?

I pause. There is so much going on that lessons with Todd are the least of my concerns. However, Minnie needs practice. The more elementals come through the divide, the more I see the necessity of her training. I want her able to defend herself if they defeat me. I write back.

Tonight, at seven.

"I arranged for a lesson with Todd tonight," I call into the hallway. Minnie appears in the bedroom door.

"I'm going to give it a miss today."

"What? Why?" I'm confused and a touch annoyed. The only

reason I agreed to a lesson was to help Minnie gain skills. There's too much going on otherwise—checking for disturbances, visiting the prisoner—that helping Todd play around with lauvan is low priority. A thought occurs to me, accompanied by a pang of jealousy that surprises me. "Are you not getting much out of these lessons? Are you going to visit the river elemental instead?"

I want to be enough for her, but I recognize that my training can only take her so far. She is half-water elemental, after all.

Understanding doesn't make me feel any less inadequate.

"No," she says simply. "It's all moving so fast, that's all. I need a break. And, honestly, I'm not comfortable around Todd. I think he's bad news."

I sigh in exasperation but check the hasty words that threaten to spill out of my mouth. I think she's exaggerating the danger Todd poses, but saying that won't help matters. Instead, I focus on something she will agree on.

"I'm nervous about you being able to protect yourself. Learning how to use your new abilities is the best way to stay safe."

Minnie walks toward me and puts her hands on either side of my jaw. She kisses my lips then leans back to consider me.

"What if I promise to practice tonight?" she says finally. "I agree, the more I know, the better."

I exhale. Minnie's strands flow slowly with her determination. I won't get anywhere by arguing.

"All right," I say. "Work hard while I'm gone."

I visit Ben again. He looks fearful but resolute, despite his cracking lips. To show him what it feels like to be satiated, I allow him a drink from the tap. He slurps with gusto but doesn't reveal anything about Xenia and her plans.

Once I replace his lauvan cage and walk upstairs, Anna stops me in the hall.

"Are you sure we should be doing this?" Her eyes are troubled. "It feels cruel to deprive him. Inhumane."

"It is, no doubt. But he has a choice. The decision lies with him. Trust me, there are far crueler ways of extracting information. He's hardly been twenty-four hours without food. Speaking from experience, the human body can endure far longer than that. We need answers from him. If this doesn't work, I'll have to resort to other methods." I sigh. "I'd rather not, but I will if I have to. We must find out how to slow Xenia down until I can contact my elemental friend for help. These elementals have no sense of humanity. The one by the ocean nearly drowned a woman for amusement's sake. It's safe to assume that the rest feel similarly."

Anna swallows but doesn't disagree.

"Okay. I guess so. I just hope he cracks soon. I tried a few times, but it was like talking to a brick wall."

I bid Anna farewell and drive to work in my little van. There are no disturbances when I check the earth strands, and feelings of uneasiness are absent throughout my workday. It's a welcome reprieve, but I wonder why no elementals are coming through. Does Xenia have enough minions now? Are the other fundamentals catching the rogues? I will stay vigilant, regardless.

At the end of the day, I gulp down a quick dinner with Minnie, during which she promises anew to practice her abilities. After a dip into the earth strand network, which is as calm as it was all day, I hop in my van and race to a park where Todd and I arranged to meet. I'm still disgruntled from Minnie's absence and twitchy from the lack of disturbances today. If I were less skeptical, I would rejoice at their absence, but I can't believe that Xenia is finished with her plans.

It's drizzling and growing dark, and the parking lot is empty save for Todd's pick-up truck. The field beside me is partly illuminated from nearby streetlights, lit well enough for our purposes. Todd leans against his car with his hood pulled low over his forehead, but he straightens and walks toward me with brisk strides when I emerge from my van.

"What are we learning today, prof?" Todd greets me. I smile at the new nickname.

"What do you want to learn? Any suggestions?"

Todd looks taken aback, as if he hasn't considered it.

"I don't know."

"Let's start by keeping dry," I say to help him out. "I'm in no mood to endure damp clothes."

Todd rubs his hands together in anticipation.

"Excellent."

The back of my mind scans for tingles of uneasiness while I instruct Todd in the art of building a lauvan barrier to ward off rain. First, we make a large dome that covers us both, then I direct him in making a skintight version over himself.

A car pulls up, and I grimace. The weather is unpleasant enough that I hoped we would be left alone this evening. I take my leather wallet out of my pocket and quickly manipulate its strands to create a passable soccer ball.

"What are you doing?" Todd stares at my wallet-turned-ball.

"Giving us a reason to be out on this dismal evening. We have company." I nod toward the car, whose passengers are expelling from the interior. It's a father and son, out to practice

111

some soccer of their own. "Come on, let's go into those trees. It will be darker, but we can work with fire lauvan for light."

Todd's face is set in a frown.

"We're hiding?" he says with disapproval. "I've been hiding all my life. That's all my father ever told me to do. I thought, now there are more of us, we wouldn't have to be so secret."

"I don't think the world will ever be ready for our brand of strange." I pat his shoulder and lead him into a copse of trees beside the field. "Our abilities necessitate hiding. There will always be those who don't understand, and when people don't understand, they fear. When they fear, they persecute. Trust me, I've seen the pattern again and again. It's simpler to keep a low profile, don't give them the chance to find out. I recommend you only tell those that you trust."

Todd doesn't look convinced by my words, and he follows me with a disgruntled expression. I don't bother to say more. He will understand the first time he tells someone. If he's lucky, they will embrace him. Chances are they will fear him.

"I haven't told you yet—I've encountered something I call 'disturbances.'"

"What's that?"

"Remember Xenia, the earth fundamental that possessed a body and is now running amok? She's now calling her fellows from the elemental plane, and they are traveling here, one by one. Every time one passes over, the lauvan gather into a huge ball and spit out the elemental, who is met by a willing human host. I can feel the disturbances as they occur. Have you felt periods of unexplainable uneasiness in the past few days?"

"Maybe." Todd looks puzzled. "I think so. That was a disturbance?"

"I've been chasing them for a few days. We finally caught one of the possessed, and I'm holding him prisoner until he talks."

112

Todd blanches.

"Seriously? That's some medieval shit right there."

I shrug.

"I come by it honestly. We need answers, and he can give them to us. I want to stop them from coming through, but I can't do that unless I know how and why." I face him fully as a thought crosses my mind. "Have I ever showed you how to enter the lauvan network?"

Todd tilts his head in question.

"I don't think so."

I rub my hands, excited to show him something new.

"Just wait. It's something else."

I explain how to descend into the network. It takes a few tries and some frowns of concentration on Todd's part, but he finally pushes himself through. I meet him there, and his orange and silver strands swirl uncertainly.

"It feels like I'm swimming through molasses," he says in my mind. I chuckle.

"Must be because you're not an earth elemental. You can try this with air. You enter it in a similar fashion, but it might be more natural to you. Follow me—I'll show you around."

We slide along the strands—Todd's right, it's slower than air, but far more comfortable to my mind—and Todd marvels at the lauvan signatures of countless people, animals, trees, and anything with energy. I remind myself to bring Minnie here, then I recall that Shannon, the river elemental, has already taken her on a journey through the river. I'm glad she has Shannon as a resource, I truly am, but I wish I could have been there for her first time.

When Todd has seen enough of the network, I draw us back to our bodies.

"Amazing," Todd says. "I love it. I can't wait to try it in air. Hey, these disturbances, why can't the elementals figure it out?

Can't they control their own?"

"It's a good question," I say. "And one I intend to broach with my contact shortly. I gather that their world is in an uproar over Xenia's actions, but I'm certain that once they are alerted to the problem, they can contain the leak."

"Maybe they don't know elementals are coming through."

"Could be. I'll alert my contact tonight."

I have a beer on the couch with Minnie when I get home—it feels like we don't see enough of each other, some days—but the balcony calls me. When Minnie disappears into the bedroom, I pull on a sweater and brave the rainy night. My fingers reach for air strands, and I send my intent forth.

Soon enough, an air cable flops into my waiting hands, and a humanoid shape emerges from the silver threads.

"Greetings, Merry," Ailu says. "I was wondering when you might contact me."

"Hello, Ailu. I'm glad to see you. Last time I tried to contact you, there wasn't a stitch of wind to be had, and I was worried you had been caught. There's a stiff breeze tonight." It's difficult to know how to compliment an element, but I can tell I hit the mark when Ailu's strands wriggle with pleasure.

"Wonderful, isn't it? I adore a good rainstorm. The elemental for autumn squalls is an ally of mine. Water, of course, but still pleasant to work with." He changes the subject rapidly, as he often does. "Something is bothering you."

"Isn't it always, these days?" I sigh. "I feel like I never contact you without an agenda. I promise, the next time we speak, I'll have Todd with me and introduce you. I should have done it today, in fact."

"I look forward to it."

"Xenia's followers are coming to Earth and possessing humans here," I say, getting to the point. "We captured one, but the rest have eluded us. Does your side know this is occurring? I need you to alert the fundamentals, or whatever represents authority on your side, and ask them to stop it from happening. I fear for the safety of this city with so many unscrupulous elementals causing havoc. I may have abilities, but I'm only a half-elemental and don't have the full powers of your kind."

My confidence in Ailu's ability to help me dissolves when he snorts with mirthless laughter.

"You think it's bad on your side? My world is in chaos. Consider yourself lucky over there. If we were functioning properly, no doubt we could detect and stop Xenia's followers from crossing over. As it stands, we have enough to contend with. I imagine the chaos will spread to your world soon enough. Until then, enjoy your relative peace. No one is coming to save you."

My leaden heart drops. I had convinced myself that Ailu had the answer. If the elementals can't protect us against their own, what am I supposed to do? Xenia shook my belief in my own abilities when she kidnapped me and almost possessed my body. I only escaped by a hair, and the next time we meet, my triumph is far from guaranteed. Can I be so lucky twice?

"Anyway," Ailu says. "Even if someone could help over here, it would be limited to this side. We would never be allowed to cross over to your side. More elementals in the physical realm would only create more chaos." Ailu's voice softens. "I'm sorry, Merry. I know you don't want to hear that. But you're on your own."

Ailu sinks into the air cable, and I let go. It leaps into the air once more and my eyes follow it with grim resignation. I feel very alone and small against these elemental giants who are all more powerful than I am with fewer morals to hold them back from doing whatever they wish.

It's only me against an army with Xenia at the forefront.

I close my eyes to sense for uneasiness before bed, but the night's threads are still and calm. Only the driving rain breaks the tranquility of the strands. There were no disturbances today, and I don't know what that means. Is Xenia finished gathering followers?

Or is something larger coming?

CHAPTER XIV

Dreaming

My breath forms a cloud in front of my face in the bitterly cold air, obscuring the camp of Franks across the valley. I stamp my feet to warm them and wish that the enemy could be squashed as easily. The Franks are renowned for their fierce fighting and cunning strategy.

I'm not frightened—not frightened enough to confess my fears to my comrades, at least—but the sight of the enemy churns my stomach with unease. This is not my first battle, far from it, but in the months of hiring myself out as a mercenary to dueling chieftains on the mainland, I have never faced a troop of Franks, infamous for their fighting prowess. A year of traveling and fighting made a man of that boy who fled from the druids, but although my palms are callused where my sword rests, they are cold and clammy against the leather grip.

My friend Ingulf slaps me on the back. The motion of his large hand, which once caused me to stumble forward with the force, now barely moves me. Months with his Gepid mercenaries has built muscles on my once-boyish frame.

"Why the long face, Merlin?" he asks. "Pissing in your boots with fear, boy? Surely not."

"I'll be pissing in their boots once this is done," I reply with all the bravado I can muster. Ingulf lets out a hearty chuckle.

"That's the spirit. You'll be fine. And if you're not, you'll be feasting with Woden and Thunor in the halls of the gods tonight. Or whatever place warriors go where you're from."

"To be reborn, if I'm lucky," I say absently, my mind on the battle ahead, not on the afterlife. "That block you used last battle, would you show me? I meant to ask earlier, but it

117

slipped my mind."

"We haven't had time to think, you mean," Ingulf grumbles. "This job came quick on the heels of the last."

"It will pay well," I remind him, and he nods in agreement.

"That it will. We'll be rolling in silver, wine, and women once we're finished here. We struck a good bargain with King Thorweald of Trehithe, and he is generous with spoils."

Ingulf holds his spear out, and I mirror him.

"Everyone expects you to hold the spear like this," he says. "But in close quarters, its use can be limited. It's still the best grip if you have a shield, but what if your shield is lost?" He tosses his to the side and I mimic the motion. "Put your free hand to good use."

He tosses the spear higher in one hand and grasps it firmly in the other. I nod my understanding.

"Use it like a staff. Of course."

"Ah, but not simply a staff. Never forget it has a sharp end. Use that." He strikes me with the spear, and I block, then he repeats. On the third hit, he swings the spearhead swiftly toward my unprotected head. I flinch when he stops the blow before contact. He steps back with a grin. "Your turn."

I take a moment to consider what I have learned. Then, with a flurry of movement, I attack Ingulf with my spear. The ferocity of my strike makes Ingulf step back, but he soon holds his ground after his initial surprise.

"Don't just stand there," he roars. "Make me bleed."

We have an audience now, and our fellow mercenaries cheer and holler at our fighting. I wait until Ingulf's eyes flicker to a loud yell on his left. With a sweeping arc of my spear, the sharp head swings toward his face. He sees it but is not quick enough to block. I stop the spear a hair's breadth from his head.

We both breathe heavily with our eyes locked on each other. Ingulf's face breaks open with a wide grin.

118

"You have it, Merlin." He steps away from my spear. "You're a quick learner. But do you know what the wisest course of action is?"

"What?"

"Don't drop your shield," he says to gouts of laughter from our audience.

An hour later, we march across the field toward the enemy encampment. They are ready for us, ranged in a double line. Those at the back hold their spears at the ready to throw at our approaching group. Brightly striped tunics peek out from fur waistcoats that make them appear even broader-shouldered, and their heads are partly shaven above grim and intimidating faces. What they lack in numbers, they make up for in a wild light to their eyes that promises fearsome feats of strength.

I swallow hard and wait for the signal from Ingulf. It comes a moment later—the horn that hangs from his belt rings clear and pure through the frosty air—and we charge. When we're close enough, spears and throwing axes fly overhead with a deadly whistling sound. Most thud to a stop in the white-tipped grass, but a few cries of pain and gurgles of ending life indicate our enemies' successes.

Those of us who are uninjured pound forward with our spears horizontal and our war cries loud. The enemy forms a shield wall with spears poking through like a deadly hedgehog, but I have worked out a strategy which has earned me the nickname "Merlin the Flighted" among my fellows. With my shield, I smash away the nearest spear then leap onto the boss of a shield and vault over my opponents' heads.

I'm now behind enemy lines, and it would be a dangerous

place if my comrades were not currently smashing into the shield wall and causing plenty of distractions. I use the opportunity to stab two men while they are occupied, but I soon turn to face spear-throwers in the second line.

I engage in battle with the enraged Frank before me who seems determined that one of us will die soon, although he doesn't appear to care who, so reckless are his movements. Before long, my shield lies abandoned on the grass. It's now or never to practice my new move, so I hold my spear in both hands and defend myself against my fierce opponent.

Within a minute, I have dispatched the man with a spearhead to the eye, and I retrieve my shield before the next man rushes my way. He carries no spear, but instead holds a small sword in one hand and a shield in the other.

I grip my spear tightly. I have fought against men with swords before, although the spear is more common in these parts. It doesn't influence my technique overly—I still need to thrust my sharp spearhead into his vulnerable body—but I do have the advantage of reach. However, if he slices my spear with his sword, the spear could be rent in two.

I'm quick, though, and I have a decent chance at stabbing him with a powerful blow before he can hack at my spear. I thrust forward, but he deflects with his shield and lunges at me. I narrowly miss getting skewered by leaping to the side. I don't hesitate with my next blow, and the swordsman dodges and parries the spear. Then, in a move that bewilders me, he tosses his shield to the side, bats my spear with his sword, and, before I can recover from the shock, he forces my spear to the ground with his free hand and steps on the end.

It snaps in half, and I am left with a broken shaft while he picks up his shield once more.

I might be flummoxed by my predicament, but I'm not one to waste an opportunity. When he bends to retrieve his shield,

I thrust the jagged end of my spear into his exposed neck. Blood immediately pours out of the wound, and the man staggers to his knees then falls over with his hand on his neck.

His sword drops with a thud onto his shield, and I pick it up. I have some experience with a sword, but not a lot. Beggars can't be choosers, though, and without a working spear, a sword will have to do.

The weapon feels strange in my grip. It is light, meant to be wielded in one hand, and it looks freshly sharpened to a fine edge, which is visible even through the blood that stains it. Using only one hand will allow me to hold a shield at the same time, something the two-handed broadsword warriors of my homeland cannot.

Before I can pick up my shield, a new opponent turns toward me. There is no time, and I swing the sword at the approaching spear to wildly block it.

I need to gain the advantage. What did my swordsman opponent do? When the enemy thrusts his spear at me again, I block the blow. I grab the spear, thrust it to the ground, and stamp on the end. With a sickening crunch, the spear breaks. My heart leaps at the success of the new move I learned in the heat of battle.

I don't step backward, which would put me in reach of the jagged spear end. I know from recent experience where that will lead. Instead, I step toward the other man.

His tawny yellow lauvan flare out in an enraged cluster at his center. Although one of my hands is occupied with a sword, the other is available. Without thinking, I slice at the man's leg then reach forward and yank at his strands.

With a strangled yell, the man collapses at my feet. I look at my sword and my free hand in consideration. I am proficient with a spear and shield, but could I be even deadlier if I use all my talents?

CHAPTER XV

No uneasiness plagues me in the night, and the lauvan network is unruffled the next morning when I check. This doesn't calm me. Xenia is working on something, and I don't know when she will strike next.

No help is coming from the elemental plane, but I can't think of what else to do to aid our cause. I check on the elemental in Ben then head to the university. My mind is agitated, but I am determined to give my lectures as tranquilly as possible.

The students yawn and take notes as if nothing is wrong, and it's only through great restraint that my worry doesn't bubble through my façade of composure. Near the end of my second class, I feel the faintest tingling in my strands that warns of approaching trouble.

"Look at the syllabus for your readings for next time," I call out as I shove papers into my satchel and race up the aisle. "Class dismissed."

The students stare at me with baffled expressions, but I don't have time to say more. Finally, the tense silence in the lauvan is broken. Another elemental is coming through, and I mean to catch this one as well. Then, it's time to get answers—the hard way, if necessary.

With a quick plunge of my hand into earth strands that swirl around my feet outside, I establish the position of the disturbance. It's a cluster of brown strands this time, small but growing fast. It's only a few blocks away, so I retreat from the threads and sprint to my van. It will be as quick to drive as to fly, and I might need my van to transport the elemental I capture. While I run, I text the others.

Big one. Now. Northeast corner of Pacific Spirit Park.

Only Anna and Minnie reply, but they are both close and

available. I race out of my parking spot, tires squealing, and gun it down the boulevard.

The sense of uneasiness is strong, even without being directly connected to the network. My stomach turns, half with the sensation and half with fear. What is happening this time? What is Xenia's plan?

I screech to a halt a half-block away from where I felt the disturbance. Anna and Minnie, already present, run toward me with looks of confusion and concern.

"I don't see anything yet," Anna pants. "Is this the spot?"

"Yes." I scan the road. "It's earth-related, but I don't know how it will manifest."

Cars zip past us on the busy road. My eyes travel up and down, searching for a sign.

"I'm going in," I say. "Watch yourselves."

Before Minnie can open her mouth to protest, I dip my hand into the earth strands at my feet. The disturbance is close and throbs with menace. It's huge, and more strands cling to its twisting surface, looking like a large ball of malevolent yarn. It's as big as the other disturbances were at their peaks, so I pull out of the lauvan.

"Anything?" I ask. Minnie shakes her head, then she grabs my arm.

I feel it too—a jolt of the Earth that buckles my knees. We glance at each other in alarm until Anna gasps.

"Look at the road," she breathes.

A grating, cracking groan rips from the tortured road. Where smooth asphalt once spread in a gray, unbroken expanse, a lengthy split yawns. It grows bigger with every passing second, first wide enough to engulf a wheel, then far larger.

Tires squeal and bumpers crunch as cars madly avoid the growing sinkhole. Minnie's fingernails dig into my arm through my coat.

"What can we do?" she squeaks. Her words galvanize me into action.

"Anna, stay here and watch for Potestas members. We must find the elemental. Yell at me if you see one. Minnie, come with me. We need to stop this hole from growing larger."

We run to the nearest point of the split, which has almost reached the sidewalk. Screams fill the air, and the smell of burned rubber wafts past my nostrils.

"Now what?" Minnie says. Her eyes are wide but determined. I point at a snarl of strands above the hole.

"Grab whatever you can and hold it together. Massage out the knots. We might slow it down that way."

Minnie lunges for a cluster and wobbles over the widening hole. I steady her arm and snatch a cluster for myself then comb my fingers through the knots frantically. The rent in the Earth slows its deep groaning on our end.

"It's working!" Minnie shouts. I start to nod, then a piercing scream turns my head.

One of the cars that screeched to a halt at the sinkhole now crosses the divide with one set of tires on each side of the chasm whose depths are hidden in shadow. A woman shrieks as she climbs from the front seat to the back. I wonder why until I notice a car seat.

"Damn it," I say to Minnie. "She has a kid in there. Stay here and work on the crack. I'll get them out."

"Careful," Minnie says with fear in her voice, but she stays with her fingers covered in strands.

I run around another parked vehicle and slide to a halt at the trunk of the woman's car. What can I do? The vehicle is a handspan away from disappearing into the sinkhole, which is disturbingly deep. Even if the child is protected by the car seat, the woman is unstrapped. Minnie is slowing the spread of the hole, but not fast enough.

124

I grab a handful of earth strands from near my feet and another from the car. Although it's an inanimate object, its position above a gaping chasm gives it plenty of potential energy and therefore lauvan. My fingers hastily twist the two handfuls together.

I need to do the other side, but there isn't much time. Without overthinking it, I vault onto the trunk of the car, slide over the roof, and land on the hood. With another twist, the car's strands are connected to earth.

That will buy us time, but it won't be long before the strands give way. I need to extract the woman and child, fast. With a sigh of resignation, I jump onto the car's roof once more and lie on my stomach to open the back door.

The woman's frightened face peers at me.

"What—" she stammers, but I cut her off.

"No time. Pass me the child, then I'll come back for you."

Her mother's instincts take over, and she shifts to grab her child. The car sways alarmingly, and she releases a stifled gasp but thrusts up a wriggling bundle in a pink onesie. I gently take the squirming baby in my hands, careful to support her head—she can't be more than a month old—and slide back to the ground. She squalls with a pitiful cry.

"Here." A spectator reaches out her arms for the baby. "I have her. Get the mother."

I don't need any more encouragement. The back tires are nearly off the edge, and the only reason the car isn't at the bottom of the gorge is due to my lauvan knots. They are already frayed, and I don't know for how long they will last. Time is not on my side.

The woman is already climbing up to the roof, but her limbs tremble so much that I'm astonished she hasn't already fallen. I slide toward her and grip her around the torso.

"Almost there," I say. "Your baby is safe. Let's get her."

The woman's face sets with resolve, and she slides with me across the roof. The car creaks under the strain of suspension, then it wobbles. I push the woman hard off the hood of the car and she collapses in a heap on the pavement. With a snap and a groan, the car drops into the chasm.

I leap off the moving hood and roll onto the asphalt. With a sickening crash, the car disappears to the bottom of the sinkhole. My heart pounds with adrenaline, and only a few sounds reach my overtaxed ears. One is the sobs of the woman and wails of her baby. The other is Anna.

"Merry! She got away!"

Damn. Anna must have spotted the elemental responsible for this mess. I push to my feet and stumble toward Anna's voice. She stands beside Minnie, wringing her hands, while Minnie's face is taut with tension.

"I think it stopped opening," she gasps. "But I don't want to let go, just in case."

"I think you're right," I say with a glance at the hole. No more strange groans or creaks emerge from the sinkhole, nothing save the occasional clod of dirt dropping into the abyss and the gush of water from a broken water main. "It must have stopped when the elemental came through. You can let go now."

Minnie releases the strands and rocks back on her heels with a sigh of relief. I run my hands through my hair.

"What a waste," I say. "Another opportunity to capture a minion of Xenia's, and they got away." I kick a chunk of asphalt into the sinkhole, and it falls with a satisfying arc.

"I wouldn't call our trip here a waste," Anna says. "You did save that woman and her baby, after all."

"My good deed for the day." I squint at the water pouring out of the pipe below our feet. "Is anyone watching me? I could try to fix that pipe, since we're here."

126

I lie on my stomach and lean over the crumbling edge. There's a weight on my legs, then Minnie's voice floats down.

"Just dangling over a precipice, are we? Sometimes you're an idiot, Merry."

"It's not the first time you've called me that." I grunt in exertion. The water strands of the torrent are furious against my hands. How can I control them enough to stop the flow? I gather a cluster and am rewarded by a jet of water in my face. After I sputter the liquid from my mouth, my hands grasp more strands and attempt to knot them to stop the flow. Within a minute, I concede defeat and wriggle back to a seated position.

"I don't know what I'm doing," I say to Minnie. The words surprise me with their poignancy. When it comes to lauvan, I used to think I knew it all. Then I met Xenia and the other elementals, and I found out that I'm a babe in the woods. Before Xenia, I would have chalked up the broken water main as a problem unsolvable by lauvan manipulation. Now I imagine what a water elemental could do, and I despair at my own talents.

"Here, let me try." Minnie leans over the edge, and I hastily grab her calves. Her arms move for a few moments, then she stiffens and draws herself up. "There, all fixed."

I look over the edge to where the pipe is now blocked with a plug of ice. It's an elegant solution. I might have thought of it, given enough time, but I wonder if I have the finesse to pull it off.

If I can't handle a simple water pipe, what the hell am I going to do when faced with Xenia?

CHAPTER XVI

A ripple of unease shivers down my spine. I ignore it until it occurs to me that the uneasiness from the sinkhole faded minutes ago. Is this a new disturbance?

My eyes widen with horror, and I kneel to plunge my hands into the strand network.

"Merry?" Minnie's voice fades as my conscious soars away from my body. I don't travel far. Mere blocks from here, an orange cluster sparks and flickers, growing more massive every second.

My body gasps when my conscious enters it once more.

"Two blocks east," I say to the others. "Fire."

"Another one?" Minnie says, but I'm already sprinting away. Footsteps pound behind me, and we fly to the fire. A pillar of smoke billows between rooftops, and my heart sinks. How did it grow so quickly? Where is the elemental?

I skid around a corner and stop in horror. One side of the house is an inferno straight from the pages of Dante's Hell. Flames lick greedily at the other side and threaten to consume it within minutes.

There's a hoarse shout that chokes off with a cough, and my stomach clenches tightly.

"Someone is still in there," I shout to the others. "Anna, any sign of the elemental?"

"I'll follow if I see anyone, and text you where they go. You get the person in there."

Anna's suggestion is a good one if we don't want to smell roasted flesh—it's an obscene scent, yet disturbingly reminiscent of a good pork roast—so I leave Anna to watch for trouble and run with Minnie toward the fire. In the seconds we spent devising a plan, the flames have licked closer to the

128

second level window where a man drapes over the frame. He looks wilted and about to pass out. Sirens wail in the distance.

There is no way we can contain this fire, but we can rescue the man. With every step forward, my mind races through the options. I could scale the wall, but then how would I bring him down? Entering through the house is not an option anymore. Even now, flickering orange illuminates the man's back with a fiery glow, indicating that the flames are already in his room.

I'll have to harness the elements.

The heat is intense, but Minnie's hand on my back reassures me. Instantly, my body cools a few degrees.

"I made the liquid in your body colder," she shouts to me above the roar of the fire.

I nod my thanks and inwardly marvel at her skill, then I reach down and thrust my hands into the earth strands below me. Pillars of earth push my feet up with an unsteady rhythm, and I rise higher and higher. The smoke is thick enough that my antics should remain unnoticed, but Minnie pulls some water out of the ground and creates a cloud of her own to cover us. It brings blissfully cool air with it, and I breathe in relief.

By the time I reach the man, he is passed out and dangles an arm and leg out of the window frame. I yank his body over my shoulder in a fireman's carry, nearly losing my balance on my earthen pillars, then wobble into a crouch to reach the lauvan once more. Sweat pours down my face at the intense heat, and I wonder what it would feel like without Minnie's help. With a crumbling, grinding sound, the pillar descends.

Minnie clutches my forearm as soon as I regain the ground and drags me away from the house.

"The ambulance is over here," she wheezes. "Bring him this way."

The paramedics rush to help when we emerge from the smoke, and I deliver my burden with relief. We back away and

Anna joins us.

"Any sign of the elemental?" My voice is unpleasantly raspy, and I can't wait to fix it at home. My mouth is drier than the Sahara and my eyes gritty from smoke.

"No," Anna says, then she inhales sharply. "Yes. Over there. The man in the red shirt."

My heart leaps. Despite our rescue detour, we might still capture another elemental. I identify the man Anna indicated, and it's clear that he's the one we seek. His eyes are alight with manic excitement as he stares, mesmerized, at the inferno before him. He lifts his hands—flickering orange strands mingle with maroon over the knuckles—and prepares to do more damage to the already destroyed house.

"Wait right there!" an authoritative voice calls out. My head turns in surprise. Jogging toward us is Officer Lee, her face set in resolve.

"Damn it," I mutter. "She's onto me. I can't let the elemental go, though. Come on."

I run away from Officer Lee, who shouts angrily behind me, and head straight to the fire elemental. He is so focused on his task, his eyes alight with glee, that I am almost upon him before he notices me. His face opens with surprise then transforms into a sneer of contempt. He turns on his heel and races around the burning house.

I can't let him get away. Xenia's elementals are too destructive. They must be stopped, and they need to answer my questions. I charge after him, heedless of Officer Lee's yells behind me. Around the corner, the elemental waits for me with wild eyes.

"Nice try," he says then pulls some sparking fire lauvan between his fingers. A tremendous crack thunders through my body, then something hits my head and I know no more.

CHAPTER XVII

Dreaming

My foot slams into the flimsy door. It swings open with a screech of broken wood, but I brush past it before splinters hit the floor. Three paces across the tiny room brings me to my hotel bed, where I carefully lay down my burden.

The woman moans but thankfully remains unconscious. I swing the door closed, prop a chair against it to keep it that way, and bend over the bed. The burns on her face are severe, and with a start I notice smoldering sparks in the remains of her singed hair. I leap to my water basin and scoop a cupful, but before I pour it over her, I pause. Her burns are so severe that I fear touching them with anything, even water.

But the fire needs to be put out. I could pinch the sparking orange lauvan with my fingertips, but there are too many for my slowness. Better to use water.

I reach to the cup and draw out water lauvan. A few droplets of liquid rise, and I carefully maneuver them to the side of the woman's head and drop them on the smoldering hair. One by one, they extinguish with a hiss.

When I am certain that no fire remains, I kneel more comfortably on the wooden floorboards and assess my new patient. Even though the battle has passed, rage still pumps blood through my veins with force and quivers my muscles as they desperately seek an outlet for the anger. Killing the woman's attacker wasn't enough. I wanted him to burn the way she burned. That would be the only justice imaginable.

Her life took precedence, though, and I recall with regret my knife slicing his neck as I reached from behind. He never saw me coming, although the woman did, her already wide eyes filled with terror, pain, and hope. I wish he had seen me. I wish he had lasted longer, so I could have taught him a lesson that might have lasted into whatever future awaits his spirit.

Pounding footsteps pass my door, drawn by shouting in rapid French. They are likely on their way to the room I found this woman in, alerted by inquisitive neighbors. This hotel near the Palais Royale is frequented by prostitutes often enough that noises and shouting wouldn't have caused alarm, but the smell of smoke always worries folk in densely populated Paris.

I ignore the shouts and instead focus on the woman. Her breathing is shallow, and her skin is pale where it is not ravaged by burns. I run my knife gently down her ripped and burned dress to expose the skin on her torso. Although her form is lovely, I have eyes only for her injuries. The burn spreads from the right side of her face, down her neck, across her shoulder to the side of her left breast, and ends at the bottom of her ribcage. The skin is red and raw, the flesh exposed in parts, with patches of white amid weeping injuries.

Fire lauvan still flicker over the angry raw flesh and terrible knots in her royal blue strands, and I consider my options. There is little more effective at counteracting the power of fire than water, but to subject her ruined skin to water makes my own skin crawl. I have tried it in the past to ill effect.

However, water doesn't have to touch her to relieve her. I position the cup on the bed beside her ribcage, propped up by her torn dress, and pull blue strands from the water's surface. Drops hover in midair, but I touch them with my finger, and they run down my hand and away from her body. Untethered lauvan wriggle in my grasp. They won't last long without their source, but I don't need long.

With a twist of my fingers, the water strands curl around their fire opposites and negate the power they still have on the woman's flesh. Over and over I twist blue with orange until every fiery thread is paired with a blue one.

The skin is still hot—my hands feel warmth emanating from her burns—so I snatch a few silvery lauvan from the surrounding air and weave them through. With any luck, the cooling effect of wind will soothe her.

All this work on the elemental strands is only a precursor to the real job, and now I'm ready to work on her knots. I massage one close to her cheekbone, resigned to the long, tedious task ahead. Her eyelids flutter, and my heart stops. Is she waking up? The pain will be intense, and her screams might awaken the neighbors. If I am to bring her back to health and reduce her suffering, I must remain uninterrupted. I reach for the strands above her head, determined to induce a state of unconsciousness, and my fingertip brushes her uninjured temple. It's cool and clammy.

She's in shock from her wounds. This is serious. If I don't calm her body, all the untangling I achieve will be for naught. I must steady her until I can heal the wounds.

I learned a trick for this a few centuries ago. The calm steadiness of earth strands, with their slow movements compared to other elements, intrigued me. Could element strands influence a person's state of mind? I usually tweak a person's human lauvan to affect their mood, but I wondered whether mixing elemental strands might produce a longer-lasting effect. The moods didn't last any longer, but I could indeed influence them with element strands.

Luckily, my room is on the bottom floor, and brown earth threads carpet the floorboards. The woman's body trembles violently. I scoop up a handful of strands and weave them quickly into her blue lauvan. In my haste, some twist amid the other elemental strands above her burns.

Instantly, the woman ceases her shuddering and her body relaxes into deeper breathing. My eyebrows raise in surprise. I

133

hadn't expected my little trick to work so quickly nor so effectively. Her eyes flutter open, and she looks around with confused and fearful eyes. Before she can scream, I shuffle closer to her head so she can see me.

"Don't be afraid," I say quietly. "I am here to help. My name is Merle. What is your name?"

Her shoulders relax when she sees my face.

"You saved me," she says in a hoarse voice. The smoke must have affected her. I make a mental note to fix the knots around her throat. Her eyes wander over my features. "My name is Celeste."

Her face contorts in a grimace of pain. I swiftly reach for the strands of her head.

"Sleep, Celeste," I whisper. "By morning, this will all be a terrible dream."

CHAPTER XVIII

Sound is the first sensation that returns to me. The swish of tires on pavement and the shuddering quiet of a vehicle in motion mingle with a murmur of voices. My mind can't comprehend speech yet, so I let it wander.

Pain is the next to arrive. My head throbs with incessant pounding, and my throat is agonizingly parched. Memories drift back to me of the fire elemental and the flaming house. The elemental must have collapsed a beam from the house on me. How am I in a vehicle? Did Anna and Minnie drag me away, or is this a police cruiser?

The murmuring voices are female, which doesn't rule out the possibility of Officer Lee driving me to the station. I bully my tired brain into understanding the words.

"That was an amazing cloud you made to cover us," Anna says. I relax. I might be in pain, but at least I'm with the right people. "The police officer had no idea where we were."

"Thanks," Minnie replies. "There's no way we can explain anything, so it's better not to stop to chat with the police. Besides, I can heal him faster than the hospital can."

A rustle of fabric indicates that Anna twists to look at my sprawled body on the back bench.

"Is he okay? Can't you fix him up now?"

"He'll be fine," Minnie says dismissively. "I want to get away from the police first. It's not the first time he's been injured—he's used to pain."

It's such a callous remark from my usually gentle and caring Minnie that I almost stop breathing. Anna must be similarly affected, for she is silent for a long moment. She must be looking at Minnie strangely, because Minnie sighs explosively.

135

"That was heartless, wasn't it?" she says.

"Maybe a little," Anna replies. "From what memories are coming back to me from the past, it seems unlike you."

"I don't know what's going on." There's a tapping sound, as if Minnie drums her fingers on the steering wheel. "Ever since I found out about my half-elemental status, I've been different. It comes out—"

The throbbing in my head increases unbearably at that moment, and it makes my ears ring so loudly that I can't focus on Minnie's words. When the sound clears, Anna is speaking.

"What if you didn't have to be like that anymore? Your human lauvan are still you, aren't they?"

"My conscious seems to travel with the elemental lauvan, but my human strands are the ones that contain my soul, or whatever comes back every rebirth," Minnie says. Her tone is pensive.

Anna wriggles in her seat, and the leather creaks.

"Exactly. What if—and hear me out, here—what if you could take away your elemental strands and put them on someone else?"

"Isn't that what Xenia did to possess people?" Minnie sounds dubious. "I'm pretty sure I would take over the body."

"But maybe your human lauvan would recover their consciousness," Anna says, excitement edging her voice. "And if your elemental strands wanted to, they could probably coinhabit with the person's strands of the body you possess. An equal partnership." She pauses then says in a diffident tone, "I'd be willing to try, if you want."

There's more drumming on the steering wheel, then the van swings to the right and stops.

"What the hell," Minnie says. "Let's try it. I hate being like this, being pulled in two."

It's time to wake up. Minnie is about to take drastic action,

136

and I'm worried she—or Anna—won't survive the experiment. I groan loudly and then regret it when my head threatens to split in two at the vibration.

"Merry," Minnie says close to my face. "You're awake. Here, let me fix your head enough for you to talk."

I let Minnie administer to my wounds. Neither she nor Anna mention their discussion. When my eyes are finally able to open, I study Minnie's face. She has always seemed excited about being a half-elemental. What changed? The altercation with Todd doesn't seem like it would warrant this reaction.

Does she truly think being like me is such a terrible thing?

After Minnie untangles the worst of my head knots, I take over and she settles in the driver's seat.

"I need to check on the prisoner," I say. "We've left him long enough. I need answers."

Minnie and Anna glance at each other with worried expressions, but Minnie shrugs and turns left toward Bethany's house. When we pull up to the sidewalk at our destination, my head is clear, and my throat can speak without rasping.

"What are you going to do?" Anna says with trepidation once we exit the van. My face tightens.

"Whatever I need to do to get some answers. If you want to stay outside, I understand."

Anna swallows and Minnie is pale, but they both shake their heads.

"We all need answers," Minnie says. "We're coming."

In the basement, Ben is still on the chair where I left him this morning. His lips are cracked, and his face is gray and sunken.

"Ready to talk?" I say without preamble. His eyes narrow

with dislike, and he shakes his head. I slide out of my coat and roll up my shirt sleeves. "So be it. Don't say I didn't give you a chance to avoid this."

I kneel on the ground and carefully pluck two human strands from his torso. He twitches and watches me with wide eyes.

"What are you doing?" he forces out of his parched throat. I grin, but there is no mirth in the expression.

"Making you talk."

Slowly but relentlessly, I pull the two strands outward. Ben shows no reaction at first, but then his body stiffens. After two seconds, a grunt of pain emerges from his contorted face, then a scream rips out of his throat. I release the strands.

"You consider yourself an expert on the elements, and rightfully so," I say calmly. "But I've lived in a body for fifteen hundred years, and I've learned a few tricks. That was only a taste of what I can do. Consider your next words carefully."

Ben pants with frenzied breaths and panicked eyes. This is his first time in a physical form, and it's not going well for him. We captured him as soon as he crossed the divide, and he's been starved of food and drink and now tortured. If he was hoping for a fun ride in his new body, he didn't get one.

I reach for him once more, and his entire body flinches.

"Wait," he says. "Wait. What do you want to know?"

I don't let my triumph show on my face, but I sense the others' relief behind me.

"What is Xenia's plan? Why are elementals crossing over? How can I stop it?"

He barks a laugh despite his nervous glance at my fingers.

"You can't stop her. She's the earth fundamental. She has more power than you can even imagine."

"Yes, yes, the all-powerful fundamental. I understand. I still want to know what she's up to."

"I don't know much. She sent out a call to her allies, offering

138

a chance to explore the physical world. I jumped at it. We haven't been allowed for millennia. She said she would need us for something, but that we would get details after crossing over." His face darkens. "Thanks to you, I haven't seen her yet. And when you cut off my access, I couldn't communicate."

"That was the idea." I tap my fingers on my knee in thought, and the elemental flinches again. "How do I stop you lot from crossing over?"

The elemental shrugs.

"I don't know how this side works."

I sigh and stand. My vision tunnels to a pinpoint before widening again. I should untangle the rest of my threads before I exert myself further.

"How many more are coming through?" Minnie asks with an edge to her voice.

"Four or five? Xenia is still recruiting, so maybe more."

I don't have anything else to say to the elemental, so I escort him to the bathroom. After I lock him in the basement once more, I meet Minnie and Anna upstairs.

"You'd better feed him," I say to Anna and pass her a few bills. "We have all the information we'll get from him."

"What do we do with him now?" Minnie glances at the basement door.

"I was doing some reading in the spirit library," Anna says. "There might be a way to banish spirits from this world. I can keep researching if you like."

"Please." I rub my hand through my hair. "I have no ideas. Anything you find is helpful. But now, I need to go lick my wounds. Who knows when the next disturbance is coming?"

139

When Minnie and I get home, I park myself on a dining chair to untangle my strands.

"Need help?" Minnie leans against the kitchen doorframe and watches my deft fingers pick apart knots.

"I'm only fine-tuning." I shake my head. "I won't be long."

Minnie shrugs and retreats to the couch with a book. Minutes later, when I pull apart the final tangle with a flourish, there's a knock on the door.

"I'll get it," I say. I amble to the door and open it with a lazy pull, expecting Alejandro or Jen.

My neighbor Gary stands in the hall. He grins affably at me.

"Hello, Merry. I forgot my sweater here last time. At least, I can't find it, and the missus swears she didn't wash it."

"Come in." I wave him into the entryway. "I don't remember seeing it, but I'll ask Minnie."

"You almost have your own missus now." Gary chuckles and enters the living room. Minnie slides a bookmark in her novel and smiles at our visitor.

"Have you seen Gary's sweater?" I ask her.

"I put it in the bedroom. I thought maybe it was yours."

When Gary isn't looking, I give her a look of incredulity—I might be old, but my fashion sense doesn't allow for an old-man cardigan—and she snickers silently.

I retreat to the bedroom, where a gray cardigan lounges on my dresser. I shake my head once more at Minnie's comment and return to the living room. Gary's back is to me while he talks to Minnie, and his topic catches my interest.

"I saw the article in the missus' magazine. Completely crackpot, I says to myself, but then I remember the cave and Merry's powers, and I read more. This woman, she says she has past lives and can remember them all. What a yarn."

Minnie makes a noncommittal noise and glances at me. I shrug and let her deal with the conversation. She deserves it

140

after the cardigan comment.

"I don't think I'd want to know," Gary continues. "Even if I could. Even if the woman wasn't a crackpot. It's been a good life, a full one, with the missus and the kids and grandkids. Lots of experiences. It was full enough, you know? I don't want more than that." Gary chuckles. "But, likely enough, she's a looney, and this is all talk."

"I found it." I hold out the cardigan to Gary. He takes it with a smile.

"Thanks, Merry. The evenings are too cold these days to be without my favorite sweater. Night, Minnie."

Gary shuffles out the door and down the hall after a cheery farewell. When I return to Minnie, she pats the couch.

"I hope I'm that content when I'm seventy," she says.

"I know I wasn't." I sit at her invitation and drape my arm over her shoulders. She snuggles closer. I briefly wonder if Gary has a past, since everyone else I know seems to. From the sound of it, Gary wouldn't touch the grail even if given a chance. "I'm glad Gary is, though."

I sleep uneasily that night and wake from a restless doze when Minnie kisses my cheek. My eyes open, and I stare at her in puzzlement.

"You're dressed already," I say.

Minnie chuckles.

"Very observant. I have an early client today. Text me if there's a disturbance, okay?"

The worries of yesterday flood back at Minnie's words, and I lie in bed with a churning stomach for a few minutes after she departs. Fretting doesn't solve anything, however, so I

141

eventually leap out of bed and dress myself for the day.

Since I'm early, I stop at a coffeeshop on the way and treat myself to a very tall, very dark roast that tickles my nostrils with delicious tendrils of scent. It smells too good to waste on distractions like driving, so I wander to a nearby park to enjoy it. I might as well dip into the lauvan network while I'm there to check for disturbances. No uneasiness has plagued me yet, but the day is young.

I sip my coffee and walk over the dirt patch of a pitcher's mound. Instantly, the ground around me churns. I freeze in horror. What is happening? It isn't me.

Was I unlucky enough to walk over a new disturbance?

CHAPTER XIX

Far quicker than I can react, the dirt shoots up from the ground and forms a wall higher than my outstretched arms, surrounding me entirely in a brown tube. The scent of freshly dug soil fills my nose, moist and heavy. My coffee spills, and part of my mind curses its loss even as I plunge my hands into the lauvan to release myself from my earthen prison.

The strands skitter around my hands, slippery and elusive. My fingers scrabble uselessly at the dirt but can't gain a hold. My heartrate spikes. This is no disturbance. This is Xenia trapping me, for reasons I don't yet comprehend.

Dirt crumbles in a circle at face height, and I flinch when Xenia's spirit in March's body gazes at me in satisfaction.

"Dear Merry," she says. "He tries so hard yet is so easy to foil. You've had quite the runabout lately, haven't you? Chasing after portals only to be waylaid at every turn."

"We captured one of yours," I spit out. My heart pounds, but now from anger instead of fear. What does Xenia hope to accomplish by trapping me? My mind flips through the possibilities, and none are promising.

"Yes, that was unfortunate," she says with a sigh. "Although, it was probably for the best. I don't need followers who can't best a half-elemental. Can't really pull their weight, can they? I want strong, capable followers. The loss of one weak link isn't much of a loss at all. Tell me, did he spill any deep, dark secrets, anything that will allow you to defeat me?"

She says this with a knowing smile, and my blood boils. The elemental didn't tell me anything I couldn't have guessed, and Xenia knows it. She chuckles.

"Your problem is that there isn't really a master plan, and what there is, I wouldn't tell my allies. They are all beneath

143

me. Why would I trust them with important information? They play their role, nothing more. Everything of note is locked in here." Xenia taps her forehead.

I close my eyes briefly in acknowledgement of the setback.

"Even if we capture your minions," I say heavily. "It won't gain us anything, except remove one more source of destruction from the world."

"Exactly." Xenia beams with satisfaction, and I want to wipe the smug expression off her face. "They are quite destructive, aren't they? Glorious when they come through the divide. They're lying low for now, but in a few days—I can tell you this, because there's nothing you can do to stop it, and I enjoy seeing the hopelessness in your eyes—we're going to let loose. The others want to have some fun, and I see no reason to not indulge them. Making my allies happy keeps the ranks in line."

Xenia traces the edge of the earthen hole while I think of a way to escape her gloating, but my mind races through the bigger picture. What does Xenia want, and how can I stop her?

"I've been working on my other element skills," she says conversationally. "Took a page out of your book. It's a work in progress, but it's rather exhilarating to try new things. You can't comprehend how freeing it is to be out of dormancy." She gazes at me in reflection. "It's a terrible state of nothingness. I was conscious, but only enough to know that there should be something more than what I had. I could communicate with others, but influence nothing. It was horrible, and for what? So you could live?" She sniffs. "But it doesn't matter now. The world might be out of balance, but I'll let the other fundamentals fret about it. I have plans, and a little chaos will only help bring my schemes to fruition."

"We will stop you," I say with more conviction than I feel. Xenia must sense my foreboding, for she laughs.

"Humans are weak, pitiful creatures, hardly different from

144

the deer in the woods. I admit, as a half-elemental you have a few more tricks, but it's nothing compared to the might of an elemental, especially one such as myself. You and your kind don't stand a chance." She smiles. "I had nothing else to say beyond that. I merely saw your signature close by, and I couldn't resist gloating. Is that petty? I can't say I mind. I could stop you, but I rather enjoy watching your feeble attempts at impeding me. It should get even more interesting in the future, when my more powerful allies come to the physical world." She steps back and waves her fingers in a mockery of a farewell. "Until we meet again, Merry."

She disappears and leaves the tube of soil surrounding me. I sigh in frustration and plunge my hands into the earth strands one more. Surely, with enough intention, I can override whatever Xenia did to turn them slippery. To my surprise, my fingers comb through them with ease. Xenia must have released whatever hold she had on them.

I rip the soil away in a frenzy, desperate to escape my earthen prison. When I emerge from the collapsed mound of dirt and brush soil off my clothes, an audience watches me.

"Are you okay?" a man calls out, but no one steps forward. The sight must have been too unnerving.

"Fine, thanks." I wave and attempt to sidle away, but a woman in a blue uniform strides forward.

"Merry Lytton," Officer Lee says in a no-nonsense voice. "I need to bring you to the station for questioning."

I hang my head for a moment. The police are the last thing I want to deal with right now. I have more important business to attend to, and going into the station is a waste of time. However, if I don't cooperate, I will have to go on the run, which I currently don't have time or patience for.

"Do I have a choice?"

"Not really." She tilts her head. "You can come quietly or

145

not." She touches the handcuffs on her belt.

I nod.

"Lead the way."

Officer Lee opens the back door of her cruiser and gestures me inside. Her partner sits in the driver's seat, sipping a coffee. I think sourly of my spilled beverage within the mound of dirt.

"Back to the station?" he says. Officer Lee nods.

"I want to ask him a few questions."

"Shouldn't we leave that to the detectives?"

"They can have him once I'm done. I won't be long. He's not on anyone's case radar yet."

Her partner glances at me before he flips on his turn signal and eases into traffic.

"Then how did you nab him? What was he doing?"

"He came willingly," Officer Lee says with satisfaction. "Just a few questions, for clarity's sake, then he's free to go."

Her partner shrugs, and we drive in silence for the short trip to the station. It's not in my best interest to speak until spoken to, so I remain quiet. Inwardly, I'm seething at the delay—I could be checking for new disturbances, warning the others of Xenia's words, reading the books that Anna discovered about banishing spirits—but instead I'm on my way to placate an overly suspicious police officer.

We pull into a spacious but utilitarian garage and Lee escorts me through a side door into the station followed by her partner. We pass by a desk with a cop shuffling papers around.

"Bringing this man in for questioning," she says to him. "Pass me the forms and I'll fill them in—it's your break soon."

"Thanks, Kat," he says with a look of relief at not having to process my details. He flips open a folder and slides sheets of paper out. "Room three is free right now."

"Thanks." Lee grabs the papers and gestures toward a hallway. My footsteps echo on the cement floor as I pass blue doors with industrial steel handles.

"Keep an eye out, will you?" Lee says to her partner when we reach a door with a white three painted on it. When he nods, she opens the door and ushers me inside. I look at her with a raised eyebrow once we're seated across from each other. The table is bolted to the floor and has sturdy loops embedded on the surface. In the top corner, a winking camera watches me.

"An interrogation room?" I say with distaste. "Really? I thought this was a friendly chat."

"I can record our conversation in here," she says without apology and presses a button on the wall. "Where else, the lunchroom? This will do just fine. So, Merry Lytton. I've encountered you at many different locations, some crime scenes, some not. The flooding by the Fraser River, the first and second house fires, the wall of dirt, and the museum. You have given alibis for everywhere except the second house fire and the dirt. Please explain what you were doing at each location and why you ran away from me at the fire."

"Today was strange. I have no rational explanation for the dirt. Were there excavator tracks? Perhaps I was dumped on by errant construction machinery. I can be very absentminded on occasion and might not have noticed nearby vehicles."

Lee's fingers twitch, as if she is trying not to drum them on the table in frustration.

"And the fire? Why did you run?"

"I saw someone smiling and holding a lighter. It was probably the arsonist. I was doing my Good Samaritan duty, but he got away and a piece of the building fell on me. My friends dragged me to safety by the time you showed."

Lee's jaw is tight. She's trying so hard to find flaws in my tales, but I'm a master storyteller.

"In addition," she says. "You were caught on security camera at the museum on September twenty ninth but were not

147

on the list of witnesses for the artifact theft. Care to elaborate?"

"I left too soon," I say with a shrug. "I heard sirens in the distance on the way to my car, but they could have been for anything. Such a shame, isn't it? A beautiful piece of history taken by an unscrupulous collector. I hope it turns up soon."

"Your phone number was on a flyer that came to the station's attention. What was that for?"

Lee must refer to the wanted flyer for March that we posted around town.

"My friend's aunt wandered away from her home and we haven't seen her for a few days. Someone said that the woman in the photo had visited her the morning of her disappearance, so we thought we would gather information."

"Why didn't your friend approach the police with it?"

"Fear of authority." I shrug. "I did try to convince him."

Lee audible grinds her teeth. I tilt my head in question.

"Anything else?"

"Please wait here while I consult my partner," she says tightly.

I don't have time for this. I've humored her long enough. When she stands, I reach for her nearest magnolia-pink strands and pour my intention into them.

"I think we're done here," I say softly. "You can let me go now."

Her eyes glaze over, and her brow relaxes.

"Yes," she says faintly. "Yes, thank you for coming in."

"It was my pleasure." I stand and nod my head. She unlocks the door and holds it open for me, and I breeze out with a jaunty wave at her partner who stares after me with a frown.

Before I duck behind a parked car to transform into a bird— my van is still at the coffeeshop—I text the others.

Round table meeting at dinner. We need to be proactive about Xenia.

CHAPTER XX

I catch my last class—the students look surprised to see me, as if they weren't certain I would show—and spend the afternoon alternating between marking and sensing for disturbances, but the lauvan are quiet. The tranquility doesn't reassure me.

Enough of my friends respond to my text that the bag of Chinese food I carry to Alejandro's door is heavy. Most are there when I arrive, and Alejandro takes the bag from me while Minnie kisses my cheek.

"What happened?" she says with concern. I take off my coat and sling it over the couch's arm.

"Xenia happened." I speak louder when I realize everyone has stopped to listen to me. "She trapped me in a prison of earth and proceeded to gloat about how weak and defenseless we are compared to her and her minions. I was then accosted by a police officer and questioned at the station for being at the disturbances for no good reason."

Minnie's grip on my arm tightens at my story. The others look shocked.

"But you didn't do anything wrong," Jen says with indignation. "You even saved a few people from dying."

"It's suspicious why I was there every time, though. I get the sense that Officer Lee doesn't like mysteries."

"Kat Lee?" Wayne says with raised eyebrows. "Patrol officer, Asian, pretty but tough?"

"That's the one. Why, you know her?"

"She's the police friend I keep talking about." Wayne scratches his neck. "I've known her for years. She was my sister's roommate—that's how I met her."

"Does she know about me from you?" This is a complication

I hadn't anticipated. Wayne shakes his head vehemently.

"No. Anything I've asked her to look up has been in confidence, and she doesn't know your name from me."

I exhale explosively.

"I don't know what to do about her except hope that she doesn't catch sight of me at another disturbance. She is so confused. It would almost be amusing if she weren't getting in my way. As it stands, I don't have time to be hauled down to the station for her questions. On that note, we need to be more proactive about Xenia. Ailu made it clear that we are on our own and can't expect elemental help." I spread my hands, palm up. "I'm open to suggestions."

"We can keep being on the scene for new disturbances," says Liam.

"Yes, but that's not getting us far. Only one elemental captured."

"And four people saved," Jen reminds me. I nod.

"And four people saved. But it's not solving the bigger problem. We need to find Xenia and her minions, and we need to stop new ones from coming through the barrier."

"I don't know about finding Xenia," says Alejandro. "Not a single person has called from the posters with March's face on them. But for stopping new minions, what if we made a trap for new ones after a disturbance? They are still human."

"It will depend on the location," I say. "But I like the notion."

"I don't know about a trap," says Wayne. "How could you be sure they would walk into it? But what about a tranquillizer gun? Take the bastards down from afar. Like Alejandro says, they have human bodies."

"I'm a good shot," Cecil says. "I was on my rifle team in high school."

"Good," I say. "I have experience as well, of course, but I

prefer to have my hands free to manipulate lauvan."

"I can source the guns tomorrow morning," Wayne says eagerly. "This is great. Nab them from a distance. Clean and safe."

"If they do get closer," Anna says. "I was doing some reading, and I found a spell that might make it harder for elementals to mess with human lauvan."

"I'm always in favor of safeguards," says Jen. "Can we try it out now, and Merry can test it?"

Anna pulls a piece of paper out of her pocket.

"Liam, do you have a sharp knife?" she asks. Liam frowns but returns from the kitchen with a paring knife. Anna takes it from him and presses the tip against the pad of her index finger.

"Blood?" I say. "What kind of spell is this?"

"I think it's used because it's a very human ingredient," Anna says with a grimace as the blade breaks her skin. A bead of red liquid balloons on her finger, and she swirls it on her forearm while chanting in a language native to precolonial South America. I watch in fascination as her strands bunch around the swirl of blood then fan out to the rest of her body.

When she stops chanting, she holds her arm out to me.

"Try messing with my lauvan," she instructs. I oblige and reach my fingers out to grab her purple strands. They skitter away from me, just as the earth strands did in my dirt prison this morning. I raise my eyebrows, impressed by the effectiveness of Anna's spell.

"It works. Teach that to everyone. I don't know how long it will work for, so best to repeat it often."

I stand to stretch my legs and collect plates for the takeout food. Liam joins me in the kitchen.

"Have you figured out how many people Alejandro was in the past?" Liam opens a drawer full of cutlery. His question

151

sounds casual, but his strands are tense and waiting for my reply.

"I believe so."

"And you were friends with him in every life?"

"For the most part. Occasionally, fate led us in opposite directions, but there was always some overlap." I lean against the counter and regard Liam who twitches under my scrutiny. "You're still not sure about whether to touch the grail or not. What's holding you back?"

Liam shrugs with unease.

"It's a big decision. I don't want to rush it."

I say nothing more and merely watch Liam take a stack of plates to the table. He doesn't want to know in case he has no past. He doesn't want to be the one apart. Before he touches the grail, there is still a chance that he is one of us. When he touches it, we will know one way or another.

When I return to the table, Alejandro is speaking with Cecil.

"Next time there is a disturbance, you shoot the elemental and I'll run in to grab him," he says. I frown at Alejandro's tone and strands, both of which illustrate his reckless streak.

"Once the elemental is incapacitated, of course," I say. Alejandro shrugs.

"Of course. But now that we have Anna's spell, there isn't much danger."

"Do not underestimate these people," I say sharply. "None of you. Just because I can't break through Anna's spell doesn't mean they can't. And they don't have to touch your human lauvan to attack you with the elements. Even the weakest elemental has far more power than I do, and Xenia is another level altogether. No heroics."

Alejandro doesn't answer and shoves food into his mouth instead. Jen glances at him in concern.

"Speaking of power," Jen says to me when I take a bite of

spring roll. "I'm tired of being the damsel in distress. I want to learn how to defend myself. Do you have anything to teach me, Merry?"

I nod slowly while I chew and swallow.

"That's a great idea. I'll show you a few moves after dinner. It won't do much against an elemental, but with Anna's spell in place, it might give you a fighting chance to get away."

After dinner, I lead Jen to the backyard. Dark clouds swirl overhead in the fading daylight, but no rain falls. Cecil comes out and hovers nearby, but I ignore him. My focus is on Jen.

"Firstly, the best way to win a fight is to not start one," I say. Jen grimaces.

"Yeah, fine, but I have you as a friend. Fights seem to follow you around."

"They do lately, don't they? Still, it's a good rule to remember. If you have no choice, then you do what you must. You, as a slight woman, don't have the luxury of muscling your way through a conflict. Wayne could probably barrel down someone without bothering with technique and still win half the time."

"I need to fight smarter."

"Precisely. There are four especially vulnerable points on a human: nose, eyes, throat, and groin. Focus on these and don't bother with the rest. Hitting one of those will buy you time to get away or use your handy pepper spray to great effect."

"Okay, show me my first move." Jen bounces on the balls of her feet with her ponytail swishing behind her, her hands at the ready. I suppress a smile.

"First, let me protect myself." I weave a barrier of lauvan over the same vulnerable points I mentioned to Jen. "I want you to hit me with the force you would need to get away from a real attack. No pretense here."

I show her a series of moves designed to incapacitate an

opponent that favor a smaller person. Jen listens intently and throws as much power into her hits as she can muster. Cecil lingers nearby and offers comments and suggestions when Jen appears to be losing her advantage. I hold my tongue for a few minutes until I back up and accidentally bump into Cecil, who mutters an apology.

"Jen is in no danger here," I say, annoyed by his hovering. "Back up, please. You're making it difficult to teach."

Cecil looks chagrined but only moves away two steps. I glance at Alejandro with an unspoken plea for assistance. He throws me a resigned look but picks up a pair of wooden swords.

"Hey, Cecil," he calls. "Want to spar?"

I continue my lesson with Jen, whose face of concentration and jagged lauvan show her determination to learn. After a few minutes of instruction, a thud and shout alert me to a battle on the other side of the yard. Cecil rubs his arm with a frown then lunges without warning toward Alejandro. A flurry of blocks and thrusts ensues, and they are so quick that I can scarcely follow the action. Alejandro's eyes are narrowed in fierce concentration, and both men's strands are tight and pointed at each other. I sneak a glance at Jen, who bites her lip.

With a jolt, their swords lock at the hilt. They push against each other with intense competition, straining to make the other give ground. Wayne strides forward and pulls at Alejandro's shoulder while he pushes Cecil's.

"Good fight," he says in a jovial tone to diffuse the tension. "There's ice cream in the freezer if anyone needs to cool off."

Alejandro breathes heavily and takes a moment to compose himself before he walks into the house. Cecil paces in a circle and wipes his forehead on his sleeve. Jen touches my arm.

"I think we'll head out," she says quietly to me. I nod.

"Probably wise." I raise my voice. "Minnie, shall we leave?

I think I've imparted enough wisdom upon Jen for one day. She'll need to ruminate on my teachings to soak up their full value."

Minnie gives a very unladylike snort at my pronouncement, and Jen kicks gently at my ankle.

"I'll consider your pearls of wisdom, oh wise one," she says.

"Sarcasm is not a good color on you," I say with a wink.

The entire night passes without a disturbance. I hardly sleep, my nerves on edge to sense the uneasiness I associate with an elemental coming to our world. I barely notice what I'm eating for breakfast, and Minnie has to ask me three times when I'm leaving for work.

I give lectures and mark papers all morning, but I'm similarly distracted. My students glance at each other when I say the wrong poet's name and tell them to open their three hundred-page textbook to page one thousand and four. It's a relief when classes are over, and I can retire to my office to fret without an audience.

Finally, a niggling uneasiness tingles my spine. I sit bolt upright then bend over and plunge my hands into the earth strands on the floor of my ground-level office. My conscious speeds along the strands toward the uneasiness, which is stronger in the lauvan. Past the flowing expanse of blue threads that indicates Burrard Inlet and up the North Shore I flow, until the uneasiness reaches a zenith. There, almost inconspicuous among human clusters nearby, is a ball of strands. It's of every shade of brown imaginable. It's tiny, but the speed at which it grows would cause my heart to skip a beat if I could still feel it.

I memorize the location and fly back to my body. As soon as I have control over my hands again, they reach for my phone to text everyone.

Big one on the North Shore. Come if you can.

I include the address and press send. My fingers waver over the screen for a moment, then I dash off a text to Todd. I could really use his help. His half-elemental nature would be a huge asset. I haven't burdened him with the disturbances yet, but I don't know if I'm enough, anymore. I need back-up, and he and Minnie are the only ones who can mimic my abilities. Indeed, Minnie can do more with water than I ever could.

Rush hour hasn't started yet, so I race through downtown in my little van and soar across the suspension bridge to the North Shore. Mountains reach to the sky, their tops already dusted with the first snowfall of the season. A twinge of uneasiness ripples down my spine, unconnected to the growing lauvan cluster. What manner of disaster will we face at the base of these intimidating mountains? I am part-earth elemental, and even I feel apprehension.

The uneasiness pulls me to a residential neighborhood at the base of a steep cliff. Although it's a workday, there are several people walking back and forth, which surprises me until I recall that a popular hiking trail passes along this back road before veering into the forest once more.

I leave the keys in my van when it stops—who knows when we might have to make a fast getaway—and push my hands into the earth lauvan. The cluster is depressingly large, although there is no sign of its presence in the physical world yet. When I emerge from the strands, Alejandro and Liam stand before me.

"Anyone else?" I ask. Alejandro shakes his head.

"The others are at work, and there's no response from Minnie. Liam and I don't have tutoring for another hour.

Where's the disturbance? Everything looks fine here."

"It's coming." I grimace and stand upright. "I don't know what it will be, though. I want to get closer to the exact point. Perhaps I can see something on this side, start untangling it. I won't know until I try. In the meantime, keep your eyes peeled for former Potestas members and danger to the public."

They nod and split up. The hikers look at our group with curiosity but keep walking toward their trailhead.

I strike out to the cluster. It must be in a backyard, for a boxy house with stucco siding squats directly in my path. I vault over the gateless fence and stride around the corner.

The sight stops me in my tracks. The cluster is here, and it glows with a warm brown light that dazzles my eyes and sends flickering light against the back porch of the house. This is the first time I have seen a disturbance in the physical world. It's huge now, as wide as I am tall and still growing. Apprehension fills me at the thought of touching it, but I must. How else can I stop it from increasing? This is my first opportunity to be so close to the source of a disturbance. I don't want to waste my chance.

I take a deep breath and plunge my hands into the ball of writhing strands. The sensation is like touching an earth cable—blissful agony overwhelms—but I master myself and open my mind's eye. How can I stop this?

There are no knots in the ball, which is unfortunate. At least with a knot, I could unravel it and hope the release would help. My fingers carefully tease apart loose strands and pull them away from the ball. When I drop them, they wriggle on the ground, lost and purposeless.

But the cluster grows far faster than I can untangle, and before long I pull away from the lauvan in dismay. Any loose threads I remove are merely a drop in the bucket. The cluster is now two heads taller than I am, and there's no stopping it.

157

I feverishly run my hands through my hair and think. What sort of earth disaster could occur in this region? I mustn't rule out earthquakes and sinkholes. My eyes wander to the mountainside that looms above the houses, so steep as to be almost sheer and covered in rocky outcrops and loose scree. My heart sinks. If there were a landslide, the results would be catastrophic.

Whatever the disaster, it will likely be localized, and that means we need to evacuate. As a bonus, a lack of spectators will allow me to focus on capturing the elemental. With that decision, I race around the side of the house and burst onto the street. Liam is close, so I shout to him.

"Liam! Get every civilian you can find and shuttle them away from this neighborhood. My keys are in the van."

Liam sprints toward my little blue van, and Alejandro comes running at the sound of my voice.

"What's going on?" he gasps.

"I can't stop it, so we need to evacuate. Quick, go door-to-door, get people out of here. There shouldn't be many since it's a workday."

Alejandro turns on his heel and runs to the nearest house. I scan the mountainside. If a landslide is imminent, are there weak points that I can shore up? I don't know how much time I have, but I can't sit idle. If I do nothing, the lives of innocent hikers and those of my friends are in danger.

A careful study of the slope and the lay of earth strands over it indicates a few weak points. My eyes trace the longest slender threads that reach to the houses. If I hold onto those, perhaps I can contain any slides that might occur.

A rumble distracts me from my plans, and my eyes flick to the far side of the slope with my stomach clenched tightly. I'm too late—it has begun.

CHAPTER XXI

Screams fill the air as loose scree on the mountainside slips toward the houses. A car door slams, and my blue van flies past with a wild-eyed Liam at the wheel and the passenger seats filled to bursting with hikers. Alejandro runs after it, piggybacking an elderly woman who grips his shoulders with white-knuckled terror.

The roaring slide hits the far houses with a heart-stopping crunch. Debris flings through the air like shrapnel, breaking windows across the street and causing the fleeing spectators to shriek and yell. Thankfully, everyone is out of the slide's path, but they are close enough that flying debris whizzes past them.

This is too big for me. If I fly closer, perhaps I can stop further slides, but I feel very helpless against the forces at work here.

"Merry?"

A familiar voice makes me whirl around with relief. Todd stands behind me with his mouth agape and stares at the destruction. Five houses are demolished, and the nearby ones haven't fared much better.

"You're here," I breathe. Perhaps now we can manage this disaster.

"Yeah. Got off work yesterday with an injury. Healed right away, thanks to your instruction, but work doesn't know that." He grins at me then frowns at the mountain. "Why are we here? We need to get to safety. We're in the direct path of the rest of the mountain."

"We can stop it. We might be the only ones who can."

"Why do you care so much? There aren't many people here, and everyone has insurance for their houses. Don't you have any self-preservation?"

I shake my head in disbelief. Survival is my middle name, but even I have some vestigial humanity.

"We're here, and we can. Isn't that a good enough reason? Slowing the landslide also gives the others a chance to look for the elemental when it emerges, and the fewer of those on the loose, the better."

"Just don't get yourself killed," he mutters. "Who's going to teach me about lauvan then?"

I'll ponder Todd's value system another day. If he's here and willing to help, I will take what I can get.

"Get into a spot you can be safe but still effective." I consider him. "Can you whip up a wind strong enough to slow a landslide?"

Todd's face cracks in a slow grin.

"I'd like to try."

"Good." I pat him on the back. "If you see a slide start, do your thing. I'm going closer to pull some strands and try to stop it in the first place. Good luck."

As I speak, I pull and knot my own lauvan. A quick glance at the street reveals Alejandro and Liam darting into harm's way to usher a few stragglers to safety. Liam looks up at the mountain with frequent frowns, but Alejandro charges ahead, heedless of danger.

My last strand pops into place, and I dissolve into my merlin falcon form. With a shriek, I lift off the ground with powerful beats of my wings and flap to the mountainside. A ledge halfway up the slope looks large enough for my human body, and I direct my wingbeats there. My body dissolves into my human form, and my fingers cling to the rock face as the substantial height, unproblematic to my bird brain, gives my human mind vertigo.

When that clears, I reach for earth strands that drape over the loose scree. Some are long enough to pass across the entire slope. I close my eyes to sense the state of the Earth.

It's not good. The slope is unstable and growing more so. The cluster is now twice my height and twitches strangely.

I must reduce the impact this cluster will have on the slope. A notion creeps into my mind, and I send my conscious over the hillside. My intention is to freeze the slope in place until the cluster has exhausted itself. It's not a huge stretch, I hope, for earth tends toward stasis, not motion. It takes a lot of force to push stubborn earth around.

Tumbling rocks cease to fall, despite the cluster's rapid growth. I allow myself a sense of satisfaction, but it doesn't last long. Strands tremble, and my tenuous hold on the instable slope fades.

Rocks roll downhill once more. I pull hard on the strands in my hands and the stones slow, but not enough. Todd's eyes meet mine, and they narrow with determination. He raises his hands.

A cloud of air strands forms above his head. My shoulders tighten in anticipation of the wind to follow, but the air isn't directed at me. Instead, the swirling mass of silver threads boils underneath the falling rocks.

Miraculously, they slow their headlong rush down the slope, although they don't stop completely. I haul on the earth strands, my forehead moist with effort. Movement catches my eye, and I squint at the figure running behind Todd.

It's Alejandro. What is he doing? Everyone must be evacuated by now. I don't know how long Todd and I can stop the inevitable destruction. The best we can do is let the slide down gently, so that rocks don't pour over streets further down the hillside and onto people who haven't yet evacuated. There isn't much time before Todd and I exhaust our strength and allow the slide to surge onto this road. My hands already shake from the strain, and Todd's face is grim.

161

My shoulders tremble, then my torso. My knees weaken, and I don't know for how much longer I can hold on. Todd must also be slipping, for the cloud of air lauvan is smaller and more diffuse. Where is Alejandro?

He finally appears from a house on the far side of the street. He clutches a small dog under one arm and sprints to the end, out of danger's path. I breathe a sigh of relief and let go of my burden, bit by bit. The rocks slide faster, but they are much closer to the roadside now and don't have far to go. Todd slowly releases his cloud of air.

The rocks pile up against the mountainside houses and rumble to a stop. Choking dust billows, and Todd's coughs reach my ears. He must summon a breeze shortly after, for the dust flows rapidly away.

I transform into a falcon and soar to his side. He jolts in surprise when I materialize before him.

"That was superb," I say. "Well done. I couldn't have done it without you."

Todd smiles bashfully, then he twists his mouth in disapproval.

"Let's not do a repeat, okay? I want us intact for a while yet. I only just learned that I'm immortal—I want to enjoy it."

I slap his back, and we walk toward the end of the street. The others run to meet us from a group of residents and hikers that mill around in fright and confusion. Liam looks relieved to see us.

"Everyone is okay," he says. "That was amazing."

"You and Alejandro evacuated the residents in record time. No sign of the elemental, I presume." They shake their heads glumly. My shoulders slump, but I keep the disappointment off my face. What a waste of another opportunity. Perhaps I should reprioritize like Todd. To distract myself, I look at Alejandro. "I have to ask, what the hell were you doing with the dog?"

"The owner was crying," he says defensively. "The dog is her family. I couldn't leave it to get crushed."

The owner and dog in question approach our group, and I nod for Alejandro to notice. He steps aside to speak to her, but not far enough that I can't hear.

"Thank you so much for saving Baron." She cuddles the dog and looks at Alejandro through her eyelashes. "You were so brave."

"How could I do anything else?" Alejandro says.

She puts her hand on Alejandro's shoulder and kisses his cheek. He blinks in startlement, and his strands twist with embarrassment and interest.

"I'd like to get to know my hero better," she says quietly. "Where's your phone?"

Alejandro digs into his pocket and hands her his phone in a daze. She quickly taps her contact information on the screen.

"Call me," she says and walks away. I wait until she's out of earshot before I chuckle.

"Now I understand your recklessness. It's a surefire way to get dates. Too risky for my liking, but if it works for you..."

Alejandro studies his phone then glances at me with a frown of confusion.

"Do you think I should go for it?" His eyes flicker toward the city, where Jen works in a downtown high rise.

"Yes," I say firmly. "I do. Don't halt your life for something that might never happen. It's not every day a beautiful woman hands you her phone number."

CHAPTER XXII

Dreaming

Arthur puts his hand on the bridle of the messenger's horse. The messenger looks at him.

"Yes, my lord?"

"You recall the message you are to relay?" he asks. I lean my head against the side of the stable in repose.

"Arthur, he knows."

"Half the troops to Ergyng to join our Saxon ally Framric," the messenger recites. "The others to Caer Magnis, where you will meet them to face the newest threat coming across the ford."

"Good." Arthur doesn't release the bridle. "I don't anticipate the Caer Magnis invasion will take us long to dampen if the troops meet us there. Scouts report only a small party of Saxons. We should be home within a week. Ergyng, however, might take longer." He pauses, then says, "Tell Lancelot that he should follow the Ergyng group."

The messenger nods, and Arthur finally releases the bridle. The horse snorts when the messenger kicks its sides, and it trots through the palisade and along the eastern path. I stare at Arthur until he notices.

"What?" he says.

"Keeping Lancelot away for as long as possible?"

"I would keep him away forever, if I could," he says flatly. "If I see his face, I will want to strike him, and losing him as an ally wouldn't help our cause."

"Fair enough."

Movement catches my eye across the courtyard. My eyes flick to Guinevere's blond braids and long work dress dyed with red ochre. She holds a bucket in one hand, clearly on her way to help the servants milk the goats, but she pauses when a warrior hails her. He sharpens his sword in preparation of our departure, but he waves his whetstone at the bucket. He must say something humorous, for although I cannot hear his words, Guinevere's light laughter reaches my ears.

Arthur's lauvan spasm in reaction. Even after Guinevere moves on and the warrior returns to his task, his strands are agitated.

"You have two choices," I say once I am certain no one is within earshot. "You must either lock her in her chambers forevermore or let her earn your trust."

Arthur silently watches Guinevere disappear into the barn.

"I don't know how to do that," he says finally. "I can't control the jealousy, the distrust, the anger that fills me at the sight of her with others. I don't know where to start."

"You start by pretending not to notice. You can feel all the rage you wish, but the moment it comes out is the moment you have failed. As for your inner struggle, well, time is the only cure. That will give Guinevere a chance to show you her sincerity."

"Time heals all wounds?" The side of Arthur's mouth twitches in mirth. "Are you reciting that old nugget of wisdom?"

"Supposedly, it is true." I pat him on the shoulder once. "We'll have to wait and see."

The sword flies in a shining arc over Arthur's ducked head and into a nearby pile of hay. I laugh heartily.

"Foiled again, Arthur. I love this new move. Here, try it on me."

Arthur retrieves his sword from the haystack and turns with a glint in his eye.

"I will, but only when you're not expecting it. One day when we're sparring, you won't know what hit you."

I laugh again and sheath my sword.

"I look forward to that day. Until then, we must prepare for our journey. I'm glad it is for a festival this time and not a battle."

"Those will come soon enough." Arthur sighs.

Guinevere appears from around the corner of the barn. Arthur smiles and holds out his hand. Guinevere returns the smile and briefly squeezes his fingers.

"Have you come to call us for the midday meal?" Arthur says. "We are finished."

"Yes, but also another thing." Guinevere retrieves her hand and twists it with the other. Her wheat-colored strands are tight with tension. "I wish to learn to defend myself."

Arthur looks puzzled.

"Why?"

"When my uncle attacked us, there was nothing I could do." Guinevere glances at me, and I recall the band of Saxons who ambushed us while I escorted Guinevere and her women from one house to another. I was pierced by an arrow before Guinevere recognized her uncle.

"There was little I could do, either," I point out. "It was an ambush."

Guinevere's forehead wrinkles.

"That is not what I mean. Still, when someone tries to hurt you, you know what to do. I am helpless. And if the attack had not been by my uncle, I would have been dead, or worse. I want to know how to protect myself."

Arthur takes her hand again.

"I promise, you will never be unprotected. You are my wife, and I will make sure that you always have strong warriors around you to fight off our enemies."

Guinevere takes her hand back and clenches her fists.

"What of Queen Boudica, or Sgathaich, the warrior woman who trained Cú Chulainn in your stories, Merlin? I am not alone in my reluctance to rely on others. Please understand, I don't want to campaign with you, but if enemies are at my door, I don't want to cower helplessly behind others."

Arthur shrugs and glances at me for help. He doesn't understand why Guinevere is asking for this. I open my mouth to speak, but a maid appears from around the corner.

"My lords, my lady," she says. "The midday meal is prepared. The stable boy bade me tell you that your horses are ready for your journey after the meal."

"Thank you, Nessa," Arthur says. When she disappears, he puts his arm around Guinevere and squeezes before releasing her. "I promise I will never leave you unprotected. Come, let us eat and then travel west. Gawaine has promised us a juggler for this festival."

He walks around the building, but Guinevere remains rooted to the spot, her strands shivering with disappointment. I turn her chin to look at me.

"We have so little time," I say quietly. "Not today, and not this summer. Perhaps in the long winter months we can teach you something, but most men start training in childhood. Truly, it is best if you rely on warriors to protect you."

Guinevere's shoulders slump. She nods and walks briskly toward the great hall, careful to avert her face from mine. Do tears form in her eyes? For the first time, I wonder how far a few well-placed knife strokes and some confidence would take Guinevere in a fight for her life. Is that a worthwhile goal?

167

The cock crows for a second time, and I curse as I roll off my straw mattress in front of the banked fire. Becoming an apprentice cheesemaker appealed to me when I tasted a slice of Reblochon in a tavern in Marseilles, but in the pre-dawn light that filters through chinks in the door of a small farmhouse in the Alps, it seems far less romantic.

Milking is the first task of the day, and cows patiently await me with full udders. When I push open the barn door, yawning until my face almost cracks open, Jeannot and his wife Annick are already seated at milking stools before two of their herd.

"Late again, Merle," Jeannot says quietly. He maintains a strict policy of low voices in the barn to keep the cows happy and producing sweet milk. "Does the oldest apprentice in the village need his beauty sleep?"

Most apprentices are in their teens, so I'm the subject of good-natured ribbing from Jeannot and his friends. I don't mind. Jeannot is a good man and a worthy companion. I appreciate his willingness to teach me his trade, although I suspect I fill a void that sons of his own would have satisfied.

"Do you think I maintain my handsome face on fine cheese alone?" I call softly back. Jeannot chuckles and continues to milk his cow with a splashing rhythm in his wooden pail. Annick smiles at me but does not break her silence.

I pull a short, three-legged stool into place beside the nearest cow. She is dark brown with wicked-looking horns, although her placid chewing does not give the impression of ferocity. I bend to my task, and the scents of warm milk, dusty straw, and cow manure fills my nostrils with a familiar harmony.

It has been thirty years since my wife Marie died, but I haven't left France in all that time. It comforts me to speak her language still, even though dialects change drastically from region to region. My current situation is pleasant despite the early mornings, and I expect to stay here until Jeannot teaches me all he knows or tires of me, whichever comes first. Jeannot, Annick, and the villagers of nearby Cognin are a hospitable folk, and I am in no rush to leave.

With my first cow milked, I pick up my stool and shuffle over to the next. Uneasiness lances my gut, unexpected this tranquil morning. Perhaps a breath of fresh air will settle me.

I slip out of the barn doors and lean against the wattle and daub wall. Magnificent Mont Granier looms above me, its rocky heights vast and imposing. The sun is finally rising, and it sends shafts of light through a gap in the rocky slope.

More uneasiness roils my stomach, and I frown. What is the matter with me today? Is it an illness within or without? I look around, but the world appears peaceful. An orange glow bathes the fields in soft light, and smoke rises from nearby farmhouses.

A mighty crack rents the air. My gaze jerks to the mountain. I blink a few times with incomprehension. Is the mountain shrinking?

When a roaring rumble reaches my ears, I understand. My heart nearly stops in my horror. The entire side of the mountain is slipping. It slides down, toward Cognin, toward the farmhouses, toward me. There is no outrunning this disaster. In a few dozen heartbeats, it will be upon us.

I shout in wordless anguish, but my hands and feet move of their own accord. Feverishly, I grasp every earth lauvan I can reach and weave it into the strongest barrier I can manage in the few moments I have. I make a wall of strands across the front of the barn that runs with decreasing strength toward the back.

By the time I circle the structure, Jeannot and Annick are at

169

the barn door. Their jaws drop in astonishment at the wave of rock that barrels toward us. It expels a cloud of dust that reaches to the heavens, and the roar of noise is deafening.

I have mere seconds before it hits us, so I desperately weave more strands into my wall then press my palms against it. To Jeannot and Annick, it must look like a futile attempt to fend off inevitable death, but I send out my intention of strength and resilience and brace myself for impact.

The force is like nothing I have encountered before. The rocks slam against my barrier so hard that my feet are pushed through the soil, almost to the barn wall. I grit my teeth and pour out my intention with all my strength. I might die one day, but I am determined it will not be this day.

Debris tosses into the air and over my barrier. Annick shrieks, but I can't look to see if she is hurt. All I can do is hold my position and hope that it is enough, that I am enough.

Choking dust makes me cough, but I don't release my hold on the lauvan. I'm all that stands between us and death, and the barrier must hold. If I prevail, the two farmers and their cows will survive. I wish I could have saved their farmhouse and fields. Cognin must be buried by now, and a pang of grief hits me at the thought of villagers lying under the rubble.

I felt something before the slide. Was it a premonition of disaster? What could I have done differently? One glance at the mounting soil and rock against my barrier convinces me that this catastrophe was unstoppable, even by someone with my abilities. If I had tweaked the lauvan on the slope in time, would that have done anything?

Finally, well after my arms start to shake with the strain, the landslide slows and quiets. The three of us continue to cough, and I release my hold on the barrier and cover my nose with my sleeve. The cows bellow in fright inside the barn, and Annick rushes to soothe them.

170

Jeannot meets my gaze with fearful, angry eyes.

"What are you?" he says hoarsely. "How did you stop the rocks? What did you do?"

I close my eyes in pain. This moment—when someone I care about looks at me with fear because of what I am—fills me with sorrow every time. My life here was pleasant, peaceful, and filled with good company. With one fell swoop from Mont Granier, that life is over. Even if Jeannot accepted who I am, which appears unlikely, the farm is destroyed. The life I had here has disappeared forever, and I mourn its passing.

"I mean you no harm," I say to Jeannot. "I am a traveler with strange abilities, that is all."

"Get out, devil." Jeannot spits on the ground as he backs away. "We are good people here. You will tempt us no longer. We walk on the path of righteousness."

I sigh from the bottom of my abdomen. There is no point in arguing. Jeannot's mind is clouded with fear and pain, and he will not listen to reason in the face of disaster and unexplainable powers.

I reach into a crack where the barn wall meets its thatched roof and extract my sketchbook. I don't know what possessed me to hide it in the barn, but it was a stroke of luck that it wasn't in the buried farmhouse. It would have taken me hours to shift the rubble.

"Begone," Jeannot shouts. I turn my back on him and climb the rubble's edge. Before me lies a wasteland of tortured ground littered with boulders, soil, and whole trees stripped of their branches that thrust naked limbs from the wreckage. No more am I an apprentice cheesemaker. Perhaps this is a sign that I am finished with France for now. I have mourned Marie for long enough. It is time to strike out for new lands and new experiences. If I keep walking east, what will I find? I have heard tales of the Silk Road. Where will it take me?

171

CHAPTER XXIII

Minnie is horrified when she finally calls after the landslide and hears the news, and she barely lets go of me all evening. In the morning, she still hasn't recovered from the shock.

"I can't believe I didn't get your call," she says again. "That particular client is a delicate one, and I have my phone set to 'do not disturb' during our meetings. But I should have been there. I don't know what I could have done, but I should have been there."

Her midnight blue strands twist with her self-anger. I stroke the cheek that isn't lying on the pillow.

"All's well that ends well. Your clients are important, too." Her anger doesn't abate, and I frown. "What else is going on?"

"I don't feel prepared to help," she mutters. "I should have come to the lesson last time. What if I missed something crucial that will save lives in the future? I need to learn more. I need to get a handle on this."

"I can call Todd and we can have a lesson today," I say calmly, but inside I'm thrilled. Whatever she was struggling with the other day seems to have passed. I hope she can tell me soon, but until then, I will happily take what I can get.

"Don't push me," she snaps. My hurt must be apparent on my face, because with obvious effort she takes a breath and pushes down her annoyance. "I'm sorry. Yes, today would be great."

She leaps out of bed and walks with quick steps to the bathroom as if escaping me. I roll onto my back and stare at the ceiling, whose white featurelessness is more comprehensible than Minnie's mood swings.

For today's lesson, we meet on the North Shore in an abandoned warehouse by the train tracks. We have been remiss in practicing our fire skills, mainly because spectators tend to react poorly to seemingly uncontrolled fires. Here, no one will watch us.

I'm on high alert for disturbances, but there has been no uneasiness since yesterday's disaster. It's not over, I'm certain, but while we wait for the next summons, we half-elementals can prepare ourselves by learning what we can from each other to thwart our enemies. The lesson also gives me a chance to redirect my nervous energy into something useful.

"Since we've been dealing with so many catastrophes of late," I say to Minnie and Todd once we're inside the shadowy innards of the warehouse, where the only light filters through dirty windows up near the roof. "I think it's time we focused on mitigation. Let's start with fire."

Todd rubs his hands together, clearly eager to play with one of his favored elements that we rarely use in lessons.

"Ready when you are," he says.

I point to a bundle of newspapers that I placed on the ground earlier.

"Create a fire, and we'll take turns putting it out. Make it challenging."

Minnie glances at me with a raised eyebrow but doesn't comment. Todd grins and bends to the newspapers. A moment later, a trickle of smoke winds its way past Todd's head, and his face lights with flickering orange from the growing flame between his hands.

Within seconds, it's a conflagration taller than Todd, and he laughs in delight. Minnie steps forward with resolve.

173

"My turn first," she says and reaches for the ground. From seemingly out of nowhere, she extracts blue water strands and yanks them upward. They draw water with them, and she coils the strands in her palms until she has a ball of water the size of her head. She throws the ball, and it lands on the newspapers with a splash that soaks Todd's pants and extinguishes the flame. Todd looks disgruntled.

"Good, Minnie," I say. "That was quick, and you found the water easily. Build the fire again, Todd, and you can take a turn. Try with air."

Todd frowns while he relights the damp newspapers.

"Air makes fires get bigger, not smaller."

"If you feed air to a fire, yes," I say with patience. This isn't the first time I have encountered Todd's lack of imagination. "But what if you move air away from fire? It might starve the flames of oxygen."

Todd nods. When the fire is as tall as it was for Minnie, he steps back and raises his hands. His brow creases in concentration. Drifting air threads that float around us are suddenly energized and retreat from the flames with Todd's motions. He circles the fire twice to gather all the localized air threads, but when the space is empty of strands, the fire flickers and dies.

"Nicely done," I say. "It will be more difficult to do with a larger fire, of course, but not impossible, especially with more practice. Now, I'll demonstrate with earth."

Todd ignites the fire again. I bend to the floor and gently pull earth strands toward me. The ones that come easily trail dirt in their wake from the grimy floor. When I have enough in my grasp, collected in an earthen sphere the size of Minnie's water ball, I release it over the flames.

The fire is smothered instantly. I dust off my hands and spread them wide.

174

"Now, let's try the methods that we aren't attuned to. It pays to be versatile."

Predictably, neither are as successful at the other elements as they are at their own. Through long practice, I have mastered air, fire, and water, although I still don't rival the ease of Minnie and Todd at their respective abilities. Minnie complains that the air is too slippery, and Todd keeps dropping earth lauvan. After an hour's practice, however, they can successfully extinguish the fire with any element, and they both beam proudly.

"Excellent work," I say. "Now, Todd, would you like to meet my friend Ailu?"

Todd tilts his head in question, and his strands wriggle uncertainly.

"I don't know. Do I?"

I smile.

"I think you'll get along. Come outside and I'll see if I can find him."

Todd and Minnie follow me out the open doorway. A cold rain pelts the side of the warehouse in a stiff breeze off the water. It's perfect for speaking with Ailu. I grasp a few drifting air strands and send out my intent. Seconds later, Todd inhales sharply when an air cable lands in my outstretched hands and Ailu's form emerges.

"Ailu," I say in greeting. "I've brought someone for you to meet. This is Todd."

Ailu's mouth-shape opens in a wide smile.

"The half-elemental of air," he breathes with his raspy voice. "At last. I was beginning to wonder if you were deliberately keeping him from me."

"Just busy, what with elementals crossing the divide and all. You know how it is."

Ailu chuckles.

"I do, indeed. Nothing has improved over here, I assure you. Come, Todd, place your hands in the cable."

"Okay," he says, his voice filled with awe and trepidation. I forgot that he has never seen an elemental before.

"Will you come with me on a tour?" Ailu asks. When Todd glances at me in question, I nod.

"Close your eyes and send your intention down your arms. Ailu, perhaps you can help him. It's his first time."

"Gladly," Ailu says. His form disappears, then silvery lauvan travel up Todd's arms. When they disappear into the air cable once more, Todd's silver strands leave with them. His peach-colored human lauvan remain, as do his orange fire strands. I peer into his face.

"Do you think he's still in there?" I say to Minnie then jump when Todd's eyes open. They are glazed over, but consciousness still flickers in them. I say softly, "Todd? Are you still there?"

"Yes," he says absently. "I'm kind of in two places at once. It's bizarre. I'm talking with you and with Ailu at the same time. I didn't know my brain could do that."

"Fascinating," I say then step back to Minnie. "Two elemental natures give him an extra ability."

"Just what he needs," Minnie mutters. "More power."

Minnie and I retreat to the warehouse door to escape the rain while we wait. Ailu returns with the rest of Todd within ten minutes, but he emerges from the cable to speak with us. Todd's eyes are lit with excitement.

"That was amazing," he says. "It felt so natural, like I belonged there. I can't wait to try it again."

"It was enjoyable to meet a half-elemental of my affinity," Ailu says. "I like you, Merry, but I can't deny your slow earth tendencies."

Minnie snorts. I wave away the comment.

"Yes, yes, you love to hate my earth nature."

"The three of you are very well balanced," Ailu says. "All four elements represented. If only my world were as balanced these days. With the earth fundamental gone, nothing works like it should. The fundamentals are a force to be reckoned with when they are balanced together. Their powers have been diminished for centuries, ever since your father was in dormancy, but with Xenia now in your world, one of their pillars is completely missing."

It's strange to be the cause of so much turmoil, even unknowingly and indirectly. I understand Ailu's comment about the balance, though. Each one of us half-elementals brings unparalleled abilities to the table that the others can't match. If we work together, what can we achieve?

A wave of unease washes over me, and blood drains from my face. I look at Minnie and she must feel the same, because her expression is one of wide-eyed horror.

"Ugh, what was that?" Todd says with his hand on his stomach.

It's a disturbance, one strong enough that even inexperienced Todd and Minnie recognize it. Ailu's strands shudder.

"I must go," he says. "The chaos is spreading my way. Good luck, my allies."

He melts into the air cable, and Todd releases it before it leaps into the air. I'm already striding to my van, Minnie trotting behind me. Todd runs to catch up.

"Where are you going?" he asks.

"There's a disturbance coming," I say without breaking

stride. "A big one. We need all hands on deck. Will you come, Todd?"

"I don't know." He rubs his neck in an awkward gesture. "It's not really my scene."

I maintain a calm façade but chafe inwardly at his reluctance. I'm not strong enough by myself—the elementals I fight have made that clear—and I need friends at my side. Todd can be a powerful ally if he wishes.

"I could really use your help," I say. "Please reconsider."

We reach my van and I turn to face him. He doesn't meet my gaze, but after a moment he sighs and shakes raindrops off his head with his hand.

"Yeah, sure. I'll come. Just don't throw yourself into danger recklessly, okay? I'm not done learning from you."

He's concerned about my welfare. Even though it comes from a self-interested stance, I can't help but warm to the sentiment. Minnie must feel the same, for she places her hand on Todd's shoulder.

"I agree with that one hundred percent. Let's do what we can safely."

"Great," I say, relieved at Todd's decision. "I'll check where it is. Minnie, you can call the others while we drive."

When I descend into the lauvan network, the uneasiness is palpable and draws me to its source. Orange strands flicker and spark in a growing cluster. I memorize the location and return to the others.

"Kitsilano, at the beach end of Cathbar Street," I tell Todd. He nods and lopes to his truck. Minnie climbs in the passenger's side and slams the door, and we race toward the suspension bridge that will take us to our destination. My heart pounds, but my head is clear. A big one is coming, but we are not defenseless. The elementals won't know what hit them.

The road is quiet when we arrive. A fine mist drizzles from gray clouds, but it won't be enough to counteract whatever fire mischief is coming. Shoppers dart between awnings and cars whip past the beach railing with glum drivers visible behind swishing windshield wipers. I park in a loading zone, and Minnie and I jump out to examine the area.

"Where is it?" she asks. I point at a construction site between two shops where a building used to stand. Now, there is only a deep hole with an excavator inside. Workers aren't present—it must be lunchtime—and the machinery waits silently.

"No fire yet," I murmur. "What form will it take? And how can we capture the elemental this time?"

"We need to focus on getting it," Minnie says. "Amazingly, everyone is coming, except for Anna. Delegate a few of us to watch for the elemental and trap it when we see it. Cecil will have his tranquilizer gun."

I nod. She's right—our track record for capturing elementals is abysmal. We need to get on top of this before Xenia has her full complement of minions. Every successive disturbance only fuels Xenia's unknown plans.

"Good idea. Look, here are the others." I wave at Alejandro and Liam, who jog toward us from the direction of their apartment, and at Jen and Cecil in Jen's Prius as it pulls up behind my van. Todd ambles our way, joined by Wayne. We form a large group when they all assemble, and a smile touches my lips before I grow serious.

"Thanks for coming, everyone. It's fire this time and growing fast. We'll need two teams, one to capture the elemental and one to deal with the fallout. As I proved yesterday, I don't know how to stop the disturbance from

179

creating chaos in the first place, so we'll have to handle whatever comes after."

"Jen and I can watch for the elemental," Cecil says quickly. His lauvan twist with worry for Jen, and I raise a brow.

"And capture it, don't forget. All right, good. I'll deal with the fire, obviously. Todd, I would like you to join me, as you're uniquely fire-resistant."

Todd doesn't look enthused, but he doesn't argue, so I move on.

"Minnie, I want at least one half-elemental watching for the minion, so you go with Jen and Cecil. The rest of you, choose a team. We don't have long."

Alejandro and Liam step closer to me, and Wayne joins the others. I nod briskly.

"Good. Team elemental, decide on your strategy. Use Cecil's tranquilizer gun if you can. When in doubt, follow Minnie's advice since she can see more. Fire brigade, follow me."

My team trails after me until I stop at the temporary fence surrounding the construction site. I bend and connect to the lauvan network to check the status of the fire cluster. It's huge, and when I reach my body again, I swallow reflexively.

"It won't be long, but I don't know what form it will take. There isn't much to burn in this hole."

"There are buildings on either side," says Liam. I glance at them thoughtfully.

"Yes, rather flammable. All right, go to each building and find a fire alarm to pull. But be quick about it."

Alejandro races to the left building and Liam to the right. A familiar figure ambles toward me, a shopping bag on his shoulder.

"Hello, Merry." My neighbor Gary's face wrinkles with his wide smile. "Strange to meet you away from the apartment.

I'm picking up Mrs. Watson's favorite dinner rolls from the bakery here. She swears by them, won't serve anything else."

"Gary." I look at the construction site then back at my neighbor. My face must display my fear and confusion, for Gary squints at me.

"Something's happening," he says in a matter-of-fact tone. "Something with the elementals. How can I help?"

"You should get away," I say hoarsely. "I don't know what's going to happen, but it won't be good. You should put as much space between this place and yourself as you can. Do you have a car nearby?"

Gary's face wears a mulish expression.

"I know I'm old, but I'm not infirm."

I rub my face with my hand then drop it to my side with a sigh of frustration.

"I recommend you leave, but if you won't, find Alejandro and Liam. They're evacuating the buildings around this construction site."

Gary nods crisply and sheds his old-man saunter to stride to the nearest building.

I glance at Todd.

"Do you feel it?" I say. The uneasiness is growing as strong as the landslide was at its peak. Alarms blare from both buildings, and Todd grimaces.

"Yeah. When's it going to blow?"

There's a jolt in the pit of my stomach, and my heart drops.

"Now," I croak. I clear my throat and shout, "Alejandro, Liam, Gary! Get away from there!"

Todd and I sprint down the road, both of us desperate to clear the area before the terrible uneasiness rips apart our physical world. I don't know what will happen, but with sensations like this, it can only be bad news.

People stream out of the two buildings looking confused and

annoyed. Alejandro and Liam race to join us with Gary jogging in their wake with a red face. I raise my voice to be heard over the chatter as I run by.

"Fire! Run!"

The crowd throws startled looks my way. When they see us running, a few panic and shamble after us. Herd instincts kick in, and the two groups run down the sidewalk and into the street. Cars honk and screech to a stop, but the panicked group is heedless to vehicular danger.

A brilliant flash of light blinds me, and vibrations in the ground shake my feet a split second before a blast of noise hits my back. A shockwave pushes me into Todd, and we both stumble.

CHAPTER XXIV

With ears ringing, I glance back. Where once there was a construction site surrounded by buildings, there are now two charred shells around a pit of fire. Even in the few seconds I watch, the flames rise higher than the buildings' torn roofs.

"What happened?" Todd shouts near me, but his voice is so muffled that I can scarcely hear him. I massage the strands over my ears in annoyance until sound returns to full volume, and Todd follows my example.

"The elemental came through. Now, the gas pipes are on fire. Come on, let's slow the flames."

I run toward the growing inferno. The whooshing, crackling roar of fire acts as a harmony to the melody of screams behind me. I slide to a halt as close as I dare to the pit and assess. My skin is dry in the searing heat. With squinting, watering eyes, I glance around the hole. The flame is fed by a broken gas pipe that juts out from underneath the road near the leftmost building. Huge flames lick the side of the building and char the hollow shell. An office chair, lit like a bonfire, slowly rolls off the second level and drops into the debris-filled hole.

Todd heaves for breath next to me. His eyes are a mixture of horror at the destruction and longing. For what, I don't know. Perhaps the sight of such a display of fire power is awe-inspiring to him.

"Todd, can you put out the flames?" I say urgently. He tears his gaze away from the inferno and focuses on my face.

"I don't know. Maybe? It's pretty big, and I'm far away."

"Let's go into the building. I'll do my best to hold it upright for us while you focus on putting out fires. Start with the ones in the building, then work on the pipe."

I take a deep breath of smoky air, ready to enter the building and mitigate this disaster, then a shadowy figure appears in the destroyed first floor. It isn't moving with panicked motions, and my eyes narrow.

"The elemental is in there," I growl. "I need to get it."

"We're really going in there?" Todd looks at the ruin with apprehension, but I charge toward the door. We have already spent too long assessing. In the short minute we discussed a strategy, the fire has crawled up walls and across the roof. There is a very real danger of the neighboring building catching fire, and not everyone has been evacuated yet. Furthermore, the elemental that caused this mess is within my grasp. I can't let it go without trying.

Todd follows me despite his misgivings. We cross the threshold, and the heat is intense. I gasp for breath and frantically manipulate my lauvan to make a fresh bubble of air around my head. When I glance at Todd, he appears unaffected. Perhaps his fire nature provides him with some immunity.

I dart through an intact doorway on the less-burned side of the building and almost trip on boxes that are stacked in haphazard piles over a storeroom floor. Another doorway beckons me from across the room, barely visible through the haze and dim light. Although my air bubble prevents smoke from entering my lungs, the heat is overwhelming, so I hunch over until my face is near my waist. I quickly pick my way through the box minefield and push through the door.

The next room is open to the sky on my right, and crackling heat makes me wince. The sweat pouring over my body heats to near-boiling, and I swiftly twist a few knots in my lauvan to cool it. Everywhere, the crackling, popping noises of a house on fire assaults my ears. A light bulb above my head shatters from overheating, and I duck instinctively at the sound.

Through eyes narrowed against searing heat and brilliant

flames, the silhouette of a woman is outlined in the open gash of wall, half obscured by shifting smoke. Some smoke trickles through my defenses, and I cough reflexively. The woman turns.

"There he is," she says in a mocking tone. Her auburn hair glows warmly in the orange light, and her slinky red dress blends perfectly with her chosen element. Her feet are bare but appear unaffected by the heat. "I was warned you might turn up. Welcome to my birthday party. I put on quite a show, don't I?"

She chuckles and teases a sparking fire lauvan around her finger. Flames follow and lick her wrist without harm.

I glance meaningfully at Todd, who nods. The elemental laughs again.

"You really think you can get the better of me? You have no idea who I am. The elemental you managed to capture, poor thing, was pitifully weak compared to me."

I don't wait to hear more. Instead, I yank on a handful of earth strands and direct a stream of soil from the exposed sidewall of the construction pit to smother the nearest fire. Todd snatches nearby orange strands and pushes them down to reduce the size of the flames.

She reacts with swift motions and grabs the nearest fire lauvan. Flames rush toward us, and the ceiling above me creaks and sags. Todd puts his hands up and hurriedly stops the flames in a circle around us, while I twist the lauvan of the support beams to provide temporary strength. The elemental giggles with girlish glee and pulls the fire strands once more.

Smoke fills the space and we cough uncontrollably. When it clears enough to see, she is gone. I curse and whirl around, but the space is empty.

"We have to get out of here," Todd gasps. "I can't hold it off for much longer."

"Run," I say, and we let go of the lauvan and race back the way we came. It's intensely hot, and my lungs sear when I chance a breath. Beams fall disturbingly close to us. By the time we burst out of the destroyed building, there is little of it left. Fire trucks screech to a halt in the street, and we stumble to the side to let them take over.

A strong hand grips my elbow and whirls me around. Alejandro stares at me with wide eyes, Liam and Gary close behind him.

"What happened?"

"Tried to get the elemental," I wheeze. My lungs are dry and uncomfortably tight. "She got away, of course."

Alejandro's face crumples with disappointment. Liam's lips tighten.

"They don't pull their punches, do they?" Gary wheezes. "Nasty buggers. What's the plan, boss?"

I open my mouth to answer, but a shout from down the street catches my attention.

Jen is bent at the waist, her hand clutching her arm and her face contorted with pain. I wonder why Cecil is not beside her in her time of need—as he often is—until I notice him hunched from his own wound. Raw flesh is visible through a charred hole in his shirt at the shoulder. A quick glance at Minnie assures me that she is unhurt. Wayne mashes his fist into his palm when I race over.

"Fire elemental," he growls. "Threw fireballs at us. I would have chased her, but she threw up a smokescreen and vanished." He glances down the road with concern. "Anna's that way. I need to make sure she's okay." Before I can say a word, he takes off, his feet pounding the pavement with rhythmic steps.

"Smokescreen exit?" I say to Jen and hold out my hand for her wound. "Par for the course. Here, let me see."

186

She extends her arm without hesitation. The skin is a mottled red and white, with patches of oozing liquid. I try to control my intake of breath at the extent of damage, but Jen hears it anyway. Her face grows grim.

"Can you fix it?"

"I can. You'll have a scar, though. Burns are tricky. I'll patch you up now, reduce the pain and heal the skin, then I can do a better job later."

"Good." Jen looks at her burn dispassionately. She has come a long way from the young woman who used to grow queasy at the sight of blood. "I don't care about scarring."

I quickly twist some of her knotted lauvan until the flesh closes over with pink, new skin and the taut look on Jen's face relaxes. I turn to Cecil. He shows me his shoulder with some hesitation, but as soon as my fingers pull strands to numb the pain, his eyes close in relief.

A wave of unease passes through me, and my body shivers.

"Oh, no," I whisper. Cecil opens his eyes and looks at me.

"What now?" he says, concern and resignation both present in his voice.

I twist enough of his strands to create a thin layer of skin over his raw burn then touch the earth lauvan below me. I don't have to travel far.

A swirling silver cluster like a herring ball twists near me. I pull out of the lauvan and grimace.

"What is it?" Jen asks.

"Another disturbance. Air, this time. And it's in the same spot as the last one."

I wave at the still-burning fire, unabated by streams of water pumped from fire trucks. The others' eyes follow my gesture. Alejandro swallows.

"Air, you said?"

"That's going to make the fire so much worse," says Todd.

187

Despite the concern in his words, he can't quite hide his interest in the phenomenon. Fire and air in such vast quantities must excite him.

I push my disquiet aside. I have more important things to worry about than Todd's questionable mental state.

"Get people to shelter," I say. "Todd and Minnie, with me. We'll need to do what we can to calm the approaching storm. Gary, go with Alejandro. He'll fill you in. If anyone sees the elemental, grab it, or follow and call me. But carefully. Each elemental has been stronger than the last."

The others peel off toward a group of onlookers and start shouting and chivvying the crowd. I ignore their antics and turn to Todd and Minnie.

"Todd, you're up again. You're the expert here. If a windstorm picks up, what do you suggest we do?"

I have my own notions—centuries of playing with the elements gave me ideas for a situation like this—but I want to hear Todd's view. He might not have much imagination, but air is his element. He frowns in thought.

"Grab a handful of air lauvan in each fist, pull down slowly, and send calm thoughts out my arms. It's simple but seems to work."

"It's as good as anything I have." I wonder if my abilities would allow that much power in air with so little action. Todd's mastery of his element is impressive. "Might I suggest also anchoring yourself to the ground, so you don't fly off in a gale?" A wave of uneasiness crashes over me, and all three of us wince and clutch our stomachs in unison. When I can speak again, I continue. "It's coming. Brace yourselves."

A breeze tickles my face with cool air. We hastily reach to our feet and twist knots between earth threads and our own strands. Just when I wonder if a breeze is all we should expect, a wall of silvery air threads sweeps toward us from the end of the street. It boils like a sirocco, terrifyingly tall and promising destruction. The sound reaches us a second before the wind does with a mixture of windy roars and bangs from unsecured items on the ground.

When it hits, I am driven to my hands and knees by the sheer force of the wind. It takes my breath away. Through constantly streaming eyes, I see Todd climbing to his feet with unsteady limbs. Although air is one of his elements, he can't withstand its force any more than I can a landslide. Roof shingles soar past me, and I narrowly avoid a metal garbage tin that rolls and bounces down the street.

As I claw my way to my feet, bent at the waist to stabilize myself, Todd raises his arms with labored movements and grasps air lauvan that whip through his fingers. I do the same. Beside me, Minnie repeats our motions once she regains her balance.

My intention pours out through my fingertips with fervor. Miraculously, the wind lessens from impossible to merely painful. Awnings flap fiercely, those that remain, and a motorcycle's wheel spins from its upturned position on the sidewalk.

"Merry," Minnie shouts at me. "Look at the fire."

I whip my head around. Todd was right—wind only encouraged the flames—and my heart sinks at the size of the inferno now engulfing the nearest two buildings. Firefighters shelter behind their trucks, and those holding hoses shoot ineffectual streams of water that flutter away in the gale. I renew my efforts with the wind. It lessens, but only marginally. When I glance at Todd, his arms are down, and he gazes around him at the multitude of air lauvan that gush past in an endless dance. He's clearly mesmerized, but we don't have time for that. I'm doing as much as I can with the skills I have, but it's not enough. Todd needs to take the reins.

"Bring the wind down further," I yell at him. "It's still too strong. I need your air affinity, Todd."

He shakes his head to clear it and raises his arms once more. With a frown of concentration, he channels his intention, and the wind relaxes its intensity slightly.

"Let's get closer to the fire," I shout. "Stop the wind around it, give the firefighters a chance."

The others nod, and Minnie and I bend to unknot our strands from our earth anchors. Todd must have forgotten, for he takes a giant step forward which only lands him on his knees. With a flick of my fingers, I release his bonds. He grimaces at the close contact, which is too intimate for our relationship, but nods his thanks before climbing to his lanky height again.

We run down the street to the fire. I spare a glance at the greatly diminished crowd of spectators. Jen and Cecil push a small group of laggards toward an open shop door five stores down from the fire. Already, the window is full of people taking shelter from the unnatural storm.

Jen has her arm around an elderly woman and practically drags her to the store. Cecil must see this and want to reduce Jen's burden, for he gently moves Jen out of the way and takes her place. Undeterred, Jen moves to the next slowest person, a man with a cane, and offers her arm. Cecil wants to protect Jen from everything, but she's determined to not fill the role of damsel in distress any longer.

Gary herds another group of shell-shocked shoppers toward the store. Alejandro and Liam race out of the building and usher in Jen and Cecil's group, then Alejandro points westward. Liam gestures, Alejandro nods, and they run in opposite directions. They must have a plan which I'm not privy to, but they are working well as a team and I trust them both. Whatever they are up to, it's for our benefit.

I blink in surprise. The police have arrived and start to aid my friends in their corralling efforts. Officer Lee stares at me, her narrowed eyes promising questions.

I don't have time to ponder her goals. In the few seconds that we are unconnected to air strands, the wind picks up once more and blasts the side of my face with pressure that threatens to pop my eardrums. Another striped awning rips from a storefront and sails down the road like a fighter jet.

I plant myself as close to the burning building as I can without getting in the way of the firefighters. The fire is now a living thing and writhes like a demon released from its bonds, lashing out at nearby buildings. Firefighters wear identical expressions of grim fear as they attempt to control the flames. I raise my arms.

"Give it everything you have," I shout to the others. "And keep your eyes open for the elemental."

Todd and Minnie raise their hands with me. I fill every finger with as much intention as I can wrangle. Little by little, the winds calm from a hurricane to a stiff breeze. Minnie and I are doing our part, I have no doubt, but Todd is the ringleader here. His abilities with air and fire far outstrip my own, even with all my experience, and I'm glad he's by my side today.

Amid the flurry of activity, a lone figure in a gray sweatshirt watches the scene with an air of watchful calm. I stare at the man, whose distinctive looks—dyed blond hair against dark skin—identify him as a former member of Potestas. When he catches my eye, he winks and turns on his heel. I let go of the air strands—Todd and Minnie have it under control by now— and run toward the air elemental, but a blast of frigid air burns my face with an arctic freeze. When I stop blinking my watering eyes, the man is gone.

Uneasiness grips my stomach again.

191

CHAPTER XXV

I curse and run my hands through my hair. This situation is out of control. The fire still rages with the gas leak and a steady wind, and two more strong elementals have joined Xenia's ranks. I have no way of stopping them, and my half-elemental weakness is clear. I don't stand a chance. Now there is another disturbance, and I don't know how to stop it before it starts, only mitigate the destruction when it happens. All I can do is keep fighting with my friends at my side.

If I'm lucky, I can capture an elemental and use it as a hostage. These elementals seem to be of a higher rank. Perhaps Xenia cares about what happens to her more powerful allies. I can only hope.

"Merry!" Wayne's voice startles me out of my dire thoughts of the upcoming disturbance. I whip my head around and watch him charge toward me, Anna in tow. "What happened? It's mayhem here. I was only gone for a few minutes."

"An air elemental came through. Today's elementals are more powerful."

"Merry." Minnie runs up to me, her face fearful. Todd follows, a grimace twisting his mouth. With the air elemental's departure, the wind must have died enough for them to leave their posts. "Did you feel the next one coming?"

"Yes," I say heavily. "Let me check what we're facing this time."

I enter the lauvan network. As before, the cluster of strands is right here. This time, it's water, and glistening blues flow fluidly past one another in a steadily increasing ball. The inevitability of growth reminds me of an inescapable tide. I pull out and heave a sigh.

"Water this time," I say. The others look downcast, but

Minnie's spine stiffens with purpose. "It will be soon, but I don't know what form it will take."

"We can do this, love," Minnie says. She takes my hand and squeezes it. "We can. Focus on what we want to achieve. Save people, stop the water, capture the elemental."

"I really want the elemental," I say with longing. "If I can have some leverage over Xenia, it would make all this so much more straightforward."

"We need to get people out of the way right now." Alejandro rubs his fist in his palm. "Get a head start, so we don't have to worry about them while we're searching for the elemental. And we need to trap the elemental. Can't you attack it with fire or earth, something that it won't be able to manipulate easily?"

"Interesting." My brain churns into action. "Fire could boil the water—I don't know how useful that would be, but keep it in your back pocket, Todd. Air can push it around. Minnie, you stick with fighting water with water. You're inventive, and the elemental will be unused to manipulating lauvan with a human body. Try messing with the water inside its body if you can get close enough. I'll trap water in the earth, perhaps freezing it. I'll think on my feet. If we can distract the elemental for long enough, Alejandro and the others can sneak in and attack it via old-fashioned grappling and Cecil's tranquilizer gun. My sword is in the van if anyone wants it, under the back bench. My hands will be too full."

"I'll tell the police to move people to upper floors," says Anna. She ties her hair up in a ponytail with swift motions. "No matter how the water comes, it's never a good idea to be on the ground floor when there's a flood. The police might not understand, but hopefully they will act proactively."

"I'll come with you," says Wayne. "Kat knows me, so I can convince her." They run toward Officer Lee and her colleagues. Uneasiness turns my stomach again, and I wince.

"It's coming," I say. "Brace yourselves."

"Is it that?" Cecil points to the ocean. Far out to sea, whitecaps froth over a huge rise in sea level. A tanker sways over it. The rise is oddly narrow, as if it will only wash over our section of waterfront. My heart leaps in my throat and I grip Minnie's arm convulsively.

"Get Anna and Wayne upstairs," I shout at Jen and Cecil. They sprint away without a backward glance. I turn to Alejandro, Liam, and Gary. "Try to corral any errant firefighters close to this truck. Don't tell them what's coming—they won't believe you. I can make a barrier for us, but we need to stick together. Go!"

I race toward the fire trucks. The workers there are focused on their task, and none spares a glance at the wave of destruction that funnels our way. When I'm near enough, I grab Todd and Minnie's arms.

"Barrier lauvan," I say urgently. "Whatever element you want, however you want to build it. Weave a wall of strands around this fire truck and be quick."

Todd looks frustrated, but he gamely pulls air lauvan from the breeze and twists them together. Minnie bends and draws blue strands out of the pools of water released from fire hoses, and I pull from the copious earth lauvan that blanket the ground.

My barrier is hastily erected, but it outlines the region to build on. The other two fill in holes with their own element strands. I don't look behind me, instead trusting the others to do their job. Alejandro is persuasive, and Gary talks enough to lower anyone's guard. The barrier stretches from one side of the construction hole, around a fire truck and most of the fire fighters, all the way to the far side. Approaching water should flow around our barrier and pour into the pit. With any luck, it will douse the worst of the gas fire. I can only hope.

194

A roar and the sound of crunching boats is the only further warning we get. Minnie clutches my hand.

"Alejandro!" she screams. "Get in here!"

Alejandro is arguing with the last two men holding a hose at the burning building. At Minnie's scream, he looks seaward and his eyes widen. He points to the approaching wave then hauls on the nearest man's arm with all his strength. The man stumbles after him, but his colleague stares, openmouthed, at the rushing spume of water barreling his way. Despite the barrier—which appears far too flimsy for such a force—I brace myself for impact.

Alejandro shoves the man through the barrier and leaps after him just as the frothing spray touches his body. The other man has no chance and is swept into the construction pit.

The water smacks into our barrier. The strands bend inward with the strain, but miraculously, they hold. Minnie's hand grips mine painfully, and Todd stares at the barrier with a tight jaw. Only now does the sound of screams and cries register in my ears over the thunderous noise of rushing water and crunching cars against buildings. The firefighters with us have no idea what is happening, but they are safe, and so are my friends. I hope desperately that Jen and Cecil found Anna and Wayne in time.

Seawater sloshes against the barrier up to my waist then to chest-level. A few streams of water squirt out from weak points in the strand-wall. Todd and I exchange a glance, and he pulls a lighter out of his pocket.

"A little extra height?" he yells over the noise. "Like barbed wire?"

"Do it," I shout back. "Minnie and I will stabilize the rest."

We get to work weaving more earth and water lauvan into the barrier where there are holes. I ignore the shouted gabbling behind me—the others can subdue the firefighters with

195

Alejandro's silver tongue, Liam's calm, and Gary's good-naturedness—and focus on the wall. The water is at Minnie's head now, and I'm grateful for Todd's height as he weaves a sparking orange extension on the top of our wall.

The water rises higher and higher, and Todd works frantically to complete the extra wall. When he reaches the final edge, the water touches the fire strands and hisses into steam.

The sea has almost filled the construction pit when it finally recedes. Chest-height, waist-height, knee-height, then down to puddles on the ground as seawater sloshes back to the ocean. I heave for breath at our narrow escape.

"It's done," I say to Todd and Minnie. "Barrier down."

"I thought you didn't like humans seeing you do this kind of thing," Todd says as he rips at the barrier with shaking hands.

"Desperate times. Besides, these people are filled with adrenaline, and they're seeing something impossible. After a few days, even they won't believe their own memories."

A stinging breeze hits my face, and my eyes narrow. I look around. The only calm person nearby is the dark-skinned man with blond hair. The air elemental is back, and his smile promises chaos.

"Air elemental is here," I yell. "Todd, Minnie, let's engage him in battle. Alejandro and Liam, sneak around to grab him."

I stamp down the last of the barrier and stride forward toward the air elemental with Todd and Minnie on either flank. The elemental grins and spreads his arms wide in a mockery of a welcoming gesture.

"What a wonderful world you live in," he says in a raspy voice. "I can't wait to explore it. But first, some fun. The earth fundamental promised us a good time, and I intend on starting now."

"Me too," a fluid voice says. I slow my steps and look

toward the sound. A slender, fortyish woman with black hair, wearing a turquoise sweater and jeans, smiles at us. Blue elemental strands slide around her purple human ones. "It has been too long since elementals have crossed over. Stories aren't enough. And now, we're here." She dips her hand near a puddle at her feet and lifts water lauvan to her waist. To us, she says, "Are you ready to play?"

"I want to play, too," a light voice calls out. From the direction of the burning building, still on fire despite the blast of ocean water, the barefoot fire elemental in her red dress minces toward us. She pretends to pout. "Don't start without me."

If my fingers squeeze into fists any tighter, I will lose circulation. Minnie slides her feet farther apart in preparation, and Todd mumbles a nonstop litany of curses. Three powerful elementals? Even if we give it everything we have, I don't know if we have a chance.

I have no time to contemplate our odds. With a flash of blue, the water elemental flicks her hand. Water in the nearest puddle rises and lashes against my leg with a sting. I stare down in disbelief. The laceration, while not deep, bleeds immediately through a gash in the thigh of my pants.

Beside me, Minnie growls. She plunges her own hands into the nearest puddle and tosses water in a rapid arc toward the elemental. Minnie's opponent isn't expecting resistance, and the water lashes her stomach. Blood trickles through the turquoise sweater, and the water elemental turns narrowed eyes to Minnie.

"So, that's how it is," she says in a low, dangerous voice. "You play to keep, here."

"Damn straight," says Minnie with no trace of wobble in her voice. My heart swells with pride, but I don't waste my opportunity. I lunge to the air elemental and hurl whatever

197

debris I can reach with the nearest earth strands. Todd can handle the fire elemental.

The air elemental is more prepared than the water elemental was, and he flicks my missiles aside with gusts of wind. I expected as much, and the debris was merely a distraction. When I'm close enough, I haul upward on every earth strand I can reach.

The ground below us shakes. The air elemental stumbles— it is his first time in a body, after all, and earthquakes are not common—and I leap forward and tackle him to the ground. My pulse thunders in a continuous rhythm, and my teeth bare in a predatory grin. Hand-to-hand combat is my arena. Let the games begin.

I pin him to the ground with my knees and punch mercilessly. The first few blows startle him, but by the third, he cushions the blow with a pocket of air that slows the impact. I switch gears and yank at his lauvan, human and elemental alike. His face contorts in pain and I leap out of the way as he vomits. I grab the back of his hair and bang his head against the pavement. My heart thumps with a joyful victory, but before I can cement my win, Minnie screams.

My head whips up. Minnie is on her back, water pouring onto her face from a tube of seawater that reaches from the shore to her. She coughs and sputters, but she's drowning and can't get away.

A powerful yank to my central strands forces an agonized yell from me. The air elemental wasn't as injured as I hoped, and he holds onto my lauvan with a manic glint in his bloodied face.

"You think you're so clever," he hisses. "But I'm a fast learner."

An arrow of air slashes across his cheek, and he lets go of my strands with an inhalation of pain. Seizing my chance, I

198

pull hard at his lauvan. He slumps to the ground, unconscious.

I turn to look at Todd, who hitches a grin on his face.

"Pretty good, right?" he says. I open my mouth to reply, but the downed fire elemental rises behind Todd. Quicker than thought, I twist the nearest earth strands.

A mound of dirt breaks through the asphalt with a cracking tear and whirls around the fire elemental like a dust devil. She shrieks, but the sound is cut off by coughing as dirt fills her mouth.

The dirt turns a glowing red then bursts outward in fiery clods. The fire elemental stands, heaving for breath, but her eyes are filled with rage.

Out of nowhere, Jen kicks the fire elemental in the side of the knee, and I recognize the move as one I taught her. The elemental screams at the pain—from the unnatural angle, the joint must be broken—and Jen grabs her arms. Cecil ties her feet together, sparing no glance of concern as the fire elemental wails with the motion to her injured leg, and Gary slips a blindfold over her eyes. The spell Anna found keeps my friends safe from possession, and if we can stop these elementals from touching other humans, we can defeat them in earnest.

One corner of my mind is full of pride at our teamwork, especially those of my friends who have no powers, but I have no concentration to spare for those feelings. I push myself off the ground and sprint toward Minnie, intending to save her from drowning.

Instead, I find Minnie on her feet, locked in battle with the water elemental beside an overturned car. Both are drenched and spraying jets of painful-looking water at each other, but neither gives up an inch.

With a yank, I make the ground under the water elemental's feet shudder. It isn't much, but it's enough to disturb her concentration. She ceases her attack on Minnie for a moment, and that's all Minnie needs to blast a jet at her face. The elemental topples to her bottom, and Wayne tackles her with a crushing hug to her torso. Liam hogties her squirming legs and arms.

I breathe a huge sigh of relief. For once, we have managed to get the better of the elementals. With teamwork between human and half-elemental alike, we took down three powerful opponents. There will be plenty of cleanup to do, but for now we have won.

Slow clapping travels to my ears. I turn, my heart sinking before my brain can comprehend.

"So valiant, Merry." Xenia in March's body walks toward me with unhurried steps. Behind her range her minions, their two-toned lauvan marking them as elementals. The water elemental in Esme's body smirks when she sees me. "Defeating all those elementals. But you forgot about me."

I instinctively tuck Minnie behind me. There are at least twelve minions behind Xenia. We might have defeated three powerful elementals, but a dozen is a tall order. And, now that Xenia is with them, my courage wavers. I don't know how we can come out of this in one piece.

My friends quickly gather near me, and I feel marginally better. If we are together, then we have a chance. At least we can fight together and fall together. I'm done being alone.

A flickering light makes my head twist. The fire elemental shakes off burning rope, tugs the blindfold off her head, and stands with a brush of her dress. She strides toward Xenia then gives us the finger. Xenia waves her hand at the minions beside her, and they scurry to collect the air and water elementals. Within moments, both are standing by Xenia's side, the water elemental still drenched and the air elemental slightly cross-eyed. Xenia tilts her head and studies me.

"It's not too late to surrender," she says in a conversational tone. "It does seem a shame to waste three half-elementals like this. With enough rehabilitation, you could become able allies."

Todd shifts beside me but says nothing. Is he interested in surrender? I hope he will stay by my side.

"You don't have allies," I say to Xenia. "Only underlings. And I've never been much of a follower."

Xenia's face twists with displeasure.

"So be it. I gave you plenty of opportunities to join me. Allies," she shouts to her people. "I am tired of dealing with Merry and his supporters. Destroy them all."

CHAPTER XXVI

I glance at my friends. Their faces are pale with fear at our terrible odds.

"Now is the time to reapply your spell of protection," I say to them quietly. "Quickly."

They hastily reach into pockets and prick their fingers with various sharp implements. Alejandro has a folding pocketknife, Jen has nail clippers, and Liam pulls out a sewing needle. They chant quietly to themselves and smear blood on their forearms in swirling patterns, and their strands spread out from their arms. Wayne takes a wide-eyed Gary's finger and slices it with my sword then whispers the words of power.

A figure in a blue uniform stands at the fire truck, her mouth agape. Officer Lee is watching, and she's too astute to brush off whatever she sees as hysteria. I debate briefly whether to relieve her of her gun—more weapons could aid our cause—but dismiss the notion. It's more important to hide from Lee, and I don't have time to answer her questions.

With a few twists of water and air strands, I form a cloud. I add more and more until a bank of fog rolls toward her. Before long, she is obscured.

I turn back to Xenia and her minions, who are hazy in the mist. She points to a few and directs them quietly enough that I can't hear her commands. Wayne passes me my sword and I close my fist around the achingly familiar hilt. Its solid presence reassures me. With one hand free for lauvan, my sword in the other, and my friends behind me, it will take more than Xenia wishes to destroy me. Cecil holds his tranquilizer gun in front of him with steady hands, and Wayne pulls his own handgun-style version out of a back pocket.

My confidence is short-lived. With a cry, Xenia throws out

202

her arm, and four elementals charge forward with their hands outspread. Cold sweat beads on my face, but I spring forward with a yell of my own. My free hand scoops up earth strands and pulls.

Three of the elementals stumble when the ground shakes, but an air elemental leaps with supernatural grace, supported by the air lauvan she controls. She floats to the ground and pushes a gust of air at me. I flatten myself on the ground and use my position near earth strands to send pillars of dirt shooting upward. They burst against the air elemental's hands, and she shrieks in pain. With any luck, I broke her fingers and she won't be able to use her element.

With the moment of respite, my head darts around to evaluate the battlefield. It's difficult to see, given the fog that swirls around each combatant, but a few figures are clear. Jen battles a fire elemental, while Cecil contends with a water elemental whose movements are slowing from tranquilizer but are still lethal. Fire bathes Jen with eerie orange light, but it merely slithers off her and she is unharmed. A swift kick to the knee and a palm near the nose, and the elemental stumbles backward with a hand clutched to his face. Cecil glances at Jen so often that he nearly misses his opponent's attacks, but he's quick enough to defend himself despite it.

Anna is to my right, and she is a surprise. Wayne must trust the protection spell, for she is on her own. She wields an amulet of power to good effect—I briefly wonder where she found it—and her opponent circles her warily, clearly uncertain how to approach the fierce woman.

Another shadowy figure grapples with an earth elemental. Liam is a force to be reckoned with, strong and with good form, but he must still contend with elemental influences. Unlike other elements, earth can affect the ground beneath Liam's feet, and the result unbalances Liam enough that he can't outright defeat his opponent.

Alejandro battles two elementals. Although he fights with reckless valor, his fists moving in a blur and his ducks and twists hard to follow, two skilled opponents always have an advantage have over a single combatant. Minnie lends a hand when she can, but she fights her own fire elemental nearby and can't spare the attention for long.

I can't see Todd, Gary, nor Wayne, although from the grunts and cries to my far right, I can guess where they are. Another elemental rushes me, and I focus my concentration on my opponent. She is an earth elemental, and she practically licks her lips in anticipation of taking me down.

"Xenia will honor me for this," she whispers. "Removing the thorn in her side. We will end you, Merry Lytton."

"Put your money where your mouth is," I say. Her brow wrinkles in confusion as she searches her host's memory for the meaning of the idiom. In the pause, I strike.

A pillar of earth—let it never be said that I can't learn from my enemies—pummels her hand but not strongly enough to do damage. She snarls and casts a barrage of broken asphalt at me. I deflect it with a barrier of air strands then throw a jet of water into her face. When she sputters with rage, I grab an errant fire strand that floats by in the form of a spark—perhaps Todd battles nearby—and follow up with fire to her hair. She screams and bats at the flames, and I tackle her to the ground.

Too late, I realize my mistake. Surrounded by earth strands, she regains her composure. She uses earth lauvan to smother the flames in her hair with soil, then she buries her hands in the brown threads at her side. I reach for her arms, but she throws soil in a constant stream hurled at my eyes, my nose, my mouth. I'm drowning in dirt, and no matter how quickly I pull earth strands away from my face, more soil bombards me. I roll away from the elemental, unable to see anyone or anything.

As swiftly as it started, the attack ends. I cough feebly and twist to my feet while I blink, determined to catch whatever she throws at me.

There is nothing. The earth elemental is gone, and my friends blink at me, bewildered.

"They all ran off at the same time," Jen says, her breath coming in gasps. "What are they doing?"

"Get together," I shout. I don't know what Xenia is up to, but she must have a plan, and I doubt I will like it.

My friends race toward my voice until all are accounted for. Most look the worse for wear, and a few limp or hold their arms or sides in pain. Jen is closest and nurses a lacerated forearm, so I grab it and massage strands while I look around incessantly. The fitter my friends are, the better they can protect themselves. Something is coming, and soon.

We wait, the silence broken only by our ragged breaths and faint shouts from distant emergency workers. None have ventured to our section of the street, perhaps unnerved by the unnatural fog. For their sakes, I hope they stay away.

A subsonic groan from deep in the Earth shivers my feet. I swallow a lump of dread. Minnie stares at me, and I nod.

"Xenia. She's joining the battle."

The ground jolts strongly enough to bring us to our knees. The shuddering continues and I rise to my feet, determined to stay upright. With a grinding, cracking sound, asphalt splits in front of us in a jagged line. Another cracking noise, and the asphalt behind us opens like the jaws of hell. The crevice grows deeper and more forbidding with every passing second, and when the cracks curve toward each other, I realize what Xenia is doing.

"She's trapping us," I yell. "Get out of here."

My warning comes too late. With a final grinding jolt, our

exit path is severed.

Gary gives a shout that ends in a hoarse groan. I twist to see him better. He has fallen into a crack in our small island of asphalt and is being slowly crushed. Pieces of pavement crumble into the moat of darkness around us. Gary shouts again and I skid to my knees at his side. My sword clangs against the ground. Gary's face is bloodless except for the red that coughs out of his gasping mouth.

"No," I say in despair. I yank at the earth lauvan that snake over the pavement, and the crack widens. Alejandro and I haul him from the crevasse and lie him on the ground. My eyes rake over his lauvan, but it's hopeless. Gary has only seconds to live, crushed by the relentless, inexorable force of earth. "You should have run, Gary."

"What kind of man would I be then?" Gary wheezes with what must be an attempt at laughter. Even at the end, he finds a vein of humor. "I'm proud I was by your side, Merry. Get the bastard, won't you?"

"I'll hit her with everything I have," I promise with fierce intent. Jen sniffles behind me, but I have eyes only for the dying man before me. A fading friend is a sight that I can never get used to, no matter how many times I see it. My gut clenches painfully.

Gary nods before a shudder wracks his torso. Another cough dribbles red from his lips.

"Get the missus those dinner rolls for me, will you?" he whispers, then his eyes dim. His head slumps sideways as his strands drift away and fade into nothing.

The moisture in my eyes dries with my burning rage. Xenia. It comes back to Xenia. She kills good men and women with no regard for human lives. She doesn't belong here.

"Where is she?" I growl. Jen puts a hand on my arm, but I don't look at my friends. My eyes try to pierce the cloud around us, but my dense fog only adds to the sense of isolation and menace.

Finally, Xenia appears at the nearest edge. March's face has never looked so cold and smug.

"What a glorious feeling of freedom," she says. "The freedom to do what I want, in the place I want to, to the people I wish to subject. You have no idea how restricting dormancy is. And now, with you gone, nothing will stop me from enjoying my time on Earth and then retiring to my exalted position as the earth fundamental on the other plane. Allies," she shouts. "Attack."

With no further warning, nine elementals that are not unconscious from Wayne and Cecil's guns rise into the air and fly toward us. They are supported by cushions of air, held steady by two air elementals on the ground with fierce expressions of concentration. My mouth gapes open.

"Can you do that?" I ask Todd. He scoffs in disbelief.

"I don't know, maybe if I practiced. Watch it!"

A fire elemental soars toward us with a look of manic glee on her face. The next few seconds are a whirl of sword, lauvan, screams, and curses. We battle valiantly, but we have no hope of surviving this.

"Take them all down," Xenia shouts, her voice eerily magnified in the fog. The elementals renew their efforts. Anna screams, and I turn. Wayne stands between her and a fire elemental. Before he can dodge the blow, the elemental lashes out with a whip of fire.

Wayne cries out and falls to the ground, clutching his face. I gather strands and hurtle asphalt debris toward the fire elemental, who avoids most but is hit on the arm. Anna bends over Wayne with tears on her cheeks.

I can't hold the elementals back. I might be the son of an earth elemental, but I'm still human. I'm not strong enough to combat these formidable foes. My anger at Gary's death and my fear for my companions don't add ammunition to my attack. My friends are falling around me, and there's nothing I can do to stop it.

CHAPTER XXVII

Xenia screams again from her perch across the divide.

"Get them, you idiots," she screeches.

The words trigger something in my brain, even as I defend against a jet of water aimed at me. Xenia regards herself as the ruler of all these elementals from her elevated position as the earth fundamental. She doesn't understand that the four fundamentals become a much greater force together. Separately, they are not nearly as powerful as when combined in a balanced whole. Ailu described this to me, but Xenia must not have received that message. All she knows is her own power and the abilities of her underlings. In her mind, none comes close to her level, and she treats them as subordinates. She relies on her own strength as the earth fundamental.

I know I have no hope of defeating Xenia and her minions by myself. Even with my friends at my side, there is little chance when we stand together as individuals. But what if we worked as a unit, the way the fundamentals used to do? What could we achieve together?

If we harness our strengths and execute a balanced attack using all four elements, we might have a chance. A memory of combined elements on long-dead Celeste's burns drifts to the forefront of my mind, and a spark of hope ignites in my chest. Surely, our unified front is more than the sum of our parts. I don't have to be enough by myself to save the day, not when I have my friends beside me.

"Todd, Minnie," I yell. "To me!"

I fend off another elemental with a shower of debris that knocks him from the immediate sky and turn to Alejandro, who battles beside me.

"Alejandro," I shout. "Protect me, Todd, and Minnie. It's our only hope."

He turns a sweat-soaked face toward me, and the light of fighting adrenaline flashes in his eyes. He nods once, his trust in me longstanding and absolute. He turns to Liam and shouts something, and Todd and Minnie scuffle toward me with wild looks.

"I hope you have another plan," yells Todd. "Because this one is shit."

Minnie doesn't say anything, but her agreement with Todd is clear. I grab their arms roughly and force them into a circle with me.

"Use your element," I say to them urgently. "We're going to join them together. Ailu said that's how the fundamentals gain more power."

"What does that mean, join them together?" Minnie snaps. Her strands flick and twist in agitation.

I squeeze her hand once, tightly. I have no idea if my plan will work, but I can't show hesitation to these two. They are too close to the edge of panic as it is.

"Weave together a rope of lauvan, all four elements together." I hold my sword up between us. Multicolored strands flicker along its sharpened edge. "Use the sword as a base to attach lauvan. Quickly, now."

Todd shakes his head but pulls his lighter out of his pocket and flicks a flame into being. Minnie reaches to a puddle, and I pull earth strands from near my feet. Swiftly, with hyperawareness of the battle raging around us, we twist the elemental strands together: orange, silver, blue, and brown.

A cable of swirling, multicolored lauvan forms around the sword. Once it reaches the width of my head, it pulls together strands of its own volition. Streams of threads flow into the cable. Todd stops gathering strands and watches the trail of orange sparks that fly from his lighter into the growing cable.

Minnie and I exchange glances, and her eyes sparkle with hope.

The cable shoots into the sky, as high as a two-level building, and wavers like a sapling in a storm. Certainty descends on me. This is our creation, air and fire and water and earth, and we must control it, together.

"Hold the sword with me," I shout. "And direct your intention to attacking the elementals."

Todd's eyes light up at the thought of action, and he plunges his fingers into the swirling strands around the sword's hilt. Minnie follows his lead, and I pour my intention through my arm with all my force.

The top of the cable wavers, hesitates, then plunges to stab the nearest figure. A scream tells me that we hit our mark, and a woman with a purple shirt and trailing brown lauvan spirals in a wide arc into the pit. Anna stares at her now-absent opponent, her amulet held out in front of her, and I remember that neither she nor any of our human friends can see the massive cable coming to their rescue.

"Again," I shout, and again we pour our intention into our attack. Minnie's eyes close in concentration, and Todd looks up at the cable with wild delight.

Another elemental is flung away from our asphalt island and then another. Alejandro looks around wildly until he catches my eye. I nod and raise my brows, and he grins in relief and leaps over to aid Jen as she kicks at a water elemental who hasn't yet noticed the loss of his allies.

"Merry!" Xenia screams from across the divide. "You will never understand the power I wield. Give up now!"

My only answer is to send one of her minions skidding to her feet. Xenia's face twists with rage, and she slams her hand on the ground. Our island trembles as if stricken with palsy, and we all stumble at the movement. Our cable wiggles, and some strands drift away from the main section.

"Keep it together," I bellow at Todd and Minnie. I drop to my knees for more stability and keep my hand on the sword. "Get Xenia!"

My eyes close in concentration, and without me willing it, I am transported into the cable. The landscape of lauvan is clear before me. The clusters of my friends surround me, and a ring of clusters lies at the bottom of the pit around us, evidence of our cable's force. Xenia glows with burgundy and brown, and I feel Todd and Minnie beside me, with me. With one mind, we slam the end of the cable into Xenia.

The impact blasts me back to my body. The cable disintegrates into a rainbow of threads above me, and I drop the sword to the ground in a daze. Minnie blinks beside me, but Todd points toward Xenia.

"Look, we got her." His voice is disbelieving. I whip my head around.

Xenia lies on the ground, but even as joy bubbles in me, she stirs and pushes to her feet. Her clothes are askew and dirt streaks her face, but her eyes glow with hatred.

"This is not over, Merry Lytton," she hisses. "One day, you will bow before me."

She limps away. The two air elementals who were at her side dart a fearful glance at us then scurry after Xenia.

Xenia's words seem too confident for her stance, and I watch her stumble into the fog without moving from my seated position. The cable is dissolved, and I don't have the strength to bring it back. Now that the area is quiet except for faraway shouts and sirens from the world beyond the fog, my body's many hurts assert themselves. I avoid looking at Gary's body.

My head turns to Todd with effort. He looks as exhausted as I feel, but our work isn't done yet.

"Now that you're not under pressure, can you bring the

elemental bodies up from the sinkhole using air lauvan? I would, but I need to make sure none of our people are bleeding out. Besides, you're a natural at air."

Todd's strands squirm with the compliment as I knew they would, but he scowls at me.

"Buttering me up won't get you anywhere." He sighs and stands. "But I do want to try lifting others. That was a nice trick."

While Todd is occupied with his task, I turn to the others. They are in varying states of distress, but I crawl to Liam first, whose blood leaks out of a wound on his side. He is ghastly pale. I glance over his injuries, and my heart lightens. He would bleed out in minutes if I weren't here, but it's an easy fix for me.

"Take heart, Liam." I reach for the knots above his wound and swiftly untangle. "You'll be with the living for a good while yet."

He doesn't answer, but his eyes lose the fear that haunted them. When his bleeding stops and I know he will survive until I can fix him up further, I turn to the others.

Jen looks relatively unharmed. Cecil must have stuck to her like a burr. Since no one else appears to be bleeding out, I wave her over.

"Jen, we need to deal with the other elemental at Anna's house. Can you get the van? I want to get us all away from here before the police detain us. The fog won't last much longer. Get Todd to lift you to the other side."

She nods and shuffles to Todd. I watch as Todd makes a cushion of air that lifts her up and over the divide. She clamps her lips tightly together with wide eyes but sets off at a run as soon as she reaches flat ground.

Minnie, despite her own bruised and bleeding body, bends over Alejandro's knee. He grimaces but keeps his mouth tightly shut to avoid releasing a groan of pain. I move toward Anna who holds Wayne around the shoulders, both their faces turned away from me. I touch Anna's arm gently above a clear break that must be agonizing.

"Let me fix that arm," I say. She shakes her head violently and turns a tear-streaked face toward me.

"Do Wayne first," she gasps. My heart drops, but I maintain a calm expression and shuffle over to see Wayne.

Half of his face is a mess of red, oozing flesh with liberal charred sections. I can scarcely see the extent of damage through dense knots of lauvan that cover the wound, but I can tell that his eye is ruined. My stomach turns over. I can heal most things using lauvan manipulation, but burns are some of the most difficult. Wayne looks at me with his one good eye.

"Pain, I can remove," I say quietly. I don't want to give Wayne false hope. "But you will never look the same again."

Wayne's eye closes, and he slowly nods.

"No pain would be good right now," he says hoarsely through unmoving lips.

Quickly, I knot his rust-colored strands to numb his face. I don't want to do more until we are somewhere comfortable. We have all been pushed past our limits, and we need to get off this asphalt island and away from prying eyes. I wonder if Todd could heal Wayne's injuries better than I, since his element is fire. I doubt it, though. When Todd burned himself on a candle during one of our lessons, his healing skills were rudimentary at best. Perhaps with time he could surpass me, but that time is not now.

I gesture to Anna, who holds out her trembling arm. With a few quick tugs at her strands, the bone snaps in place, accompanied by a stifled scream from Anna. I grip her uninjured arm until she stops swaying.

"I'll fix the bruising later," I say.

"I can wait." She looks pale but steady.

"Todd," I call to him. He is finished bringing up bodies, and now there is a row of them on the far side. He looks at me in question. "How much energy do you have left? I could make us a bridge of earth, but I'm fading fast. Can you lift us over there?"

Todd give me a lopsided grin.

"Yeah. This is the only fun part of this terrible day."

One by one, Todd floats us to the row of bodies. Not everyone manages to stay as silent as Jen did. Liam lets out a grunt of surprise, and Anna gasps in fright. When I land on shaky legs on the other side, I swiftly glance over the bodies. Gary lies at the end of the row, separate from the others. The outline of a wallet is evident in his pocket.

"What about Gary?" Minnie says quietly to me with a hitch in her voice.

"We'll have to leave him, let the police explain to Mrs. Watson. They'll have a story, some explanation for her. It will be far more palatable than her neighbor turning up with his body and questionable injuries. He will be identified."

"I suppose." Minnie squeezes my hand quickly. "It feels wrong to leave him there."

"I know." My stomach twists when I gaze at his still form, naked without its lauvan. My eyes travel over the other bodies and widen in surprise. "Two are still alive. We'll have to take them with us."

"What for?" Todd says. "We killed the others. Why are you going soft now?"

"That was in the heat of battle. Killing in cold blood is not something I enjoy doing. Anna is researching how to banish them from this plane, and it's possible that the possessed humans can regain their autonomy. Your parents did, after all. Xenia only killed the bodies she possessed because her

215

fundamental nature was too strong for them."

Todd shrugs but doesn't argue further. I push thoughts of his cold-bloodedness aside as my blue van screeches to a halt before us, Jen at the wheel. Already, the fog is drifting away, and the fire truck is almost visible. Shadowy figures advance toward us.

"Quick," I hiss. "Everyone into the van. Don't let them see your faces."

Jen tosses the keys of her Prius to Cecil, who darts into the fog. Todd lifts his arm in a wave to me and disappears after Cecil in the direction of his truck. Anna gently helps Wayne into the front seat and squeezes in next to him. Alejandro and I haul Liam onto a bench, then we unceremoniously shove the two unconscious elementals in the back and Alejandro sits on top of the bodies. I slide my sword under the bench and am about to climb in when a firm hand grips my arm. My stomach drops and I turn to see Officer Lee's hard face peering into mine.

"I don't know what you're doing, or who the hell you are," she says. "There have been too many unexplained disasters, and you're always there. And today I saw some weird shit. I need answers."

I position myself so that she faces away from the row of bodies. Autopsies will show no explainable injuries pointing to murder except for Gary's crushed torso, but I don't want to get wrapped up in an investigation, at least not until after I heal my friends. If I can make a quick getaway, I will.

"I don't have any answers that you will believe," I say. "But if you won't trust me, will you trust Wayne?"

I point to Wayne in the front, whose battered face turns our way. Officer Lee's jaw drops.

"Wayne? What the hell happened to you?"

"Let us go, Kat," he whispers. "Please. We've done nothing

216

wrong, I promise. We can talk later."

Lee's mouth works, but it's not until she turns to me again that words come out.

"There's nothing I can charge you with," she says finally. "Yet. But I'll be watching you. And you'd better believe I'll get answers from Wayne. If you're smart, you'll be there when I do."

I salute and swing into the van. When the door slams behind me, I knock on the floor.

"Hit it, Jen."

Jen peels away from the scene. The fog is dissipating quickly now, and from my window Officer Lee's face is visible. When she spots the row of bodies, she shouts in surprise, but we are already barreling down the road. Jen dodges emergency workers and dazed-looking civilians until she reaches an unaffected road. She turns a sharp corner and Liam groans.

"Not far now," I say. "We'll pick up the last elemental and then take you home. Healing at the round table."

Liam nods with his eyes closed. He's still as pale as a fleecy cloud, but his lauvan are strong. His blood will replenish in time.

Jen slams on the brakes outside of Bethany's house, and I leap out and run to the door. When I pound down the stairs, the elemental in Ben looks up in surprise.

"You look terrible," he says. "What happened?"

"Your fellows arrived." I grab his arm and haul him roughly up. "We killed most of them. Come on."

Ben gabbles in shock, but I ignore him and push him up the stairs and to the waiting van. It's a tight squeeze in the back, but we manage. I pull curtains over the windows to conceal our overloaded state, and Jen drives to Alejandro and Liam's home.

On the way, I untangle the head strands of the unconscious

217

elementals. Alejandro rearranges himself with a grunt of displeasure, and the elementals sit up, blinking in confusion. While they recover, I knot their lauvan so they can't connect with the elements.

"You have a choice," I say to the three of them. "I can send you back to your plane of existence right now, and you must never return. Or, I can knot your strands and keep you a prisoner in this body, disconnected from your element while you remain on Earth."

"Send me back," Ben says with a shudder. "I can't last another day in that basement. It's terrible being unconnected. No elemental should ever have to bear it."

"I only came for some fun," grumbles another. "The earth fundamental said this would be a good time. She never said we'd have to battle half-elementals. I want to go back."

The other elemental nods fervently. I shrug and tap Anna's shoulder.

"Did you find a way to banish spirits from this world? Please say yes."

Anna nods and rummages in her pocket to extract a torn piece of paper.

"It's only words, but it should work. You have to touch them, that's all."

I read the words in Latin with my hand on Ben's shoulder. His face looks surprised at first, then his eyes roll into his head and he slumps against the wall of the van. One by one, air strands that were entwined with human lauvan disentangle themselves and dissipate into nothing. I repeat her spell twice more, and earth strands drift through the floor while fire strands spark into orange threads.

I sigh with relief, then a confused voice cuts through the quiet.

"Where the hell am I?"

218

The humans are awake and aware. I glance at Alejandro. He nods out the door.

"Drop them off here. They'll figure it out."

"That sounds like something I would suggest," I say with a raised eyebrow in his direction.

He shrugs.

"I'm too tired to care much. It was their choice to be possessed. They aren't injured, and Vancouver is safe enough. They'll survive."

Jen pulls over at this pronouncement, and I slide open the door.

"Out you get, you three." I point at the previous elementals. Their expressions vary from fear to outrage, but I wave them out and they comply. I give each of them a twenty-dollar bill from my wallet. "Grab food, a cab, whatever you want. Good luck."

I slam the door in their faces, and Jen pulls into traffic once more.

"Where to?" she says.

I lean against the wall, drained.

"To the round table."

When we arrive at our destination, Alejandro supports Liam through the door of their suite, and the rest of us follow. He lowers Liam gently to the couch, and Anna leads Wayne to a chair. The rest sit at the table while Jen phones for some delivery food and Minnie and I go from person to person, fine-tuning our healings. By the time we fix the worst of the injuries, our food has arrived, and the rest are eating pizza at the table. Liam remains on the couch, but he munches slowly on a slice from his supine position with his eyes closed.

Minnie sighs, slumps onto her chair, then picks up a pizza box. She grabs a slice, hesitates, then offers the box to Anna.

"Would you like another slice, Anna?"

Anna looks at Minnie with surprise but takes the box after a moment.

"Thanks, Minnie."

The two exchange a silent moment of respect. I look down and swallow my mouthful. Minnie must feel that Anna has proven herself enough to forgive.

Minnie turns to Wayne, who sits next to Anna and attempts to chew with his mangled jaw. I did my best, but my skill is limited. Even when Minnie was Celeste and suffered disfiguring burns, I could never restore her to her old self, despite the weeks I spent trying. The left side of Wayne's face is mottled and rumpled, as if the skin has melted and reformed over a different mold. His eye is gone, burned beyond repair, and I sealed the hole to keep it from infection. He hasn't yet looked in a mirror, and I'm certain he wants to avoid it for as long as possible.

"How are you feeling, Wayne?" she says softly. Wayne grimaces with the side of his face that still moves properly.

"Surviving," he says. "I shouldn't complain. I didn't have to go through months of painful healing like most burn victims do. I only have to contend with my new face. Maybe I should get a mask, like the Phantom of the Opera. I can't sing worth a damn, though." His attempt at humor falls flat when even he doesn't smile. Minnie shakes her head.

"You can voice your feelings as much as you wish. Your trauma is real, and you are allowed to mourn the loss of the face you knew. You don't have to be stoic for us."

Anna throws her arms around his neck and gently kisses his burned skin.

220

"We're here for you," she whispers in his ear. Wayne's good eye blinks rapidly, and he leans his forehead against Anna's for a moment. I take another slice of pizza. Minnie and Anna have said everything that needs to be said, and Wayne wouldn't appreciate me getting sentimental on him. Nevertheless, I catch his eye and nod, and he nods back.

"Oh, Merry," Anna says to me. She pulls a bunch of keys out of her pocket and unwinds a key from the chain. "You should have this. It's the key to March's house, the one with the library in it. You need it more than me. I don't want a connection to the spirit world, not anymore, not for myself." She swallows and takes Wayne's hand. "The power scares me now. I don't want it. But if it can help you protect the rest of us from elementals, then you should have full access."

I take the key and pocket it. Anna is full of surprises. I truly didn't know if she could ever let go of her ambition to gain spirit powers. It bodes well for her relationship with Wayne, who gazes at her with a besotted expression, and the others, who look at her with approval.

"Thank you, Anna." I turn to the others. "And thank you, all. You came when I called, and you put your lives on the line for a cause that isn't yours. And Gary." I take a moment to let the lump in my throat dissipate. The others' faces grow despondent, and there is more than one set of moist eyes. "Gary Watson truly did lay down his life to protect others from the scourge that is Xenia. Remember him and his sacrifice."

"We will," Anna whispers, and the rest nod fervently.

"I owe all of you a debt of gratitude," I continue. "Every single one of you has earned their place here at this table one hundred times over. I am proud to call every one of you a friend."

I look at each person in turn, and I'm gratified to see Cecil and Liam's strands relax with acceptance. Liam, in particular,

221

has struggled with his place in this group if he has no past. It appears that those fears have been assuaged. Alejandro throws Liam a happy nod, and Liam smiles from his place on the couch.

Jen hugs Cecil and beams at me with shining eyes.

"Xenia is still out there, but we really cut her down, didn't we?" she says.

"We did," I say. "She will be licking her wounds for a while. I expect that we took out many of her staunchest followers. It will take time for her to rebuild, and we'll be watching."

Cecil places his palms on the table. His lauvan twitch with anticipation, and I frown in his direction.

"I want to touch the grail," he says in a loud voice. "Today. Right now. I don't want to wait any longer."

Jen glances at him sharply. I take a deep breath then reach under the table and unhook the fabric bag that holds the grail. Its dull metal bowl with enameled reds, blues, and turquoises rests in the center of the table. Liam stares at it from his place on the couch.

"It's your choice," I say. "If you feel you're ready, by all means."

Cecil stares at it, his breath coming fast. Jen grips his arm.

"Only if you're sure," she murmurs, but her golden strands twitch in anticipation. She wants to know as much as he does.

Cecil doesn't look at her but merely gazes at the cup for a long moment. I hold my breath, and the rest of the table silently waits. Cecil inhales, then snakes his arm out and grasps the grail.

The now-familiar rictus takes Cecil over, and I steeple my hands to wait for his fit to end. Jen grips the table, wide-eyed, and Minnie watches the spasming lauvan in fascination. When Cecil finally droops over the table and releases the cup, I wait a beat before speaking.

"Well, Cecil? Any revelations?"

Cecil raises his eyes to Jen's.

"Can you guess?" he says quietly. Jen tightens her lips and her brow contracts.

"Lancelot," she whispers. At the other end of the table, Alejandro puts a hand over his eyes.

"I feel odd," Cecil says at a normal volume. "I think I'll go home."

Jen stands when he does.

"I'll come with you," she says quickly. She's careful not to look in Alejandro's direction. I stand and walk them to the door.

"Minnie is always happy to counsel," I say to Cecil. "If you need to talk to someone."

Cecil nods tightly then opens the door. I look expressively at Jen, who returns my gaze with an agonized one of her own then hurries after her boyfriend.

When I turn inside again, the others are standing and talking among themselves, clearly preparing to leave. Alejandro wanders toward me.

"Well?" I ask him. "It's finally confirmed."

"I had my suspicions," he says in a hollow tone. "It's hard to hear it proved, that's all." He breathes deeply. "I have to accept that Jen might stay with Cecil, don't I? For half of our lifetimes, it's not me she spends her life with. I was only a passing fling in many lives. For all I know, Cecil was her partner at those times. He might be her destiny, too."

I place my hand on his shoulder, but there's nothing to say. Alejandro is right—Jen might end up with Cecil, or Alejandro, or neither now that she knows the whole truth.

"As I said before, don't wait for something that might never happen," I say. "I know it hurts to hear, but it's true."

Alejandro taps his fingers on his arm then comes to a

decision that causes him to frown in determination. He thrusts his hand in his pocket and pulls out his phone. I wait for a beat before I speak.

"Are you going to share what you're doing?"

"Asking out the woman whose dog I saved at the landslide," he says, his thumb busy on the screen. "You're right, it's time to move on. I have to do it now before I lose my nerve. If Cecil is Lancelot, I don't have a hope in hell. It's a fifty-fifty draw who she ends up with every lifetime, and she's obviously chosen in this one."

He presses send then looks queasy. I pat him on the shoulder again.

"Glad to hear you're moving on. Although you probably should have slept on that decision."

Alejandro swallows, angst clear on his face, but he moves off without another word. Minnie comes up behind me and slides her hands around my waist.

"Ready to go home?" she says. "I'm about to drop."

"Yes." I exhale away the day. The threat, although not entirely extinguished, is suppressed for now. My friends that are still alive are safe, if not completely in one piece. We can breathe again. "I'm ready."

CHAPTER XXVIII

I sleep until mid-morning. Minnie is in bed, but she must have risen earlier, for she leans against her pillow with a mug of coffee in one hand and a book in the other. I groan and reach for her mug, which she relinquishes only long enough for me to take a brief sip. I rub the sleep from my eyes.

"Is it truly over?" I say to the ceiling. "I don't need to leap from my bed and plug into the lauvan network to search for disturbances?"

"I haven't felt anything yet," Minnie says, taking another sip then putting down her coffee and book. "And Xenia looked pretty beaten up. We shocked her with that lauvan trick."

She snuggles into my side and I hug her close while I sift through memories of the past few days. One of them makes me frown.

"Do you remember the conversation you had with Anna, after I was knocked unconscious at the house fire?"

Minnie's strands stiffen.

"Yes," she says slowly. "Why, do you?"

"Parts of it. I tuned in as I was waking up. You were frightened of being a half-elemental, and Anna offered to take it away from you. Not possible, by the way, as far as I understand. I don't know—" I stop to find the right words to express myself. "I don't understand why you wanted that." *Why you didn't want to be like me*, is what I mean, but I don't voice that out loud. Minnie must hear my subtext, for she squeezes me tightly.

"It's not the powers, and it's not the revelation about my father," she says. "I'm thrilled that I can be a part of your world, that I can finally see what you've described for centuries. It's astounding. And I love being able to defend myself and others with my abilities and feeling so empowered."

"Then what is it?"

She is silent for a moment while her strands twist courage into her.

"I'm changing," she says finally. "You must have noticed. We've fought a few times over it. A different personality comes out sometimes, and it's happening more and more since I found out about my heritage. It feels like it's taking over, and that scares me. I don't want to lose myself. Who would the new person be? Would I forget my old self entirely? Would you still love me?"

There it is, the true source of her fear. After centuries of finding her in every form she took, do I really seem that fickle? I wrap my arms around Minnie as tightly as I can without hurting her.

"I will always love you," I murmur into her hair. "Haven't I proven that to you, lifetime after lifetime? I have lots of practice loving different versions of you. You are mine, and I am yours. I don't care what the elements are doing to you. I will be by your side every step of the way."

Minnie relaxes into me and presses her nose into my chest. A warm tear tickles my side.

"Perhaps it's your elemental lauvan," I continue. "They might bring their own quirks. Still, your human lauvan are intact. Your underlying essence is the same, no matter what you layer on top. I've never known the difference between mine. Perhaps I'm a kind and gentle person when stripped of my elemental side. Who knows?"

Minnie pokes my stomach, and I laugh.

"You're terrible," she says.

"That's what I'm trying to tell you."

Wayne comes over this morning at my request. I might not be able to fully heal his burns, but I can do the best damn job possible. My stomach tightens when Wayne appears in my doorway, his shoulders low and his hood pulled over his head. The mottled, rumpled skin looks angry in the morning light.

"How are you doing, Wayne?" Minnie appears at my elbow and pulls him inside with a gentle tug on his arm. Wayne allows himself to be led to the dining table.

"I'll survive," he says with a grimace and drops into a chair. "I won't deny, it's hard to get used to the new man in the mirror."

Minnie squeezes his hand.

"It will take time. Be gentle with yourself. You're allowed to mourn the loss. I know you're used to being strong, in every lifetime, but it's okay to lean on others."

"This is why I keep her around," I say. "So others can have a shoulder to cry on, and I can keep my shirt dry."

Wayne chuckles, but he pats Minnie's hand before she withdraws it.

"Thanks, Minnie. Anna said something similar last night. I appreciate it."

"I'll let you two be," she says. "I have some papers to read."

Minnie disappears to the bedroom, and I kneel on the floor for easier access to Wayne's face. He endures my handwaving with a stoic expression, only grimacing with discomfort when I massage out a larger change to his skin.

"Does it hurt at all?" I ask, my fingers busy on a knot.

"Not much unless you're prodding it. It's more the look. I'll get used to it, I guess."

"It's a battle wound. The mark of your courage to stand up

227

for what's right. It's a banner you should wear proudly as a memory of when you stood side by side with your friends to protect others from injustices." I twist another strand, aware of Wayne's intense concentration on my words. "Others might stare, and children might point, but you and the important people in your life will know the truth."

Wayne is silent while I finish my adjustments. Finally, I stand back and admire my handiwork. Minnie left a handheld mirror on the table for this moment, so I offer it to him.

"The texture will always be there, I'm afraid, but I fixed the color and the nerves. You should have full feeling in the skin, but no pain."

Wayne's eyes rake over his reflection.

"It's good," he says after a minute. He touches his cheek in exploration. "Much better than it was." He sets the mirror down and sighs.

"What does Anna think of all this?" I ask. "She surprised me yesterday when she renounced her desire to gain a spirit traveler."

Wayne sighs again, but it's with happiness. As I hoped, his drooping strands perk up at the mention of his girlfriend.

"She's amazing. She's so supportive of this." He gestures to his face. "And she seems genuine about not wanting the powers anymore. Yesterday really scared her, I think. She had built up a vision of what elemental powers would be like— even without having her Potestas memories—and the reality crumbled that vision."

"I agree, she appears genuine. I caught no hint of deceit when she spoke yesterday. And what of your concerns about destiny, that there is someone else for you out there?"

"I only had to look at Alejandro's twisted love triangle to appreciate what I have," Wayne says with a snort. "What a mess. When I compare that to what I have with Anna, I know

228

what I would choose, every time. Even if a woman destined for me exists, she might come with more strings than I can handle. And Anna's great. I want to see where we go from here. Especially if she doesn't mind this." He gestures to his face, and I nod in understanding.

"She has proven herself. A word of advice, though? Take her traveling. She's dying to see the world."

Wayne nods with a thoughtful look.

"I'd like that."

Wayne leaves a few minutes later, but when he shrugs his coat on, the hood remains flat on his back, and he holds his head high.

I'm happy for him, both that a few words from me can change his outlook, and that his faith in Anna appears to be well placed. I am coming around to Wayne's conclusion that Anna can be trusted, but suspicion is a difficult feeling to release completely. Anna still doesn't have her full Potestas memories back. If, by some error, she ever retrieved them, would she still be the woman that Wayne is falling in love with? For his sake, and for us all, I hope so.

I meet Jen at a doughnut shop near her house at midafternoon. It's unusual lately for us to meet up, just the two of us. I have missed it.

"Sprinkles?" I hold up a paper bag when she walks up with her ponytail swinging. She grins.

"Obviously."

She digs into the bag and extracts a puffy doughnut covered with rainbow sprinkles. I accept the bag back and grab my own, a chocolate cake doughnut. We chew in contented silence as we wander down a side street with no particular destination.

"I feel like all I tell you these days is my relationship woes," Jen says at last. "But I don't want you to be the last to know. Cecil and I broke up last night."

"Ah." I take a contemplative bite of my doughnut then glance at her. She stares at me, as if waiting for me to say more. I shrug and say through my mouthful, "Condolences? Congrats? I've been expecting this news for some time. It's not a surprise."

Jen releases her breath in an explosive sigh.

"I guess it was the right call if people expected it. It was mutual, sort of."

"That means you broke it off with him, and he held back his tears until you left."

Jen hangs her head.

"I hope not, I really do. No, he brought it up first, honestly. Mentioned how he felt weird about being together in the past, and what that means to us now. I agreed and asked if he wanted to take a break while he figured it out. He said yes. Just because I don't feel horribly sad about it doesn't mean it was my fault."

"He was probably testing you." At Jen's suddenly pale face, I elbow her in the side. "I'm only teasing. You said you weren't torn up about it."

"I still have a conscience," she retorts. "I don't know, maybe I need to take a break from dating for a while. Or maybe forcing myself to fight against destiny will cost me my happiness. Maybe I should stop fighting my feelings."

I want to ask Jen which man she is fighting her feelings for, but I desist. At this juncture, she might not even know herself. A glance at the strands that connect her to Alejandro and to Cecil tell me the answer, but I keep it to myself.

"Anyway, enough about me," Jen says brightly. "We kicked ass yesterday, didn't we?"

I grin at her words.

"We certainly did."

"I'm glad you found Todd. It must be nice for you to have another half-elemental around. I don't know what we would have done without your fancy element-joining trick." She shivers. "It was a close one, wasn't it?"

"Too close. And Gary paid the price."

We're silent for a moment. I recall the quiet sobs emanating from the Watson's closed apartment door this morning after their grown daughter arrived to visit with her mother. My foot scuffs the pavement in a fit of pique against the age-old unfairness of good men dying for bad ones. I cast about for something else to say.

"You held your own, I must say. Hardly a scratch on you."

"Cecil stayed close," she says. "But I pulled out a few moves of my own. It felt good to be able to defend myself. Really good. I never want to go back to being helpless."

"We'll keep training you." I squeeze her shoulders briefly. "You'll be like a Viking shield-maiden of old."

"Did you know any?" Jen narrows her eyes in thought. "I don't recall any memories of Scandinavia at that time."

"One or two."

We walk in comfortable silence for a moment.

"Xenia will come back, won't she?" Jen says at last.

I sigh and nod. Another reckoning is inevitable, but it will not be today.

I leave Jen at the door of her car and saunter toward my van. The rain held off for our walk, but now the gray skies release fat droplets that splat on the pavement. I stride quickly and pull

231

out my phone. The rain reminds me of elements, which makes me think of lessons with Todd. I know Minnie is keen, now that she has come to terms with her elemental side, so I dial his number and wait for him to pick up.

"Todd," I greet him once he speaks. "Did you heal yourself fully? Are you interested in another lesson today? We could go over what we did in the battle, perhaps discuss what we could have done to improve our actions. It would be an instructive exercise."

There's a pause on the line.

"I think I'll pass for today," Todd says slowly. "I met with Ailu this morning. He asked me to tell you that they've tightened up who crosses over on their side, so Xenia shouldn't be getting more minions anytime soon."

"That's excellent news." Finally, the elementals did something useful on their end. It likely wasn't for our benefit, but I will take the win.

"Ailu was helpful this morning, teaching me lots of things. Since he's an air elemental, he has some great ideas for the wind. I might keep doing lessons with him from now on, actually."

"Oh." This news is a surprise, and not a welcome one. I suppose Todd has a point—Ailu is an expert in air, after all—but there is much that I can still teach him. Having a physical body is a different experience than manipulating lauvan as a full elemental.

He probably needs some space. The battle yesterday, with Xenia and a whole host of elementals from a world he scarcely understands, likely frightened him. Gary's death would have rattled anyone. I can give him time if that's what he needs.

"All right," I say. "If that's what you think is best. Anytime you want to resume lessons, let me know. And stay in touch. We half-elementals need to stick together."

"Sure." Todd sounds relieved that I have taken his pronouncement well. "Will do. See you around, Merry."

I hang up and stare at the rain dripping down my phone. I don't want to give up relations with one of the few half-elementals I know, but I understand his reluctance to engage further with my crazy world. I hope he learns to trust me.

I hope I can trust him.

ALSO BY EMMA SHELFORD

Immortal Merlin
Ignition
Winded
Floodgates
Buried
Possessed
Unleashed
Worshiped

Nautilus Legends
Free Dive
Caught
Surfacing

Breenan Series
Mark of the Breenan
Garden of Last Hope
Realm of the Forgotten

www.emmashelford.com

ACKNOWLEDGEMENTS

A big thanks as always to my readers Wendy and Chris Callendar, Gillian Brownlee, Gabby Skelton, and Martha Rasmussen. Another thrilling cover was created by Deranged Doctor Designs. Thanks to Tristan Williams for fact-checking. A special thanks to my reader's group, the Fantastical Lair, and especially Léon Lémieux, Red Ravenwood, Krista Danielle Casada, and Tahnia Griffin for brainstorming names with me.

ABOUT THE AUTHOR

Emma Shelford feels that life is only complete with healthy doses of magic, history, and science. Since these aren't often found in the same place, she creates her own worlds where they happily coexist. If you catch her in person, she will eagerly discuss Lord of the Rings ad nauseam, why the ancient Sumerians are so cool, and the important role of phytoplankton in the ocean.

Apart from the Immortal Merlin books, Emma is the author of the Nautilus Legends (a marine biologist discovers that mythical sea creatures are real) and the Breenan Series (a young woman follows a mysterious stranger into an enchanting Otherworld).

Printed in Great Britain
by Amazon